CRAZY Hot LOVE

A DIRTY DICKS NOVEL

K.L. GRAYSON

Cover Designer: Kari March Designs
Editor: Jessica Royer Ocken
Formatter: Champagne Book Design

To all of the moms in the world ...

Cry.
Love.
Smile.
Laugh.
Hug longer.
Love harder.
Play in the rain.
Put your phone away.
Self-care is not selfish.
Get on the floor and play.
Forgive yourself for your mistakes.
Forgive your kids for their mistakes.
Don't get angry over the small stuff.
Be who you needed when you were younger.
We're all struggling. Every. Single. One. Of. Us.
It's okay to step away or put yourself in timeout.
You don't suck, even though your kids sometimes tell you that.
Take a deep breath...take twenty deep breaths if you need them.
You're not the worst mom in the world, even though they say that too.
Your child will follow by example and they're always watching and listening.
Love your stretchmarks and cellulite, because they make up you, and you are amazing.
If you yell, they will yell. If you lash out, they too will lash out. If you show compassion and forgiveness and love, guess what? They will follow in your footsteps. You are their leader and their cheerleader and no one can do the job better than you, so put your hair in a bun, drink coffee and handle your life and kids like the boss you are!

CHAPTER
One

Claire

"I can't believe I let you talk me into this."

"Stop it," Mo admonishes, her voice cracking via Bluetooth through the speaker of my car. "He's nice."

Monroe Gallagher has been my best friend for as long as I can remember. She's seen me through every up, down, twist, and turn life has thrown my way, and I love her to pieces, which is why I don't strangle her every time she tries to set me up with some guy.

"He's your accountant, Mo. This is so cliché."

"And he's a damn good accountant. Plus, he's cute, and nothing about this is cliché."

"What if he has some weird foot fetish you don't know about?"

"He's not weird—although the foot fetish is entirely possible. I did notice him paying extra attention to my shoes during our last meeting."

"I'm calling him to cancel."

"I'm joking." She laughs. "You're not canceling. Come on, Claire, trust me. I wouldn't set you up with a weirdo. Joseph is a nice, stable guy."

Joseph Berry. Twenty-seven. Accountant. Never married. No kids. And I let Mo talk me into going on a date with him. It's the fourth date I've been on in four months—with a different guy every time. Each one has been better than the last, but still no one with potential longevity.

I guess this is what happens when you're pushing thirty and your best friend decides to settle down; she suddenly feels the need to play matchmaker.

I think back on all the guys I've dated over the years. Each one was dependable, with a steady, safe job that would ensure he came home every night, and enough social politeness to get along with my group of friends. What more could a girl ask for? Except maybe some wild, hot sex and orgasms that aren't self-delivered. Unfortunately, those relationships failed due to lack of attraction. Mostly on my part, but whatever.

Maybe Joseph will be different.

Oh hell, who am I kidding? He's the same type of guy I always go after; there's no way he's going to be different—suit pants perfectly pressed, hair coifed with just enough gel to leave you wondering if he used any, and a bright smile. How do I know this? Instagram. Yup, that's right. I stalked him before agreeing to this date, and the only thing I could find wrong was an overabundance of pictures of him and his mother.

But that's not always a bad thing, right?

Shit. I haven't even met Joseph, and I already know things with him will fall into the same boring category as they do with every other guy I meet. My love life is absolutely pathetic.

Maybe it's time I step out of my box. With each date I tell myself this, yet nothing has changed.

"Maybe I don't want nice or stable," I announce, unsure if I'm trying to convince myself or Mo.

I can practically hear her roll her eyes through the phone. "Come on, Claire. We all know that other than the teeny-tiny crush you've had on Trevor, you've never had a thing for anyone who doesn't fit into your neat, perfect box."

Trevor Allen. Twenty-five. Firefighter. Ladies' man. Little brother to two of my best friends—Cooper and Rhett Allen—and he's been in my life for years. Most people wouldn't find anything wrong with Trevor's statistics. In fact, he's one of Heaven's hottest bachelors, but to me they read more like this: Trevor Allen. Four years younger than me. Unsafe job that doesn't guarantee he'll come home at night. Afraid to commit. And to top it off, he also works at his dad's ranch, and I'll have you know ranching is listed as one of the top-ten most dangerous jobs in America.

I never thought of Trevor as anything more than my friends' little brother. I thought he was cute in a scrawny sort of way—until I moved back after college. I'll never forget walking out of the grocery store and running into him. Literally. My fruit went flying, along with my brain cells when I looked up and up into his bright blue eyes. That puny kid had turned into a chiseled hunk of man. Square jaw, straight nose, thick black lashes, and a smile made to drop panties.

I haven't quite been the same since.

I frown. Putting on my blinker, I make a left turn. "There is no neat, perfect box."

"Bullshit. What about Hot Cop? Remember him?"

How could I forget? Phillip Rodriguez—also known as Hot Cop—pulled me over for speeding. With a sexy smile that probably ensured he got whatever the hell he wanted, he offered me a date or a citation. Much to Mo's dismay, I graciously accepted the ticket and vowed never to speed again.

"And what about Dean Weathers?"

Sigh. Dreamy Dean. He was three years older than us. After high school, he went off to become a professional race car driver—and succeeded. Everyone in town worships him, proudly supporting his #2 car on their hats and T-shirts. I even jump on the bandwagon from time to time. I've tuned in to a few of his races. Anyway, Dean came home last year for his grandmother's funeral. We met up at the coffee shop, had a delightful conversation, and when he asked me out, I politely declined. I could see that relationship speeding down the wrong track from a mile away.

No pun intended.

"Blake Mathews," Mo says, ticking off another name on the long list of Opportunities Missed by Claire.

Beautiful Blake. Typical surfer. With long blond hair most women would swoon over, he practically invented the man-bun, long before it ever became a thing. Tall, broad shoulders, blue eyes, and a perfect sun-kissed tan, he is every woman's fantasy—mine included, until he went off and became a pilot.

"Tucker Adams."

"Okay, okay, I get it. You can stop with names."

I realize I've been a tad irrational, but I've also seen what the death of a spouse looks like. My father was a firefighter. Thirteen years ago, his crew responded to a school up in flames. He saved several children's lives that day and was killed when the building collapsed. His death left a gaping hole in my life—and my mother's.

For years I lay in bed at night and listened to my mother cry. She cried for hours until her sobs turned into hiccups, and she'd eventually cry herself to sleep. A few times I snuck into her room afterward to find her clutching a picture of them on their wedding day.

I was constantly reminded of how much she lost. I lost my

father—a man who had been a solid presence in my life for sixteen beautiful years. But Mom lost so much more than her husband. She lost her best friend, her confidant. She lost the person she ran to every time something good or bad happened in her life. They had twenty years of marriage between them and ten years of dating on top of that.

He was her hero—still is.

He's also a town hero, a household name around these parts, and I miss him every single day. He looked out for Mom and me like we were the most precious beings in the world. I can still hear my father's voice in my head telling me to be safe. It didn't matter if I was going to school, outside to play, or the movies with friends.

Just be safe, Claire Bear. Whatever you do, use a level head and be safe.

I've carried those words with me, and somewhere along the way they morphed into so much more than a memory. They've become the golden rule in my life—one I try to live by every single day.

I could never survive that sort of loss and pain again—and I want to make my father proud—which is why I've made a conscious effort to follow his advice, even when it comes to dating. That's why I date men whose jobs lean away from hazardous and more toward pencil pusher.

"Are you sure?" she says, laughing. "Because I've got several more I can throw out there."

"Yes, I'm sure. I don't need you to remind me of all the gorgeous men I've let slip away. But just because I prefer to date guys with nine-to-five desk jobs doesn't mean I have a perfect little box."

I've never been one to discriminate. I like men of all shapes, colors, and sizes as long as they have a job on my approved-occupation list.

"Fine, you don't have a box."

"Thank you. Now, I have to go because I'm almost to the restaurant."

"Wait. You're meeting him there? He didn't come pick you up? Asshole. Just wait until I—"

"Whoa there, Fido. Calm down. He offered to pick me up, but I felt more comfortable meeting him since it's our first date and all. You know him, but I don't, and I'll feel much safer knowing my car is in the parking lot if something goes wrong."

"Good call. Although I don't think anything will go wrong. Where are you guys eating?"

Oh boy. "Dirty Dicks."

"What?" she screeches. I cringe, her voice piercing through the speakers. "Are you kidding me? He's taking you to Dirty Dicks?"

"What's wrong with Dirty Dicks?"

Not only does our best friend, Cooper, own the local tavern, he's also the twin brother of Mo's boyfriend, Rhett. The four of us were inseparable growing up, and while Mo and Rhett eventually ended up together romantically, Cooper and I did not. I couldn't be happier for the lovebirds, except for the fact that now they think I need to be just as deliriously in love as they are.

"It's a *bar*."

"It's a restaurant." My argument is weak, but Mo is ruthless, and I'll take what I can get.

"It's a tavern, Claire. There will be drunk people everywhere, a DJ set up in the corner, and ten different sports playing across the TVs. That is not a good location for a first date. He should've taken you somewhere romantic, with low lighting and a corner booth."

"I picked Dirty Dicks."

There's a pause. A *long* pause.

I look at my phone to make sure the call didn't disconnect, and then Mo speaks.

"Of course you did," she says, flatly.

I blow out a harsh breath as I pull into the parking lot. Putting the car in park, I shut off the engine and rest my head against the headrest. "I don't like those stuffy restaurants for a first date. They hold too many expectations when I all I want to do is have fun and talk."

"Coop will be there," she says, probably trying to deter me.

"I figured he would be."

"Probably Rhett and Trevor too. Maybe Rhett's buddy Lincoln."

My skin prickles at the thought of seeing Trevor. My only hope is he's not there with a woman. It sure would suck to be stuck on a boring date and watch him having fun from afar.

See? I already know Joseph is going to be boring. Damn it. I should've backed out when I had the chance.

"Good. I'll know there are four strapping men to protect me if something goes awry."

"Jesus, Claire. He's an accountant. What could possibly go awry?"

"You'd be surprised," I mumble, remembering my date with Chad O'Reilly and his obsession with smelling my hair. I thought things were going well until I found him picking loose strands off of my coat and shoving them in his pocket. The memory makes me cringe, and I pray to any god that will listen that Joseph isn't like Chad.

"Just promise me you'll try. Give him a real shot."

"Fine. I will. As long as you make me a promise."

There's another pause.

"What?" she asks.

"If things don't work out with Joseph, I want you to back off. No more blind dates, and no more bugging me about my love life."

Mo huffs. "I don't bug you about your love life, and if I do it's only because I want you to be happy."

"I am happy, Mo. I love teaching first grade and volunteering at Bright Start, and I love helping you at Animal Haven. What I don't love is constantly stressing over the fact that I'm almost thirty and single, and you make that stress worse."

"I'm sorry," she says, her voice much softer than before. "I'm not trying to stress you out."

"I know you're not, and I appreciate your valiant effort, but promise me, no more."

"I promise."

"Thank you. Now, speaking of Animal Haven, do you need my help tomorrow morning?"

Animal Haven is a local no-kill shelter Monroe inherited from her father, and since I don't have much of a social life outside of work and Mo, I volunteer a lot of my free time there. Plus, who doesn't love animals?

"Well, I guess that will depend on how tonight goes, won't it?" she says with a little too much pep. "If things go well with Joseph and you know...you end up taking him home, then don't worry about coming in. I can handle it."

"You're a slut."

She barks out a short laugh because everyone in town knows that before Mo and Rhett found their way back to each other, she was never a slut. Far from it. In fact, some of us wondered if she'd ever date again.

"Only for Rhett," she purrs.

Lovesick fool. "I'll be in tomorrow morning as planned."

"Fine. I'll be there. I might even stay the night tonight. I've got a horse getting ready to deliver, and I need to be there when she does."

"If you need me sooner, let me know."

"I won't need you sooner. Go, enjoy your date, have fun, and I want all the details."

"Yeah, yeah." I end the call, stuff my phone in my purse along with my keys, and step out of my car.

Here goes nothing.

CHAPTER
Two

Claire

I walk into Dirty Dicks and, thanks to my incessant Instagram stalking, I spot Joseph right away. He's standing at the end of the bar, sipping on a drink with one hand tucked casually into his pocket, and sure enough, just to the left of him sit Rhett, Trevor, and Lincoln.

"Hey, Claire, what can I get ya?"

I turn my attention to the bartender, Sarah. "I'll have a Bud Light, please."

She reaches into the cooler, pops the top off a bottle, and hands it to me as her gaze follows mine to the opposite end of the bar. "Are we staring at Trevor and Lincoln or the sexy stranger next to them?"

"The stranger."

"Do you know him?" she asks.

"His name is Joseph, and tonight is our first date."

"Ahh. Mo got to you again, huh?"

"I hate her." I look at Sarah, and we both start laughing. "Why does she do this to me?" I fake-whine.

"The real question is why do you let her to do it to you?"

I take a drink of my beer and shrug. "Because I can't say no. Because I'm an idiot. Because I've got nothing better to do. Because I would love to find a good, dependable, strong man. Should I continue?"

Sarah chuckles. "No. I think I've got the picture. For what it's worth, he seems nice. I waited on him when he first got here."

"How long ago was that exactly? I mean, I'm twenty minutes early, but my best friend owns the place. What's his excuse?"

Lifting an eyebrow, Sarah examines me. "You're already looking for something wrong with him, aren't you?"

"I am not."

"Are too."

"Don't you have someone to wait on, customers who could use a refill or something?"

I'm totally joking and she knows it, which is why she puts her elbows on the bar and leans toward me. "I'll tell you what, when things go south with Joseph at the end of the bar, find me, and I'll set you up with a real man."

Well, that's an interesting offer, and I'm intrigued as to who she would consider a *real man*.

"I just might take you up on that. But first…" I tilt my bottle toward the end of the bar and stand. "Do me a favor, would ya? Keep the three stooges focused on anything but me and my date."

"I'll do my best, but you know as well as I do that as soon as they spot you, they'll be watching like a set of horny ladies in the front row of a Magic Mike show."

The vision makes me laugh. I tip my beer at Sarah and walk away.

I'm halfway across the room when Joseph looks up and spots me. I have no clue if he knew what I looked like, but he pushes away from the bar and strides toward me.

"You must be Claire." His smile is warm and friendly when he reaches for my hand. I slip my fingers around his for a quick shake.

"And you must be Joseph. It's a pleasure to meet you."

He points to the beer in my hand. "Have you been here long?"

"Just a couple of minutes."

He smiles knowingly. "And you decided to order a beer and watch me from afar to make sure I wasn't a creep."

"How did you know?"

He laughs. It's a husky sound, sort of like Trevor's laugh. I wait for it to reverberate straight to my toes, but nothing. Absolutely nothing.

"I have a sister. She does the same thing. It's actually really smart. You can't be too sure these days."

"Yes. That's exactly how I feel."

"Should we grab a table?"

There might not be tingles in my toes, but there's a definite flutter in my belly, and I find myself smiling back at him. "That would be great."

Joseph guides me toward a booth at the back of the bar. I slide in, and he sits opposite me.

"Do you come here often?" he asks, picking up the menu.

"Actually, I do. My friends and I come here all the time. One of them owns the place."

Over Joseph's shoulder I see Rhett, Trevor, and Lincoln spin on their barstools. Rhett stares daggers at the back of Joseph's head, probably ready to pounce if I show any signs of distress, Lincoln smiles and waves, and Trevor...well, I'm not sure what's going on with Trevor because he's looking at anything and everything in the room except me, which is about normal for him. When I'm around he either flirts or avoids me like the plague.

There isn't a whole lot of in between.

I wave back at Lincoln. Joseph turns around, following my gaze across the room.

"I'm guessing those are your friends," he says, facing me.

I nod and smile.

Joseph doesn't.

"I'm sorry. Is that weird? We can leave and go somewhere else if you'd like."

"No. No." He shakes his head adamantly and then starts to nod. "Okay, yes, it's a little weird." Reaching across the table, he places his hand on mine for a brief second before pulling it back. "But I don't want to leave. I just hope your friends aren't putting me under the microscope. That would be awkward for a first date."

"Oh no, not at all. And I promise they won't come over here."

"Thank God."

I furrow my brow, and Joseph corrects himself.

"Not that I wouldn't want to meet your friends, because I absolutely would," he explains. "But you know…first date and all."

"I completely agree."

Well, if that didn't make things awkward. Taking a moment to myself, I concentrate on the menu—even though I already know what I'm going to order. But Joseph doesn't let me hide for long. He hooks a finger over the top of the menu and pulls it away. His smile is hesitant.

"Can we start over?" he asks. "I feel like I just made things weird right off the bat, and I didn't mean to."

"I'd like that."

We're interrupted for a second when our server arrives. I've known Sean for years, and he smiles when he says, "Good to see you, Claire."

"You too, Sean. Mo told me you started taking classes again. How's that going?"

He rolls his eyes. "Exhausting. But I'm getting through it."

"Hang in there. It'll be over before you know it."

"Let's hope." Sean's gaze cuts to Joseph. "What can I get you two tonight?"

"I'll have my usual with another beer and a water," I say, folding my menu and handing it to Sean.

"What's your usual?" Joseph asks.

I open my mouth to answer, but Sean does it for me. "Turkey club on a croissant with mayonnaise, no tomato, and a side of fries."

Joseph's eyes widen. "You do come here often. That actually sounds really good. I'll have the same."

Sean tucks our menus under his arm and walks away.

"So, Claire, tell me about yourself. Mo says you're a teacher."

"I am, first grade."

"Wow. Young ones. That must make for some interesting days."

"You have no idea." I smile and shrug. "But it's not bad. They're at the age where they're still eager to learn, and they haven't quite developed an attitude."

"I don't think I could teach. It takes a special person to have that sort of patience with a child."

"Thank you." His words warm me from the inside out, and I find myself relaxing against the seat, enjoying his company. "I won't lie though, there are days I come home and need a stiff drink."

Joseph's eyes light up when he smiles. "Oh, I bet there are. We all have days like that. Myself included. Although my work can't yell back at me."

"Or spit at you or throw things or put a whoopee cushion on your seat."

"No way. A student put a whoopee cushion on your seat?"

I nod, laughing.

"I bet you were pissed."

"Not really. It was actually kind of funny. All the kids got a good laugh out of it."

"And the kid who put it there, what happened to him?"

"He got sent to the principal's office."

"I bet he'll never do something like that again. I never would've thought to do something like that to my teacher."

"Yes, well, times have changed. Kids these days are a lot bolder than we used to be. But that's the worst that has happened."

"For now."

"Touché." I tip my beer at him. He does the same, and a comfortable silence surrounds us as we each take a drink.

"What do you do for fun when you're not teaching?" he asks.

"Really? You want to know more about me? Because I'd love to hear about you and what you love."

Joseph waves me off. "I'm boring. And we've always got date number two for that, so for now, let's concentrate on you."

Can this guy get any sweeter? I'm going to owe Mo an apology by the time the night is over. "I volunteer at Bright Start Learning Center and at Animal Haven with Mo."

"What is Bright Start Learning Center?" he asks.

"It's a tutoring facility. I work with kids who need a little extra help."

"Wow. A teacher and a tutor and volunteer. I think I hit the jackpot with you. My mother would absolutely love you. I think she's getting tired of the women I've been bringing home."

"Oh. Do you live with your mother?"

His eyes widen. "No. God, no. I meant that figuratively."

Whew. Not that there's anything wrong with living with your mother, but we're pushing thirty, and getting it on with Mama in the next room would be extremely uncomfortable.

"But the few women I have introduced her to wouldn't hold a candle to you."

"Well then, I'm honored," I say, remembering all the photos I saw of him and his mom on Instagram. "Are you and your mother close?"

"Very. She was a single parent. Worked her butt off to raise me and my sister. Maybe one of these days you'll get to meet her." He winks playfully and takes another drink of his beer.

"I guess we'll see how tonight goes, huh?"

"I guess so." Joseph looks around Dirty Dicks. "Is there a bathroom around here?"

"Past the bar down the hall."

"Thank you." He stands, and I watch him walk toward the bathroom. I wait for him to turn the corner before I pull my phone out of my purse. I send a quick text to Mo.

You were right. He's nice.

Her reply is quick. *I told you so. But if things are going well, why are you texting me?*

He stepped away to use the restroom.

In that case, tell me everything.

There isn't much to tell. He's courteous and sweet. I could definitely see myself going on a second date with him.

That's great! And I won't even say I told you so.

You already did.

There's a pause. I wait to see if Mo will reply, and then I catch sight of Joseph walking toward me. *He's on his way back. Gotta go. I'll tell you everything tomorrow morning.*

"Who were you talking to?" he asks, nodding toward my phone as I slip it into my purse.

"That was Mo. I figured she was dying to know how things were going."

"And...what did you tell her?" Joseph slides into the booth.

A giddy feeling bubbles up inside of me, and I decide to go for complete honesty. "I told her I could see us going on a second date."

Joseph slides his hand across the table, resting it on mine. "I'm glad to hear you say that, because I have a surprise for you after dinner."

"You do?" My mind races with all of the things it could be. An evening stroll in the park followed by dessert at the local ice cream shop and a sweet kiss on my doorstep, maybe?

"Yes, but it's going to have to wait until after we eat."

We're interrupted a second time when Sean drops off our food.

"This looks wonderful." Joseph removes his hand, squirts ketchup onto his plate, and offers me the bottle, but I wave him off.

"You won't be disappointed."

We fall into easy conversation about everything under the sun as the patrons around us bustle and laugh. Joseph, who asked me to please call him Joe, tells me about college and what it was like growing up in New York, and I tell him all about growing up in a small southern town.

I always swore I'd get out of Heaven, Texas, and when it came time for college I ran fast and far. But it didn't take long for me to realize small-town living wasn't so bad. Coming home was an easy decision, made even easier when Mo's dad had a stroke.

We finish our dinner and politely decline Sean's offer of

dessert. Shortly after he walks away with our dirty dishes, a woman approaches our table.

A familiar woman.

Where do I know her from?

I try to place her, but Joe answers my question when he stands up and pulls the woman in for a warm and perhaps slightly too long embrace.

No. Freaking. Way.

His mother is crashing our date?

Is this some sort of joke? I look around, expecting a crew of cameramen to jump out and yell, *Gotcha.* Because who does this? Who brings their mother on a first date? Well, Joseph Barry does obviously. He was worried about being interrogated by my friends, and yet he thinks it's okay to introduce me to his mother?

"Claire," Joe says, motioning for his mother to slide into his side of the booth. "I'd like you to meet my mother, Lorraine."

I draw in a shaky breath as I reach across the table to shake her hand. "It's a pleasure to meet you," I lie.

"You too, dear. Joseph has told me so much about you."

"Really?" I laugh humorlessly. "Because we just met tonight. Seventy minutes ago, to be exact."

I reach for my beer, downing it in three gulps. Lifting my arm, I signal Sarah for another.

Joe's mom watches me for a few moments. She tilts her head and smiles. "Do you drink often, dear?"

"Only when it's necessary... Thank you," I say to Sarah as she drops off another beer.

Silence descends on the table, and then Joe's mom leans in and whispers in his ear. "I don't think it's the best idea to date a woman who drinks so much."

"It's only her third one," he replies, softly.

"I can hear you."

Mother and son look at me.

"Can we have a moment alone?" I ask Joe, giving him a tight smile, one I hope tells him exactly how wrong this is. So, so wrong.

"Uh…" Joe glances between me and his mom before sliding out of the booth. "Sure."

I step around him, careful not to brush his shoulder. He follows me to the bar and stumbles back when I whirl around on him.

"What were you thinking? You invited your mother on our date? Our first date, no less. You do realize that's date suicide, right?"

Joe looks shocked. "But you said we would see how tonight went, and tonight is going well. When I went to the bathroom, I shot Mom a text and asked her to drop by. I really don't see the problem here, Claire."

"The fact that you don't see a problem is a *huge freaking problem*," I whisper-hiss, my voice rising with each word.

"You're making a big deal out of nothing. She just wanted to meet you. She'll ask you a few questions, get to know you, and be on her way."

"I don't want her to ask me a few questions."

"Too late. Here she comes. Smile," he whispers.

I glance to my right and sure enough, here comes Lorraine, striding across the floor. And she doesn't look at all happy that we left her high and dry at the table.

"Joseph, honey," she says, putting her hand in the bed of his elbow. "I'm not sure it was a good idea for me to come tonight."

"I know, Mother, I'm sorry. I didn't expect Claire to be so… so…"

"Choose your words wisely, Joe," I warn, unafraid to shove

my boot up his ass.

He gives me a worried look. "Uneasy," he finishes, smiling at his mother. "Go home, and we'll talk about this later."

"You should go too," I say, crossing my arms over my chest.

Eyes wide, Joe looks at me. "Come on, Claire. The night was going so well, and obviously I made a mistake, but this doesn't have to change anything."

"Obviously," I mutter. "And it changes *everything*. You need to go. Goodnight, Joseph."

I hear a gasp, probably from Lorraine, when I turn around and walk back to the booth to retrieve my purse. Tossing a few twenties on the table, I head back for the bar, bypassing the mother-son duo who are still standing there whispering.

Sarah must've caught part of that little conversation because she waves me down to the opposite side of the bar where Rhett, Trevor, and Lincoln are sitting in all of their sexy cowboy glory.

"Date over already?" Trevor asks.

Instead of answering, I park my ass on the stool between him and Rhett and look at Sarah.

"Another beer? Maybe an appletini?" she asks.

"Just a water, please." The last thing I need right now is alcohol. I'm going to sit here with the guys, bitch about Joseph for a few minutes, and then I'm going to go home, open a tub of Ben and Jerry's, and take a nice, hot bath where I can ponder what in the world is wrong with me.

Except I already know the answer to that.

"Uh-oh." Rhett presses his hand to my forehead, and I slap it away. "Are you feeling okay? You never turn down an appletini."

"No, I'm not okay."

"Is this about your date and the woman he's walking out with? Because for the record, you're way hotter than she is," he says.

"She's his mother," I growl. "Who brings their mother on a first date? How is that even acceptable?"

Sarah slides my water across the bar, and I take a drink.

"Kinda hot for an older chick," Lincoln says, quickly holding his hands up when I glare at him.

"Yeah, that's odd." Rhett leans back in his seat and runs a hand through his hair. "But why did they leave so quick?"

"Probably because she thinks I'm an alcoholic and unfit to date her son," I say, taking another sip of my water. "And I told them to leave."

"Want me to kick his ass?" Trevor asks.

"No." I pout, slouching against the bar. "But I appreciate the offer."

Rhett rubs a hand over my back, and I lean into him, grateful to have such a wonderful friend and even more grateful that he and Mo were able to find happiness in each other. I'm also secretly jealous and worried I'll never find that for myself.

"What do you need, Claire? Want me to call Mo?"

"No. I'm just going to go home."

"You sure?" he asks. "We can go shoot some pool, maybe throw some darts?" I shake my head, and he continues. "Wanna relive our teens? I'm not opposed to cow-tippin'."

Laughing, I look over at him. "Those were fun times."

"The best."

I'm jolted on my stool when some busty blonde squeezes between Trevor and me. She leans in close, whispering something in his ear, and then giggles.

And that's my cue to go.

"Goodnight, Rhett. Linc," I say, tapping him on the shoulder when I stand up. He gives me an obligatory nod, but he's too engrossed in a texting war on his phone. Grabbing my purse from the bar, I fling it over my shoulder. Trevor's heated gaze catches mine over Blondie's shoulder.

"'Night, Red," he says when I walk by.

I hate that nickname. Hate. It. Just because I have an untamable mane of red hair doesn't mean I need the obligatory nickname. Usually I'd rip him a new one for using it, and maybe he's trying to draw that out of me, but tonight I don't have the energy.

"Goodnight, Trevor." I keep walking. The weight of the evening sits heavily on my shoulders as I head for the front door. I reach for the handle and then stop to steal one last glimpse of Trevor, needing a reminder of why I shouldn't lust after a guy like him—a guy who oozes testosterone, has had more women than I've had pedicures, and whose idea of fun is running into a burning building. Only when I look back, Blondie is long gone, and Trevor is watching me.

It shouldn't make me feel better that she's no longer perched on his lap, but it does. Maybe the next time I date, it'll be a guy of my own choosing—someone who isn't a pencil pusher. Someone more like Trevor.

Smiling, I duck my head and walk out.

CHAPTER
Three

Claire

"Morning. I come bearing gifts."

Mo drops the rake and looks up at me.

"And by gifts, I mean caffeine in the form of coffee," I say, handing her a steaming cup.

Mo brings the cup to her nose, closes her eyes, and takes a big whiff. "You're a godsend."

"How's Peanut? Did she have her baby yet?"

Mo looks exhausted, and I'm certain she's covered in horse shit, but I refuse to comment on her state of disarray.

"She did." Mo smiles proudly, as if she herself had given birth. "Mama and baby are doing great."

"And Mo? How's Mo doing? Because you look like a feather could knock you over."

Using her arm, she pushes a chunk of hair out of her eyes. "That's pretty much how I feel. I haven't slept in thirty-six hours."

"Jesus, Mo. You should've called me sooner. I would've come last night to relieve you for a while."

"I know you would've." Mo blows across the top of her cup

and takes a sip of her coffee. "Do you have any plans today?"

"Nothing other than helping you."

"Good," she sighs. "Because I really need you to take over here so I can go home and get some rest."

"Of course. That's why I'm here. You don't even have to ask."

Her shoulders relax as she blows out a sigh of relief. "Thank you. I owe you one. And you won't be entirely on your own. Trevor is here."

My hand stops midway to my mouth. "Oh." Slowly, I bring my cup the rest of the way and take a drink.

"Rhett had to drive back to Houston this morning—he and Lincoln are training for their next ride—so Trevor offered to come help out. He's going to mend a few fences for me and then help you with whatever you need."

An entire day of ogling Trevor? Yes, please. And if I'm extra lucky, he'll take his shirt off, and I'll get to see all of those tight, defined muscles soaked in sweat.

"Sounds good. We'll get it all done."

"Are you sure? Because you'll probably be here until late this evening. I need you to lay new shavings down in Peanut's stall. She made a mess last night. Plus, I received seven more dogs yesterday, as well as two cats, and then there's the foal—"

"Mo…" I place my hand on her shoulder and gently turn her toward the front of the barn. "I know how to take care of Animal Haven. I've done it many times while you've been gone."

"Yes, but never with this many animals."

"I'm going to be fine. And if I have any questions, I'll ask Trevor. Together we'll get through the day."

She sighs. "Okay. I'll show you the newbies before I leave." She leads the way out of the barn. We walk past my truck, and I look around for Trevor's, but it's nowhere to be found. Maybe he isn't here yet.

I follow Mo into the kennels, listening intently as she introduces me to all of the new animals, telling me their stories and what kind of care they need.

"Don't forget to keep the new ones away from the others until I get them checked by the vet. Plus, I haven't had time to evaluate their behavior, although none of them has shied away from me or tried to bite."

"I remember. What's his deal?" I ask, nodding toward the cage on the end.

Animal Haven is huge. Mo's kennels are big enough to house two dogs to one pen but luckily, she hasn't needed to do that.

"Someone left this little pup in a box by the front door two days ago. No collar or chip." She opens the cage and crouches down, inching her way toward the dog. "A little skittish, but I would be too if I were blind."

"Blind?" I follow her into the pen and join her on the floor. The tan fur ball hasn't moved. He's curled up tight.

Mo talks softly before petting the pup, and when her hand makes contact, the dog flinches. His lids pop open, and now I see it. His eyes look cloudy as he tilts his head toward the sound of Mo's voice.

"Name?"

"Nothing yet."

I scoop the little guy up and cradle him on my lap. At first he shivers, and I'm not sure if he's cold or scared, so I cuddle him close, and he relaxes.

"Looks like a Pomeranian," I say.

"That's what I thought too."

I kiss the little ball of fur on the head before setting him back down. "Anything else I need to know before you go?"

"No." Mo stands up and brushes her butt off, and I follow

her out of his cage, making sure it's locked before we step back
outside. "Not that I can think of."

"Where's Ruby?"

Ruby is Mo's dog. They rescued her as a pup and she became the resident pet at Animal Haven. Now she shares that
role with Pickles, a snobby cat that I can't help but love.

Mo frowns. "Rhett and I decided it was time to move her
home with us. She's just getting too old to run around out here
by herself. Last week another dog plowed her over and I didn't
think she was going to get back up. She just can't keep up with
the life here."

"Poor Ruby. How's she doing being at your house?"

"Well, considering she's only ever lived here, she hates it."
Mo laughs but lacks humor. "But she'll get used to it. She has
to."

"She will. It just might take some time." She nods and I continue. "You said Trevor was here, but I didn't see his truck."

"Oh," she says, grabbing her keys off the hook by the door
before we step outside. "He's around here somewhere. He had
to haul some lumber out to fix the fence. You probably won't
see much of him today…unless you want to. And no one would
blame you for watching that man work. He is sex on a stick."

"Really? You haven't even asked me how my date went with
Joseph—a date you set up—and you're already suggesting I ogle
Trevor?"

"You were going to ogle Trevor whether I suggested or
not." Mo shrugs. "And I already know how your date went with
Joseph. I'm so sorry, Claire. I can't believe he invited his mother.
I mean, I knew they were close because he has a ton of pictures of her in his office, but I had no idea he would take it that
far. And then for them to suggest you drink too much…" Mo
shakes her head.

"Rhett is such a blabbermouth."

"It wasn't Rhett. I'm the one who told her."

Mo and I turn at the husky sound of Trevor's voice, and my tongue nearly rolls out of my mouth. Trevor is coming across the yard in nothing but a faded pair of jeans, cowboy boots, and a pair of dirty gloves. *Lord have mercy,* I think my panties just melted.

Trevor stops at the barn, grabs a piece of wood, and hoists it onto his shoulder. My mouth waters as I try not to stare. But it's hard. So, so hard. Literally. His chest is a work of art, almost inhuman, like a sculptor chiseled away on a block of stone until his piece was absolutely perfect, and then he named his artistry Trevor.

Mo nudges me in the arm. I blink and clear my throat.

"Maybe you should mind your own business, Trevor." My voice is way too shaky for my bite to do any good.

"And maybe you should wipe the drool from your chin."

My lips part, and I scoff. "I am not drooling."

"Nothing to be ashamed of, Red. If you were parading in front of me without a shirt on, I'd be drooling too." Trevor winks and disappears around the building.

"I hate it when he calls me Red."

"No, you don't. You secretly love it because he's the only one who does," Mo says.

"I'm not arguing with you about this right now. I have work to do." Grabbing Mo's shoulders, I direct her to her truck, open the door, and shove her inside. "Go home. Sleep. I'll call you later."

"You sure you'll be okay here today?"

"I'm good. Now go."

CHAPTER
Four

Claire

"This is your own fault. I warned you that you'd get a bath if you ran through the mud, but you didn't listen."

Murphy looks at me with the most adorable, soulful eyes I've ever seen. He's a mutt—the perfect mixture of what I believe to be a Boxer and Labrador with floppy ears, big brown eyes, and a playful temperament.

"Don't look at me like that. You're not getting out of this."

I lather him up, but Murphy is having no part of it. Once he realizes his cute looks won't get him out of a bath, he thrashes around, trying to make a run for it.

"Oh, no you don't." I clip his leash to the pole above the wash basin, and once he's settled down, I finish scrubbing. "See, this isn't so bad? And now you're going to smell good, and all the lady dogs are going to go crazy." Murphy whimpers. "I know, baby," I coo, rinsing the soap out of his coat. "I'd be scared of them too. They only want you for your good looks. They have no idea you're just a big, sweet teddy bear."

With a steady stream of baby-talk and the promise of lots of treats, I'm able to finish bathing Murphy. I dry him off, lift him out of the tub, and walk him back to his kennel.

"There you go, Murph. Your food bowl is full, your blanket is clean, and now you smell like mangos." I give him a good rub down before shutting the door.

I step back and take a deep breath, letting it out slowly as my eyes sweep the room to make sure I didn't forget anyone. The morning flew by. I've cleaned all the kennels, changed out the water bowls, and fed all of the animals. I've done a load of laundry, washing all of the blankets and towels, and I've let the first group of dogs out in the pasture to run.

You'd think I'd be almost done, but that's not even half of it. I still have to take out the newbies individually, give four more baths, take care of the horses, and then take the bigger dogs on a longer walk. But first, lunch.

Taking care of Animal Haven without having Mo here used to stress me out. The endless, back-breaking work, plus keeping all of the animals straight—who gets what medicine and how much food and outside time. But the more I do it, the easier it gets, and I've come to enjoy my alone time here. I can see why Mo loves her job. Don't get me wrong—I love teaching, and I love my kids, but taking care of an animal is rewarding in a different way. These innocent little creatures don't expect a thing, and they give every bit of love in return while they wait for their forever homes.

Speaking of innocent little animals...

Before heading to the front office to make my lunch, I decide to check on the blind pup one more time. He's standing at his food bowl. His legs are like tiny sticks, barely visible under all that hair, and I can't help but laugh. The pup freezes, then lifts his nose in the air and sniffs.

Maybe he recognizes my scent. I imagine since he's blind, he uses his other senses to acclimate himself to his surroundings.

"Hey there, little guy," I say, unlocking the pen. "Did you finally decide to get a bite to eat?"

I stand back, waiting to see if he'll come to me, and sure enough, after a few moments he sniffs the air again, following his nose toward me. Remaining still, I allow the pup to get familiar with my scent, and when he stops sniffing and sits at my feet, I take it as an open invitation to pick him up.

Bending down, I scoop him up by the belly. "We should give you a name," I say, scratching the soft spot behind his ear. "I can't keep calling you fur ball and pup, it just doesn't feel right. How about Max?" I look at his face. He sneezes. "Nah. You don't look like a Max. How about Milo? That's a nice, strong boy name." The pup licks the top of my hand, obviously in agreement. "Well, okay then. Milo it is."

When I bend down to set Milo on the floor, he lets out a high-pitched bark.

"So you can talk. I was starting to wonder." Milo lifts his head, and if he could see, I imagine he would be looking at me. "Do you want to hang with me a little more?"

"Arf."

"Fine, fine. You don't have to beg." Milo gets settled in my arms as I walk to the main office. The bell chimes when I open the front door, and Milo yaps again. He wiggles in my arms, and when I set him down, he takes off running. His little stick legs carry him as fast as they can until he rams head first into a chair.

Pickles lifts his head from his bed in the corner and blinks heavily but doesn't get flustered at Milo's presence.

"Oh!" I cringe when Milo stumbles to the side. Maybe I was wrong about his other senses; maybe he hasn't figured that part out yet. "You've got to be more careful," I scold, picking him up.

"You're blind, remember?" Milo blinks up at me as I rub the spot on his head where he hit and then lower him to the couch. "Stay here with Pickles while I make myself a sandwich. And don't pee. Mo will kill me if you pee on her couch." I turn my attention to Pickles. "And you play nice."

Pickles stretches his arms and legs out as far as they'll go and rolls over without a care in the world.

"Fine, ignore him, that works too."

The main office of Animal Haven isn't much of an office. It's more like an apartment since Mo stays here on occasion. There's a couch, table, desk, and TV all in the front room, as well as a bathroom and a semi-stocked kitchen off to the side. Thank God she keeps food in the kitchen, because I forgot to make a lunch.

Whistling, I throw together a turkey sandwich for myself and two for Trevor. I haven't seen him since this morning, and there's no lunch box in the refrigerator, so I'm guessing he either forgot his lunch or he's planning on leaving to get food. No sense in that when I'm here.

I polish off my sandwich, a bag of chips, and a soda, all while Milo snoozes on the couch.

"Come on, sleepyhead," I call when I'm done.

Milo lifts his head and drops it back down, clearly too exhausted from a long day of doing nothing to get up.

"Fine, lazy butt." I grab the pooch along with the sack lunch I packed Trevor and walk outside. It would be easier to hop on the four-wheeler to find him, but it's nice out, and I could use the exercise.

Hooking a leash to Milo's collar, I start walking, but he has different plans. He plops down on the soft grass and rolls over, revealing his underbelly.

"Get up." I tug on the leash a bit, but the dog doesn't move.

"Carrying you around is getting old." But I do it anyway, and he rewards me with a slobbery lick across the face.

With Milo in one arm and Trevor's lunch in the other, I make the short walk across the back forty, following the tire marks Trevor's truck left in the grass. When I find him, his Chevy is parked off to the side, giving me a gorgeous view of the man himself. Slowing my pace, I allow myself time to drink him in, studying the way his muscles shift and flex beneath his skin as he swings the hammer.

Trevor swipes his arm across his face, mussing up his dark hair in the process, which makes it look better than it already did. *Damn him.* Men like Trevor should be required to walk around with a flashing neon sign above their heads, warning all women of their potent sexuality.

When I'm within an earshot, I put Milo down and call out to Trevor. "Hungry?"

His arm is raised to swing the hammer when looks back at me. Lowering the tool, he pulls out the rag hanging from his back pocket and wipes off his hands as he walks toward me.

"That depends."

My back stiffens. If he even says he wanted ham instead of turkey, I'm going to slap him. "On what?"

"Are you on the menu?"

I tilt my head. "Are you flirting with me?"

He watches me while I wait for his answer, and then he laughs. "No, Claire, I'm just messing with you."

"Oh." *Damn.*

CHAPTER
Five

Trevor

I 'll be damned if she doesn't look disappointed by my answer.

Every time I see Claire, I tell myself to play it cool. No staring. No flirting. And absolutely no smokin' hot fantasies. Nine times out of ten I succeed, but today is that tenth time, and I can't seem to control what comes out of my mouth. Oddly enough, she doesn't seem to be bothered by it, which I find fascinating.

I've seen the way women look at me—like I'm a piece of meat, someone to show them a good time. I can hardly be mad because that's the vibe I've given off. But with Claire, it's always been different. When she looks at me, it's as though she's looking through me, tempting me to open myself up and tell her all my secrets, secrets I need to keep her away from. It's unnerving to say the least, and yet peaceful in a way I don't quite understand.

My reputation as a ladies' man is true. It's also a thing of the past. I've never been interested in a committed relationship, but lately the thought of taking home a beautiful woman, only to have her walk out a couple of hours later, never to be seen again, isn't as appealing as it once was.

Mom always said one of these days I'd feel the need to settle down. That need hasn't hit full force, but maybe this is the start of it, maybe it's somewhere on the horizon.

I have a feeling I could settle down with someone like Claire. Unfortunately, I'll never get the chance. Rhett and Coop would kill me if I laid a finger on her. And while I'm certain I could kick both of their asses with my hands tied behind my back, I have my own reasons to keep her at arm's length. But those reasons seem to fade when she's standing this close to me.

Tucking the rag into my pocket, I take a step back, hoping I'll be able to regain some of my sense. "Whatcha got for me?" I ask, nodding toward the brown bag in her hand.

Claire sets the bag on my tailgate and pulls out two sandwiches, chips, and a soda. "Figured you didn't bring lunch."

"You're right. I didn't. But this is great. Thank you." I grab the first sandwich and take a hearty bite.

"Were you planning on working through lunch or what?"

"This fence isn't going to mend itself, so yeah, I was plannin' on working through lunch."

Claire shakes her head. "All you Allens are so much alike. Work, work, work."

She hit the nail on the head with that one.

I have three brothers and a sister; Beau is the oldest brother, a freelance photographer who bops around the world. Then there are the twins, Cooper and Rhett. Coop owns Dirty Dicks, a local tavern and restaurant, and Rhett is a bull rider with the PBR, and he also works on the ranch with Dad. Aside from our blue eyes and mutual affection for the one and only Claire Daniels, the only thing we boys have in common is our work ethic. None of us knows when to quit or step back. We're always pushing ourselves beyond our limits. It seems the only one who has been able to find balance is Rhett, and that's all thanks to his relationship with Mo.

Then there's my baby sister, Adley—smart and sweet with the mouth of a sailor and more balls than most of the men in my fire department. Plus, she's got a heart made of pure gold, which explains why she's studying to be a nurse.

"Work isn't a bad thing. Keeps me out of trouble."

Claire raises a brow. "And by trouble you mean someone like Blondie who was trying to mount you in the bar last night?"

Is she jealous? I want to call her on it, but if I found out she was, in fact, jealous, that would add fuel to the fire already raging inside of me. "I didn't touch Ella."

"Ella? She has a name."

"She does. And the only reason I know it is because I used the jaws of life to get her out of a mangled car about a month ago."

"Oh." Claire blinks and looks down.

I follow her gaze, and that's when I notice the dog she's brought with her.

"Sometimes I forget you save lives for a living," she says.

"I don't save lives for a living. I'm a firefighter, Claire. Who's your friend?" I nod toward the fuzz ball prancing around in the grass like she's got a stick up her ass.

"Nice deflection," Claire says. "And this is Milo. He's blind, so be careful."

I squat down, offering the dog my hand to sniff. Milo prances toward me, sniffs around, and licks the tip of my finger before bouncing off to the next best thing. She gets tangled in the leash and falls down, but gets right back up.

"Sorry, sweetheart, but Milo is a girl. No male would flounce around like that."

"Excuse me," she scoffs, bending down to cover Milo's ears. "He doesn't flounce, and he is definitely a *he*."

"Oh yeah?" I lift a brow.

"Yeah."

"And you know this because..."

Claire opens her mouth to tell me how she knows, but nothing comes out. Probably because she knows I'm right.

"Because I just know." Turning away, she leads Milo back the same way they came. "How dare he question your masculinity?" She talks to the dog as if it's a person, and I laugh, following after her.

She only makes it about ten feet before I snag Milo off the ground.

"Hey. Give him back." She reaches for the dog, but I'm much taller than Claire, and I keep the pooch raised above her head.

She jumps several times, her breasts rubbing against me in the process, and I'm tempted to hand the dog back before I get a hard-on, but Claire feels too damn good, and I can't bring myself to do it.

Eventually she gives up. "Damn you for being so tall."

"If you stop, I'll prove to you Milo is not a boy."

"Fine." She crosses her arms over her chest, fluffing her tits to perfection, and watches me.

I flip Milo over, tucking her in the crook of my arm. Her tail hangs down, her legs parting as she graciously accepts a belly rub. There's a ton of fur down there, but when I push some of it aside Claire can easily see.

"No penis or balls. Your little friend Milo is a girl."

Milo wriggles at the sound of her name, scrounging to crawl up my chest, and I maneuver her accordingly while smiling proudly at Claire. Milo finally reaches my neck and licks a slobbery path from my collarbone to my ear.

"Awww… She loves you."

"Most women do."

Claire rolls her eyes and takes the dog from me. Milo commences licking Claire's neck the same way she did mine. *Lucky bitch.* That's what I'd like to be doing.

"Goodbye, Trevor."

Claire walks away, her denim-clad ass swaying from side to side and fueling every single fantasy I've ever had about her.

And damn it, now I'm going to have to work the rest of the day with a hard-on.

CHAPTER
Six

Claire

"Sorry, sweetie." I put Milo in her cage, giving her one last pat on the head before I lock it up. All of the dogs are cuddled up on their beds with full bellies, perfectly content to be in for the night. Not one of them lifts a head to bid me farewell... Well, no one except Milo. She's still yapping away, wondering where her new sidekick is going. I felt guilty putting her away earlier so I carted her around with me the entire day.

I shut off the light on my way out of the kennel, hoping she'll get the hint and go to bed like the rest of the animals—like I want to do. Today was exhausting. I don't know how Mo does this day in and day out. She's in tip-top shape, that's for sure. Me? I ache in places I didn't know a woman could ache, and I scratched my arm on a nail in the barn. Damn thing bled for almost an hour. I should probably get it checked out, but I don't do hospitals, so that's a big no-go. I'd rather end up with a scar than chance a silly doctor trying to stitch it up.

By the time I do one final walk-through, the sun is setting, my stomach is growling, and Trevor is walking out of the barn.

"Heading home for the night?" he asks, pulling his gloves off. He tosses them in the back of his truck before walking toward me.

"Yup. You?"

"Nah. I'm going to grab a bite from Dirty Dicks and then come back out here and do a few more things before calling it a night."

"Mmmm," I moan, letting my eyes drift shut. "A juicy burger from Dirty Dicks sounds amazing."

"Careful, Claire."

Trevor's gravelly warning wraps around me, and I go perfectly still. Slowly, I open my eyes. He's taken a few steps back, his body drawn tight as though he's physically holding himself back from something.

But from what? Me?

Next thing I know, he's barreling toward me, his eyes clouded with determination.

He grabs my arms and *oh God*, this is it. He's going to kiss me.

"You're bleeding." He twists my arm to get a better look, but the touch of his hand causes a zap of energy to race up my arm, and I pull away.

"Huh?" I say, looking at my arm to see if his touch burned me. But there's nothing but a dusting of goose bumps.

"You have a cut on your arm," he says, nodding toward the blood.

"Oh. Uh…" I look at my arm again, trying to collect my thoughts.

How foolish of me to believe Trevor would kiss me out of nowhere. I've known him for years, and not once has he tried to put the moves on me, why on Earth would he do it now?

I shake my head. "It's nothing. Scratched it in the barn earlier."

"It doesn't look like nothing." He reaches for my arm again. "That's deep. You might need stitches. And a tetanus shot."

"No and no."

"What do you mean no?"

"I don't do needles." I try to pull my arm away again, but this time he has a firm grip.

"Let me clean it up, get a better look at it, and I'll be able to tell."

"It's fine. I'll clean it up when I get home."

"Quit being difficult and let me help you." Grabbing my hand, Trevor leaves no room for argument. With my fingers wrapped in his so I can't get away, he unlocks Animal Haven and leads me to the bathroom.

Standing beside the sink, I watch carefully as Trevor pours peroxide on a cotton ball and brings it to my arm.

"Shit," I hiss, flinching away from him.

"Sorry. There's a lot of blood, some of it dried, so this might take a minute or two."

I grimace. "Just make it quick. I don't have a high pain tolerance."

Trevor grins and looks up. "You never have. Remember that time Rhett, Coop, Beau, and I took you, Mo, and Charlene hiking, and you twisted your ankle? You cried like you lost a damn limb—"

"Yes, Trevor, I remember," I admonish. "No need to remind me."

"I didn't mind carrying you down the hill that day."

What? "You didn't carry me down the hill, Beau did."

"Nope. Pretty sure I remember that day because it was the first time I ever got to touch you, and I was on cloud nine. Walked as slow as I could just so I'd get to hold you a little longer."

My jaw drops open. I don't even know how to respond to that as I work my brain, trying to remember the details of that afternoon.

"Don't think about it too hard, sweetheart." He laughs when I roll my eyes. "Where's Milo? I thought for sure you'd end up taking her home."

"No. I don't really do animals."

"What are you talking about? You love animals."

"I never said I don't love them; I just don't own them. Never have."

Trevor's stops dabbing at my cut. "You've never had a pet? How did I not know that?"

I shrug. "Nope. My parents said we didn't have time for one."

"It's never too late. You could get one now."

"I know, but I'm not sure I'm ready. They're a lot of work. I couldn't imagine doing this sort of thing day in and day out."

"You're ready." He says, wiping away more dried blood. "And you've got to remember, you'd only have one, not the twenty or thirty you take care of out here."

"Yeah, I guess you're right. Maybe I'll think about it. Sometimes it gets lonely coming home to an empty house."

"What about all the guys Mo has set you up with? They could come keep you company. Maybe next time Joseph wouldn't bring his mother."

I slap Trevor's shoulder, and he laughs.

"You are not allowed to make fun of my love life, Trevor Allen."

There's a pregnant pause. I watch Trevor's smile transform into something wistful. "For what it's worth, Joseph doesn't deserve you, and it's his loss. Any man would be lucky to have you, Claire. Don't ever think differently."

My heart swells at his kind words. Trevor and I have known each other for ages, but we aren't alone together often, and I don't think we've ever just sat down and talked. But I like it.

A little too much.

"That's worth a lot," I tell him. "Thank you."

He nods. "I also think you're ready for that dog and you'll make a great pet owner."

I smile to myself. "I'll think about it."

Neither of us says a word as he finishes cleaning my wound. After he's applied the triple antibiotic ointment and Band-Aid, he looks at me. "It's not as deep as it looked. I don't think you need stitches."

"Good," I sigh. "That's good. Because that would not have been pretty."

"But you will need a tetanus shot."

"I'll add it to my list of things to do."

"I'm serious, Claire." He gives me a firm look. "Soon. You need to have the vaccine within twenty-four hours of the injury."

My eyes drop to where Trevor's hand is wrapped around my arm. His thumb makes slow, circular movements just above my elbow, and I wonder what it would feel like to have his hands touching other places on my body.

I draw in a shaky breath and look up. "Okay. I'll go after work tomorrow."

"Good."

His smile is so potent that I have to suck in a shaky breath. His lips are ruddy and full and look so damn soft—and screw his hands, I wonder what is mouth would feel like trailing across my skin, latching onto my breast, traveling down my stomach. And is it just me or did he move closer?

"Promise me." His warm breath fans the side of my face, sending a shiver down my spine.

Even after a long day of work, he smells amazing. I want to yank him in, bury my face in his neck, and smell him some more, maybe take a little taste. Instead, I stand motionless, afraid that if I move he'll move, and I definitely don't want that. But I do have to squeeze my thighs together to suppress the growing ache. It doesn't do any good.

"I promise," I whisper.

I force my eyes to his. Tension thickens, heat creeping between us, and as if he's reading my thoughts, Trevor's eyes dip to my mouth. I'd give anything to know what he's thinking, but judging by his erection, which is pressing against my hip, I think I have a pretty good idea.

"Good. That's good." His hand slides down my arm, and his head drops. He watches his fingers slip off my hand and land on my hip. When he looks up, his eyes are hooded, and I silently urge him to do it—just do it already.

Kiss me.

He takes a breath.

Sweet baby Jesus, this is it.

"Claire?"

"Hmmm?"

"Tell me not to kiss you."

I should. You know it, I know it, but… "I can't."

Trevor leans in close. My lips part, and I close my eyes.

"Last chance," he warns.

Curling his fingers around my hip, he tugs me forward until my body is flush against his. My heart beats rapidly, and there isn't a doubt in my mind he can feel it against his chest.

There's a pause, and then his hand is gone from my body. A second later he's cupping my jaw as though my face were made of porcelain. I hold my breath, waiting to feel whether his lips are as soft as they look.

"Breathe, Claire."

I do, and on my next breath, Trevor's lips brush mine. It's gentle and sweet, and I try to tell myself it's no different than any other first kiss I've had with a man. But I'm lying. It's different because with this kiss, I melt. With this kiss, my heart thunders inside my chest, and my toes curl in my boots, and I dig my fingers into his shirt as I hold him to me because I can't get enough.

This kiss is everything I've hoped for and everything I've told myself I didn't want or need. But I want it, and I want it with Trevor. Far too soon, the kiss ends, and I open my eyes.

Trevor's blue eyes are wide, pupils dilated, and all of the desire coursing through me reflects in his gaze.

"What are we doing?" he asks, rubbing absently at his bottom lip.

"No clue. But I want to do it again." I push up on my toes, sealing my mouth over his, and when he groans, I push my tongue inside his mouth. His tongue brushes against mine, exploring my mouth while I do the same, and you'd never guess that this was our first dance because Trevor kisses me like it's something he's been doing for years.

Wrapping an arm around my waist, he hoists me onto the sink. He uses his knee to push mine apart and steps between my legs. I wrap my thighs around his hips, pulling him to me. Trevor threads his fingers into my hair.

No kiss has ever felt this good, this right. I get lost in his touch, in his scent, in him, knowing I'll never be the same. With one kiss, Trevor Allen has ruined me for all other men.

Like all good things, this kiss comes to an end, and Trevor rests his forehead against mine. It takes a couple of seconds for me to catch my breath, but when I do, I smile.

"I have no idea what just happened there," he says.

"It's called a kiss," I quip.

He pinches my side, and I giggle, my knee jerking up.

"*Ooomph.*" Trevor winces and doubles over.

CHAPTER
Seven

Trevor

"You kneed me in the junk."

Claire's eyes widen, her pink lips part. "Oh my God. I'm so sorry. Are you okay?" She reaches for my cock as if she can somehow make it better.

Standing up, I band my arm around her back and hold her to me. The last thing she needs to see is my erection, which is growing by the second with her tight little body writhing against mine.

"I'm fine," I answer, realizing that rather than seeing it, she's now likely feeling it.

Screw it.

I refuse to apologize for the way my body reacts to hers. Oddly enough, she doesn't seem affected by it.

"Are you sure?"

"Positive." I drop my head to her shoulder, needing a moment to catch my breath and process these…these strange feelings coursing through me.

Claire Daniels is the only woman in this town who gets my blood pumping. I've been lusting after her since the fifth grade when she showed up at the rock quarry in a purple bikini. Until tonight, I thought she looked at me as nothing but a distant friend, which worked perfectly, because if that's all I was to her, there was no reason to tell her my secret, a secret I've carried around for thirteen years. But clearly, I was wrong. It's one thing to watch Claire from afar, but it's entirely different having her in my arms and knowing that the giant secret I've kept for so long could ruin us before we've even started.

I want to blurt it out right now just so we can move forward without anything between us, but I'm not ready for that—and I'm not sure Claire is ready for that. I'm not even sure there'd be anything left between us after I spoke. But my only other option is to walk away now, and after getting a taste of her, I'm not sure that's an option.

You have to, I remind myself. Something between Claire and me could never work. There are too many things working against us, too much history between us—history she doesn't even know about.

But I'm a selfish bastard, and even though I know I should climb in my truck and never look back, I'm finding it increasingly difficult to do.

When I look up, she smiles. Her green eyes are shining with a brightness I haven't seen in far too long, and I'll be damned if that doesn't make me feel ten feet tall.

"Hi," she says.

"Hi."

"We were talking about that kiss," she adds, softly.

"Best damn kiss I've ever had."

Claire's cheeks turn pink. She rests her forehead to my chest and laughs.

"Most women don't laugh when I compliment them."

My words only make her laugh harder, and after a couple of

seconds I find myself laughing along with her.

"Why are you laughing?" I ask.

She looks up, her eyes wet with tears. I sweep a stray hair from her face and tuck it behind her ear.

"Because I finally get you in my arms, and I knee you in the balls. Only *I* would do something like that."

The smile falls from my face. This is another reason I find Claire so incredibly attractive. She's honest to a fault. But that's not what has all coherent thought flying from my brain—it's the other thing. The really important and shocking thing.

"Finally?"

She pulls her bottom lip between her teeth and watches me. Lifting my hand, I tug on her chin until her lip pops free.

"I sort of, maybe have a thing for you," she whispers.

"I know."

"You do?"

"Figured it out when you attacked my mouth."

"What?" Her jaw drops, and when I smile, she punches me in the shoulder. "You attacked my mouth first, mister."

Wrapping my fingers around her wrist, I hold her in place. I shouldn't tell her I feel the same way. It'll only make what I have to do that much harder, but I'll be damned if I let her share her feelings and walk away thinking I don't feel the same.

"You're damn right I did, because I sort of, maybe have a thing for you too."

Claire's lips fall open. "You do?"

I laugh. "Why do you find that so hard to believe? You're a beautiful woman, Claire. You're smart, funny—"

"Old," she inserts.

"Old? You are not old."

"I'm four years older than you."

"Are you serious right now?"

She pinches her lips together and glares at me. This is the first time I've seen her flustered, and I like it.

"When I was twenty, you were only sixteen."

"Well, you're not twenty anymore, and while I still have the stamina of my sixteen-year-old self, I assure you I've matured physically and emotionally."

She swallows, all humor gone from her face as she looks down at my erection nestled between her legs. "I know."

I've never seen nervous Claire either, and I like her just as well—although the last thing I want Claire to be around me is nervous.

"Is that why you never told me? Because of our age differ- ence?" Not that it matters, but I want to know.

"Mostly that—and because you're Rhett and Coop's little brother."

"Yeah, I'm pretty sure they'll want to kill me when they find out about this."

"You don't look too worried."

I grin. "I'm not."

"What now?"

Now comes the hard part, sweetheart—the words that will likely kill me to say. "Despite how both of us feel, we can't act on it."

She blinks, and then blinks again. "We can't?"

I shake my head. Pressing my palm against her cheek, I move my fingers through her hair and curl them around her head. Slowly, gently, I pull her face to mine. Her eyes dart to my lips, and the need to taste her, one last time, is too strong. My lips find hers, and Claire's eyes flutter closed as she falls against me. Her lips are soft, and she tastes so damn good, but that's all this is—all it can be—a taste.

Claire peels her eyes open when I pull back. "Are you sure

you don't want to change your mind? Because I'd really like to explore that a little more."

I groan, pressing my lips to hers again, wanting her to feel how hard this is for me, to know that walking away from her is the hardest thing I've had to do in a damn long time. She opens to me on a sigh, and I stroke her tongue with mine until her body relaxes against me.

"I've got to admit, Trevor, I'm not sure where you're coming from," she mumbles against my lips.

I place my forehead to hers and smile. "You're making this so hard."

Her body wriggles against mine. "That's not a bad thing."

"It's a very bad thing," I say, watching her smile die. "Because we can't be together."

"Remind me again why that is."

Because I'm a coward. Because I don't deserve your attention, let alone your affection, although I crave it more than you'll ever know. "There are so many reasons I don't even know where to start."

"Humor me."

"There's Rhett and Coop for one."

"I can handle them."

"How about the fact that you're relationship material, and I'm the farthest thing from it."

"Who said anything about a relationship?"

"Come on, Claire, you're a relationship kind of girl, and that's not a bad thing. And what about your rule? You don't date firefighters, remember?" *And for a damn good reason.*

"Oh, right." The hope drains from her face. "That pesky little occupation." She worries her bottom lip for a few seconds. "I'm starting to wonder if my rules are stupid."

"Your rules aren't stupid. They're logical, and you have

them in place for a reason, and while I believe that someday you will move past them, I don't think today is that day. And I'm not sure I want to be the test dummy."

Her cheeks flush, and she looks down. "Maybe you're right."

"Small steps, Claire. Maybe you should start with Milo."

"So where do we go from here?" she asks, looking up.

"We go back to doing what we've always done."

"And what's that?"

"I flirt and annoy you, and call you Red, and you ignore me. It's our thing."

"I've never been able to ignore you."

"Pretend."

"So, we just forget tonight happened? I'm not sure I can do that."

"I hope you don't forget it, because I sure as hell won't. Tonight becomes a fond memory—one of many between us— that we'll file away like all the others."

She nods, her wistful smile transforming into a yawn.

"It's been a long day." I brush a thumb across her plump bottom lip. "It's getting late. You should head home and get some sleep. You're probably going to be sore tomorrow."

Claire slides off the bathroom counter. She's halfway out the door when she turns around. "Tonight wasn't a mistake, right?"

"Not at all." *I'm protecting you, Red. I'm protecting both of us.* Because losing Claire over what I did would be far worse than never having her at all. "It just can't happen again."

She flashes me her beautiful smile one last time. "See you around, Trevor."

CHAPTER
Eight

Claire

"What are you doing here? You do realize you aren't on the schedule to volunteer tonight, right?" Mo says, swirling in her seat when I blow by her.

"I know." I disappear into the back room where Mo keeps the animal supplies she gives away with an adoption. Doggie bed. *Check.* Food bowl. *Check.* Adoption blanket. *Check.* Treats. *Check.*

"Would you like a box for all of that?" Mo asks.

"That would be great. Thank you."

She looks at me strangely and then disappears, returning a couple of seconds later with a cardboard box. I dump everything in my arms into the box and take it from her.

"Um…Claire?"

"Yeah?"

"What are you doing with all of that?"

"I've decided to adopt Milo."

Mo furrows her brow, but I don't have time to stop and explain because I have a million things to do today, and I still need to go buy a collar and a leash.

"Who's Milo again?" she asks, following me out to my car.

I put the box in the back seat. "The blind Pomeranian."

I've thought about Milo several times over the last week. Trevor's encouraging words about getting her have been ringing in my head, and I think maybe he's right. Maybe I need to start with something small like adopting a dog—which I've always wanted to do—before I go rearranging all of my well-laid plans about life and love and who I'll date. I finally figured, why not? What am I waiting for? My life to get on track? Because it's about as on track as it's going to get.

Sure, Trevor derailed me a little bit with those sinful lips of his, but ever since that encounter, I've felt rejuvenated and ready to take on the world.

"Wait a minute. *You* want to adopt the blind Pomeranian?"

I nod.

"And you named her Milo?" Mo asks.

What about this is so hard to understand? I nod again.

"You do realize Milo is a boy's name, right? And she's a girl."

"Yes, Mo, I know. Trevor made a big spectacle of pointing that out." I step around her, intent on getting Milo and taking her to her new home. "Now if you'll excuse me, I have a million things to do today."

I can hear Mo's footsteps behind me as I walk into the kennel, but they're quickly drowned out by the ear-piercing sound of a dog's cry.

"Is that Milo?" I ask, rushing toward her cage.

"She's been crying for days, and nothing I do makes her better. I've changed her bedding, tried different foods, taken her to the vet…I have no idea what's wrong with her."

I flick the lock and fling the door open. Milo is sitting in the corner, her little body shaking as she howls blindly at the ceiling. It's as though she trying to get someone's attention, and I think I know who that someone is.

Squatting down, I call out to her. "Milo, come here, girl."

Milo stops howling at the sound of her name. With her nose in the air, she angles her face toward my voice.

"Well, I'll be damned." Mo looks at me. "That's the first time she's stopped crying in a week."

"Because she missed me." Milo inches toward me, veering off to the side, but rather than pick her up, I let her find her way to me, and she does. Her tongue darts out, tasting the tip of my finger, and then she spins in a circle and barks.

"That's right. You remember me," I say, picking her up. She nuzzles her wet nose to the side of my neck. "You missed me, didn't you, girl?"

"Arf."

"That's what I thought." With Milo against my chest, I step out of the cage. "We bonded last Monday."

Mo is smiling. "I can see that."

"I want her, Mo."

Mo's smile wanes. "Are you sure? Because I've tried to get you to adopt a dog before, and you've always resisted. I just don't want you to get her home and change your mind; that would break her little heart."

"I'm positive, and I won't change my mind."

"Then I guess she's yours."

"Did you hear that?" I coo. "You're officially mine. Milo Daniels. Has a nice ring to it."

"It's not official yet. I still need you to sign some paperwork."

"Absolutely. And I'll pay the adoption fee."

Mo waves me off. "You help me out so much around here, I could never take your money. Consider Milo an early birthday gift."

My birthday isn't for months, but I'll take it. "Thank you, Mo."

Mo gathers all of the appropriate paperwork, which I fill out and sign, and then we redo the paperwork for Milo's chip, assigning me as her owner and contact if it ever gets scanned.

"That's it." Mo shuts the manila envelope. "Milo is officially yours."

I look down at Milo, who is sleeping comfortably in my lap, and scratch the top of her head. "I think we're going to do great together."

"I think you will too. Is there anything else you need before you go? Any supplies to get you started?"

"I don't think so. I've got what I stole from your supply cabinet, and that should get me going until we get settled."

Milo doesn't move a muscle when I stand. She's limp in my arms as I carry her to the car, but when my step falters at the big truck parked next to mine, her head pops up.

Trevor climbs out of his truck, tucks his hands in his pockets, and leans a hip against the driver's door. "Whatcha got there?"

"I took your advice. As of sixty seconds ago, Milo is mine."

A knowing smile pulls at the corner of his mouth. Pushing away from his truck, Trevor walks over to me and pets Milo. She licks frantically at his hand but can't quite catch a finger before he pulls back.

"Good choice." His eyes sweep the length of my body. "Lookin' good, Red."

"You don't look so bad yourself."

I hear Mo gasp beside me as Trevor does one of those sexy nods that men do. He walks away, and I can't help but call out to him, needing to see that sexy smirk one more time.

"Hey, Trevor?"

He turns around and grins but keeps walking backward.

"I got my tetanus shot."

His grin stretches across his face. "Good girl. Would you like some sort of prize?"

I shrug, feeling bold and beautiful in his presence. "You could do us all a favor and take your shirt off."

"You first, sweetheart."

"In your dreams."

"Don't I know it." He laughs and steps into the barn.

I look at Mo, and her jaw is practically dragging the ground.

"Umm…what was that?" she asks, putting her hand on my forehead.

I swat her hand away. "What?"

"First the dog and then whatever that was between you and Trevor. Are you feeling okay?"

"I'm fine, and *that* was nothing."

"Mmm-hmm. Try again."

Laughing, I open my car door and climb in. "Goodbye, Mo."

"You're really not going to tell me? Come on, Claire, we're best friends. You can tell me if there's something going on between you and Trevor."

"There's nothing to tell. I'll call you later."

I shut the door, set Milo in the front seat, and check my rearview mirror as I pull out of Animal Haven. Sure enough, Mo is still standing there, hands on her hips, but it's Trevor's eyes I catch a glimpse of, and they hold mine as I drive away.

CHAPTER
Nine

Claire

"Knock, knock." I push open the front door at my mom and Phil's house and poke my head around the corner. She's standing at the sink doing dishes, but as soon as she hears my voice she turns around.

"Hey, sweetheart." Tossing the rag over her shoulder, she walks into the living room and pulls me into a warm embrace.

Sharon Daniels is the best mother a girl could ask for. After Daddy passed away, our lives weren't easy, but you'd never know it. She pulled up her pants—figuratively, of course—and despite her grief, fell easily into the dual role of mom and dad. And I sure as hell didn't make it easy on her. To say that I handled my father's passing poorly is a huge understatement.

The denial stage didn't last long for me—a few days tops. And not long after Dad's funeral came the anger. I was angry at him for going back into that building. Angry at myself for being angry at him. Angry at Mom for being seemingly unaffected by the whole thing—although I know now she was putting on a front to stay strong for me. I spent days in bed, crying my eyes out, and then throwing things around my room. But Mom was always right there with a gentle touch and enough encouraging words to coax me into the shower or to eat a hot meal.

The bargaining and depression phase was nothing but a big blur of emotional mess. Tears. Crying. Screaming. Sleeping for days. Refusing to go to school. Refusing to see my friends. Refusing to live. Not even Mo could get through to me.

And then, somehow, came the acceptance. It took years, but with my mother's unwavering support and love—and her example of bravery and perseverance—I finally came to accept that my father was gone. Some days—especially holidays or birthdays—I still expect to see the fire truck pull up in front of the house. I'm not sure that'll ever go away. I'm not sure I want it to. Because unlike when I was younger, I can look back on those memories—the memories of my father dressed in his turnouts barging through the door, scooping me up, and tossing me over his shoulder while he gave my mother a kiss; Mom and me taking Christmas cookies to the firehouse and listening to the guys all fawn over my mother's baking skills—and feel something other than devastating emptiness. I can feel the joy I had in those moments, though they're long past, and they remind me of the duty I have to be the woman my father would have wanted me to be. Careful, loyal, brave, strong.

A smile tugs at the corner of my mouth. Maybe I should bake cookies and take them to Trevor.

"Where's my grandpup?" Mom asks, looking around at our feet.

"Oh, um, she's still outside." I turn around and whistle. "Come on, Milo. Do your business already."

Milo doesn't pay me any attention. She simply walks in circles, sniffing the ground.

"I don't know what she's looking for: the dog can't see."

Mom laughs, and about that time Milo drops a load, kicks

at the grass with her hind legs, and darts toward the porch—except she forgets she's blind and runs face first into the base of the step.

I can't help it, I laugh. One of these days she'll learn that she has to use her other senses to find her way around. I walk down the steps, scoop her up, and go back into the house, shutting the door behind me.

I've only had Milo for a couple of weeks, but I'm learning so much about her and how she maneuvers through her world as a blind dog. And what I'm learning is she doesn't do it well. Her biggest tool is her nose, which she's using now.

Milo juts her snout into the air, and I know she's familiar and comfortable with her surroundings when she starts to squirm. I let her down, and she sniffs her way to Mom.

"Yeah, you know who your grandma is, don't you?" Mom lifts Milo up and walks into the kitchen. "Do you want a treat? I bought some just for you."

Milo barks and then barks again, showing her approval.

"She's already had two treats."

Mom shakes her head. "This dog is the closest thing I've got to a grandchild, and until you settle down and decide to pop out kids, don't tell me I can't spoil her."

"Fine." I roll my eyes. "You just had to throw that in there, didn't you?"

"I'm not getting any younger, Claire Daniels, and neither are you." She grabs a treat from the bowl in her cabinet.

Mom went a little crazy when she found out I'd adopted Milo. Turns out she always wanted a dog; it was Dad who didn't. I asked her why we never got one after his death, but she said it was hard enough managing me. She couldn't imagine throwing a dog into the mix.

"Don't rush me, Mother. Mo is bad enough. The last thing I

need is you on my case too."

"I'm sorry, sweetheart." She feeds Milo the treat and turns to me. "I'm not rushing you. It would just be nice to see my only child settle down."

"I am settled down. I have my own home, a great career, and a dog. It could be worse; I could be whoring myself around town, sleeping with every Tom, Dick, and Harry who looked my way."

"Okay, smartass," she quips. "You know what I mean."

"I do, and I promise that if and when I find a good man, you'll be the first to know."

I don't bother telling her that I think I've already found him, because I don't want to get her hopes up—or my hopes, for that matter. I still have to find a way to snag him. And by him, I mean Trevor.

It's been three weeks since our heated kiss, and I've thought about him every second of every day. I've thought about the touch of his skin against mine, his soft lips, and the way he held me as if I was the most precious thing in the world. I've never felt so alive and wanted, and it's made me think long and hard about what I'd begun to realize about my rules even before my disaster of a date with Joseph. I've bubble-wrapped the passion right out of my relationships. Of course I need to be careful and responsible, but maybe relaxing my stringent standards a bit would be worth it if it meant getting to experience what I felt in that bathroom with Trevor again.

That thought alone makes my heart race and my palms sweat, but it no longer gives me the urge to throw up. I'm left wondering if those sensations are of anticipation rather than dread.

There's only one way to find out.

The only problem? I haven't seen Trevor to tell him, and it

hasn't been for lack of trying. I've done all the things I normally do, including dinner at Dirty Dicks with Mo and Rhett, and I even had an impromptu girl's night out with Mo, Tess, and Trevor's sister, Adley, hoping I'd catch a glimpse of him at the bar. But he was nowhere to be seen either time.

I could pick up the phone and call him, but what would I say? *Hey, remember that kiss we shared? I haven't been able to stop thinking about it. Wanna do it again?*

"You better get going or you're going to be late."

I look down at my watch. Crap. "I have three classes tonight, and the last one gets over at eight, so I should be back here to pick up Milo by eight fifteen."

Milo is spoiled rotten, and I learned the hard way that when I come home from work, she expects me to stay there and pamper her. And by the hard way I mean she destroyed my favorite heels and we went three days without speaking to each other. Needless to say, from now on, when I volunteer in the evenings, she comes to Mom and Phil's, who don't seem to mind one bit.

"Okay, sweetie, go do your thing."

I kiss Mom on the cheek, then Milo, and I slip out the door.

CHAPTER
Ten

Claire

"Tara, keep your eyes on your own paper."

"Yes, Ms. Daniels." She bites her bottom lip and drops her eyes to the worksheet in front of her.

"Ms. Daniels, can I use the restroom?"

"Me too."

I look at the identical little faces. Troy and Marcus have light blond hair, pale green eyes, and porcelain skin. If I didn't know better, I'd swear they were angels. But they're not, which is why they spend two hours a week here with me. If any of the kids in my class are going to move their clip down for talking, it's these two.

"I don't know, can you?"

Marcus smiles and tries again. "May we use the restroom?"

Troy shifts around in his seat, crossing his legs. If I don't give them an answer, I'll be stuck cleaning up the mess.

"Troy, you go first and then Marcus can go."

Troy jumps from his seat while Marcus' eyes grow wide. "I

can't hold it," he whines.

I sigh. "Fine. Both of you go. Be quick, don't play, and wash your hands when you're done."

You'd think first graders wouldn't need detailed instructions on using the bathroom, but you'd be surprised.

The twins scurry off. I peek my head out the door and watch each of them walk into the bathroom before I pull the door shut and allow my gaze to travel across the classroom. Although it's not really a classroom—not like the one I'm used to.

During the day I teach first grade at Heaven Elementary School, and on Wednesday nights I volunteer here. Bright Start Learning Center is in an old home that's been refurbished into a tutoring facility. The number of kids I tutor varies based on child need, but I have a consistent group of ten, all of whom are present tonight. They range from first grade to third and come from both the public and private school, and three of them, the twins included, are also in my regular first grade class.

Laughter drifts through the thin walls, drawing the attention of Josephine and Tara. I clear my throat, and both girls look at me before shifting their eyes to their papers. The house is small, with six different rooms, each filled with anywhere from five to ten kids. On some nights, with kids being kids, it gets a little loud in here.

Cecelia raises her hand, and I make my way across the room to kneel next to her desk.

"Can you help me with this?" she asks.

I spend the next several minutes showing her how to regroup numbers. When we're done, I look for the twins, but they're still not back.

"Class, keep working. I'm going to check on Marcus and Troy."

I'm three steps from the door when the fire alarms start blaring.

You've got to be kidding me.

The kids cover their ears against the shrill sound. A few of them jump from their seats, but I hold up a hand.

"Stay in your seats. I'm sure it's a false alarm." Wouldn't be the first time, and I'm sure it won't be the last.

The junior high kids are the worst. At least once a month one of them gets the wild idea to pull the fire alarm in hopes of going home early. Unfortunately, it usually works. By the time everyone evacuates the building and the local fire department sweeps the house, it's usually time to leave.

Normally it doesn't take long for the teacher of the offending kid to figure out what happened and shut the alarm off, but tonight that isn't the case. I stride across the classroom and yank open the door to find out what's going on, and that's when I catch the faint smell of smoke.

Kids are running through the building—a few of them crying, others covering their mouths with their hands—and that's when I realize this isn't a false alarm.

One of the other teachers comes barreling down the hall yelling, "Fire! Fire! Everyone out!"

Shit.

I spin around. "Leave your bags. We need to get out of here," I say as calmly as I can.

But it's too late, my kids are scrambling toward the door, knocking Tara over in the process.

"Slow down," I holler, rushing after them. I lift Tara into my arms and race after the kids. The smell of smoke is getting stronger, and a few of the kids are coughing. We make it to the closest exit, which happens to be the back door. Sirens bellow through the air, alerting us that help is on the way.

Setting Tara on her feet, I usher her out the door, along with the other students.

It's chaotic to say the least, with kids running around screaming and a few of them pulling out their cell phones while the teachers struggle to keep everyone in one area.

"Ethan, get over here!" I yell, moving my group away from the building. I snag his wrist before he can run off, and then I scan the group to make sure all of my kids are present.

One. Two. Three. Four. Five. Six. Seven. Eight.

Eight.

Shit.

I count again, this time looking at faces rather than counting heads.

Christopher. Ethan. Josephine. Tara. Eleanor. Cecelia. Ava. Phillip. Drew.

Eight.

Shit. Troy and Marcus!

"I need you guys to stay here, okay?" Their little heads nod while I reach for the arm of one of the high school students. "Stay with this group. There are eight. Don't let them out of your sight. Got it?"

Before she can answer, I'm running through the yard, scanning the crowd in hopes that the boys ran out when they heard the alarm. My eyes sweep left to right, and when I don't immediately find them, panic sets in.

My heart pounds violently in my chest as I look at the house. I don't see flames, but smoke rolls from a few of the windows, and my adrenaline kicks in as I dash toward the door.

I can't leave the boys in there.

Please be okay.

Please be okay.

I chant those three words as I run through the back door, the same way we came out, and down the hall past my classroom. When I round the corner, I'm hit with a wall of smoke so thick it pulls me to my knees.

Jesus, how did it get this bad so fast?

For a split second I'm rendered helpless, and then, as if he's here with me, I hear my dad's voice in my head.

Cover your mouth.

Drop to the floor.

Get out.

Coughing, I lift the bottom of my shirt over my mouth and lower myself to the ground. The sound of the boys screaming powers me forward. I expect to hear my dad's voice yelling at me to turn around, to save myself, but I'm met with the distant sound of a fire roaring and another ear-piercing shriek.

With my belly on the floor, I crawl to the bathroom, kick the door open with my feet, and then I see them. Troy and Marcus are huddled in the corner beneath one of the sinks. The brothers are holding onto each other for dear life, and when they see me, Troy bursts into tears.

A billow of smoke follows me in, and I quickly kick the door shut, grateful that smoke hasn't saturated the small room. I take a deep breath as I scurry across the floor and fall to my knees in front of the boys.

Troy reaches for me first, locking his arms around my neck. "Are we gonna die?" he cries.

"No, sweetie, we're not gonna die, but I do need to get the two of you out of here. I need you both to be really brave for me, okay?"

Marcus nods.

Troy's grip tightens.

I pry his arms off of me. Tugging my sweater over my head, I hand it to Marcus and then peel my shirt off and hand it to Troy, grateful that I still have on a camisole. It's usually nice in Texas in early spring, but the evenings can get cool—and so can this old building—which is why I dress in layers.

"Hold these over your mouths. Stay as close to the floor as you can get. We're going to get out of here."

Eyes wide, Troy frantically shakes his head. "I can't. I'm scared."

"I know you are, but we're going to be okay. I promise I will get you out of here."

My father was the best damn firefighter in the county. When I was young, he taught me all the basic knowledge someone would need to survive a fire—although running back into a smoldering building would've been a huge no-no. Each one of those warnings and instructions—not to mention my perpetual desire to make him proud—rages through my head as I look at the door handle. It doesn't look hot, but that doesn't mean shit, and the door only swings one way: in. I borrow the sweater I gave Marcus, wrap it around my hand and open the door.

A lick of fire darts in front of me, and I reel back, pulling the boys with me as the door slams shut.

"What do we do?" Marcus asks, scooting close to his brother. His wide eyes watch me as he covers his mouth and begins to cough.

Smoke starts to seep under the door, and all I know is we've run out of time. I need to get these kids out of here, but it isn't safe. The fire has clearly spread, and I can't risk our lives by going out there. Our only hope now is that the fire department does a sweep and gets to us before the flames do.

"Boys, I want you to sit together in that back corner," I say, pointing toward the opposite side of the room.

I shove my sweater under the faucet, drenching it in water until it's heavy and saturated. Rolling it up, I stuff it in the small crack between the bottom of the door and the floor. That won't do much, but it might buy us a few minutes of cleaner air, and right now those few minutes might mean the difference between life and death.

CHAPTER
Eleven

Trevor

"Shit," I hiss under my breath when we roll up on scene. "This doesn't look good."

We got the call for a first-alarm fire less than ten minutes ago. We've been called to this address several times—three times this year already—and it's always a false alarm. Usually some punk who thought it would be funny to pull the alarm. But not tonight. Tonight there are flames shooting out the windows, and I'm instantly on high alert when I see a number of kids huddled around crying. My crew piles out of the three trucks while Chief doles out orders.

I'm wrapping blankets around a group of kids while other members of my crew prepare to fight the fire when I hear the chief ask someone if everyone made it out. Pushing to my feet, I turn toward him. He's talking with a young woman who can't be but a couple of years older than me.

"I...I think so," she stammers, looking around. "Some of the classes came out the back door, so maybe check back there to be sure."

"I'm on it."

Chief gives me the nod, and I weave my way through the young bodies toward the back of the house. Kids are milling around, crying. Maybe fifty or sixty of them, if I had to guess. They're all lucky they got out when they did, because this fire is raging, and the scene in front of me could've been much, much worse.

I find the first adult, a middle-aged man. There's a phone pressed to his ear, but he hands it off to one of his students when I approach.

"Are all of your kids accounted for?"

"Yeah," he sighs, stuffing his hands in his pockets. "All of my kids made it out."

"Great." I clap a hand to his shoulder before I turn to check the next group of kids.

"Wait!"

I turn to the right. A young girl, maybe fourteen or fifteen, is standing next to a group of kids. She shakes her head frantically, tears streaming down her face.

"Their teacher," she cries, motioning toward the group of kids huddled around her. "She went back in."

I close the distance between us. Everyone is running on high emotions, so I speak in a clear, steady voice. "Who is the teacher?"

"Claire Daniels," a little blonde girl says, looking up at me.

Shit!

My heart races in my chest as I squat down in front of the little girl. I put myself at her eye level and do my best to stay calm, though everything inside of me is screaming to run into that damn building and save Claire.

"Do you know why she went back in?" Claire is a smart girl—level headed—and there's no way she'd run into a burning building unless she felt she had a damn good reason, not after what happened to her father.

Her tiny head bobs. "Because she only counted eight of us, and there should've been ten."

I look at the group of kids, doing a quick count of my own, and sure enough, there are only eight. "Do you know who's missing?"

The little girl looks around at the other kids in her group as they watch the house go up in flames, and she nods. "Troy and Marcus. They're twins. They went to the bathroom before the fire alarm went off."

"Which way did she go in?"

The high school girl points to the back door. "Just a couple of minutes ago."

Smoke curls from the back door. This fire is escalating fast. There's no way Claire will make it out of there with two boys on her own.

Not alive anyway.

I hear the little girl burst into tears when I turn away. Chief is standing with a group of kids, but he steps away when I walk up.

"Three people are missing, a teacher and two boys. She couldn't find them after evacuation, so she went back in for them."

His jaw clenches as he looks at the charred house, no doubt thinking the same thing that's racing through my mind. I'm tempted to run in whether he likes it or not, but I'm not stupid, and I know if I want to get Claire out of there alive, I've got to keep a clear mind.

"We don't have much time," I urge.

"The structure is unstable. It isn't safe." Chief's words are clear, yet I hear the *but* in the tone of his voice.

"I know, sir. We can go in through the back. It doesn't look as engulfed."

His eyes are hard, but he nods. "In and out, Trevor. Take Mikey with you."

Mikey and I suit up while Chief shouts out directions to the rest of the crew.

Mikey and I grab a hose. Together we run along the house, breach the back entrance, and move through the building as quickly as we can. Thick black smoke hangs in the air, and if it weren't for our breathing apparatus, we'd never make it.

My chest constricts at the thought of Claire and those two boys sitting somewhere in here, struggling to breathe while they wait for us to find them.

Hold on, Claire. I'm going to get you out.

I swallow hard, pushing the fear away as we inch through the house. My mind keeps reverting back to the kiss Claire and I shared, but I shove the thoughts away because my main focus—my only focus—is getting her and those boys out of here.

Mikey stops at the first classroom, but I wave him on. "To the bathroom," I yell. My voice is muffled by the mask, but he nods, and we move forward, examining each door until we find one labeled *Boys*.

I reach for my ax, prepared to knock the door down if it's locked, but when Mikey pushes, it opens. He pushes again, but something causes the door to jam. Mikey gives the door a solid shove, dislodging a dark chunk of material. A sweater or jacket maybe, and I just know Claire put it there.

Good girl.

Flames ripple along the ceiling. I tap Mikey's shoulder, motioning for him to take the hose and douse the ceiling, covering me as I search the bathroom. Even in turnouts, the heat is hot, and I pray Claire and the boys haven't passed out.

I cut my way through the heavy smoke until I can see them.

Claire has the boys tucked in the back corner of the room. They're facing away from me. She's huddled over them, shielding their bodies as best she can, and the tightness in my chest eases just a fraction.

"Claire!" I yell, moving toward them.

Her head whips around, an iota of relief in her terrified gaze.

She opens her mouth, but all that comes out is a strangled cough. Pointing to the boys, she slides out of the way. One of the boys is unconscious, lying in a ball on the ground. The other peels his eyes open to look up at me, and I know he isn't far behind the other.

Mikey steps up and checks the boys' pulses while I pull out the extra oxygen masks. We place them over the boys and hand one to Claire. She situates it on her face and takes a few hits of oxygen.

I pull it away, allowing her time to cough before guiding it back to her mouth. "Slow, deep breaths," I instruct. "We're going to get you guys out of here."

She squeezes her eyes shut, tears falling down her face, and I fight every instinct I have to keep from pulling her into my arms. Right now she doesn't need affection or comfort, she needs to survive, and I'm ninety-nine-percent certain she has no idea who I am with my mask and gear on, which is probably a good thing. We both need to stay focused.

Mikey grabs the boy who's still awake, and I grab the other. "Are you okay to move?" I speak loudly so she can hear me through the mask, and she nods.

We turn toward the door, but the smoke is heavy, cutting our visibility to nothing. Mikey looks at me, and we lower ourselves to the floor, each of us cradling a boy against our side. Claire follows suit without guidance.

"I'll go first. Claire, you stay between me and Mikey." I grab onto the hose, motioning for her to do the same.

Slowly, we move along the wall and out of the bathroom. With the young boy tucked under my arm, I keep moving forward, knowing Mikey is behind Claire.

Every few seconds Claire coughs, but when I look back, she gives me a thumbs up. Debris is falling around us, but we eventually make it down the long hallway, and when the back door becomes visible, with specks of sunlight slicing through the dark clouds, I send up a silent prayer.

I can't see my fellow firefighters, but I know they're out there, keeping the flames at bay while we make the rescue.

"Almost there," I yell.

The closer we get to the back door, the better my visibility gets, and when the roar of the fire starts to die, I make a split-second decision to get us the hell out of here. Pushing to our feet, Mikey and I stand up. I reach down for Claire to help her up, but she doesn't move.

"Can you stand?"

She coughs, shaking her head. She blinks up at me, her lids sluggish, and I know she's running out of time.

I pass my boy off to Mikey. He hoists them both, making sure he has a good grip, and then he runs, following the hose out of the house.

I scoop Claire off the floor, and with her limp body in my arms, I make a mad dash for the back door.

A loud crack resonates through the air. My crew is yelling, waving at us through the doorway, and I keep plowing forward as I hear it again—another snap followed by a pop. I look up as the ceiling crumples, and I have just enough time to curl my body around Claire's, acting as a human shield against the falling debris, before it hits.

Chunks of the ceiling land on top of us with enough force to steal my breath. My body crumples over Claire's. My vision blurs, everything around me going black. I blink rapidly, struggling to stay awake, but it's too much. With a ragged breath, I press my mask to Claire's forehead, offering a silent apology for failing her yet again.

CHAPTER
Twelve

Claire

A tickle in my nose pulls me awake. I blink heavily against the florescent lights and swipe a hand across my face, but it gets caught on something plastic. I sit up in bed, pulling at the offending object.

Oxygen tubing?

Air hisses out of the nasal cannula. I stare at it, blinking, and then it hits me. The fire. I collapse against the pillows. My mind races to remember everything that happened, but it's all fuzzy.

"You're awake." Mom rushes into the room and wraps me in her arms. "Oh, baby, I've been worried sick about you." She kisses my forehead and my cheek, and then pulls back. "How do you feel?"

I take a deep breath and blow it out, taking stock of my body. Nothing feels out of the ordinary except a burning feeling at my forehead, but when I lift my hand, there's no bandage, so I must've imagined it. A glance under the blanket shows my legs and arms intact and sans any sort of cast. "I think I'm okay. What day is it?"

She frowns. "Thursday. You were in and out all night. The doctors said you hit your head pretty hard, but they don't believe you suffered a concussion, only smoke inhalation. You should make a full and quick recovery. But I think you took ten years off of my life. Thank God I have Phil. He kept me sane through all of this."

"I'm sorry, Mom."

She shakes her head and blinks away tears. "Don't be. You're here, and you're okay, and that's all that matters. Do you remember what happened?"

"There was a fire." Pressing my lips together, I close my eyes and try to access the details. As I talk, the fog starts to lift. "The fire alarms went off. We evacuated. I remember counting the kids and then…*oh God*!" I dart back up in bed. "The boys. Marcus and Troy."

Mom holds my hand in hers. "Shhhh… It's okay. The boys are okay."

My eyes open. "They are? Are you sure?"

"I'm sure. They were kept overnight for smoke inhalation and released this morning. They're doing great."

Oh, thank God. My heart rate begins to slow and then kicks back up as the little details flood in.

I'm the reason the boys were in that situation.

When the fire alarms sounded, I hesitated. I shouldn't have wavered even for a second, knowing lives could've been on the line—that's something my dad taught me. Except I did. I let my guard down, and by the time I realized what was going on, all I could think about was getting the class to safety.

I wasn't even thinking about the boys in the bathroom, not until I was already out of the building. I failed.

All of the kids made it out unharmed, and for that I should be happy. I *am* grateful. But that doesn't erase the barrage of remorse. I put those kids' lives at risk—especially the boys in the bathroom—and the thought of them getting hurt because of me makes my stomach churn. I am so much more than a teacher. When they're with me, away from their parents, it's my job to protect them. I failed them, and I also failed my father.

Be safe, Claire Bear. I hear his words in my head. But I wasn't. I wasn't safe. I didn't heed his warnings and look at where that got us.

Squeezing my eyes shut, a soft sob pulls from my chest. Mom wraps me in her arms, holding me close.

"Oh, sweetheart. You've been through so much. I know how scary that must've been for you especially after..." Her words trail off.

Wiping my face, I look up. "After Daddy," I say, finishing for her.

A wistful smile pulls at her lips. "You remind me so much of your father. You get your bravery from him."

I swallow past the sour lump in my throat. I want so badly to tell her she's wrong, that I wasn't strong, and I didn't act the way Daddy taught me to, but I can't get the words out. I don't want to disappoint her too.

"I'm not brave," I manage, wiping the tears from my face.

Mom's brows dip low. "Claire, you ran into a burning building to save two children. Most people would never do that. You put your life on the line to help someone else. If that isn't being brave, I don't know what is."

Her words penetrate deep inside of me, causing a new wave of guilt and frustration. I could've died—the same way my father did. What would that have done to my mother? And Milo.

"Milo."

"She's fine," Mom soothes. "She's at my house."

That doesn't make me feel better. If anything, it makes me

feel worse. Tears drip down my face. I wipe them away, but they keep falling, and I bury my face against Mom's shoulder.

"I'm sorry, Mom," I cry, my voice muffled by the soft cotton of her shirt.

She shakes her head. "Sweetheart, don't apologize. You have nothing to be sorry for. I think you're just overwhelmed and probably in shock. Let me go get the doctor."

It's on the tip of my tongue to tell her it's not shock that has me so worked up, it's guilt. I want to tell her what happened— all of the things I did wrong.

Instead, I nod. "Okay."

"Mo is out there. Would you like me to send her in?"

If there's one person in the world I need right now besides my mother, it's Mo.

"Yes, please."

"Okay, sweetie." With a kiss to my forehead, Mom walks out, and a second later, Monroe rushes in.

I don't even have time to process the thoughts racing through my head, let alone get control of my emotions, before she throws herself at me.

"You scared the shit out of me." When she pulls back, I can see that her eyes are red and puffy. "Between you and Trevor, Rhett and I are about to have a heart attack."

"Trevor? What happened to Trevor?" I ask, furrowing my brow, and there's that burning feeling again. I rub against the tingling sensation and pull my fingers back, but there's nothing there.

"What's wrong?"

"Nothing. My forehead feels funny." I shake my head. "I'm sure it's nothing. What happened with Trevor?"

Monroe blows out a harsh breath and studies me for a second. "You don't remember?"

"Remember what?" And then it hits me. *Trevor is a firefighter.* "Oh my gosh, was he there? Please tell me he didn't get hurt putting the fire out."

Monroe shakes her head. "He didn't get hurt putting the fire out. He got hurt saving your life," she says softly, as if her tone could lessen the blow. But it's too late. Monroe's words are a sucker punch straight to the gut.

"*What*? What do you mean he got hurt saving my life?"

"Claire." Monroe looks at the door. "Maybe the doctor should explain this, or your mother. I really thought you knew," she says, bringing her gaze back to mine.

"I remember going in after the boys. I can recall bits and pieces of crawling through thick smoke, and the last thing I remember is a big body slamming down on mine." I gasp, covering my mouth with my hand as the words pass through my lips, a fresh wave of tears sliding down my face. "That was Trevor?"

Monroe grabs some Kleenex. She hands one to me and then wipes the wetness from her cheeks. "Yes. I'm so sorry; I thought you knew."

I shake my head. "No. How could I? The smoke was so thick. I could barely breathe, let alone see, and those firefighters—there were two. I couldn't see their faces because of their masks, and their voices were muffled. God, Mo, all I could think about was getting out alive."

Goosebumps race across my skin, the knot in my stomach from earlier growing with each passing second. "Is he okay? Please tell me Trevor is okay. And the other guy—do you know who he was?"

"Mikey. He's fine. He got out with the boys, and Trevor stayed behind to help you up, only you two didn't make it far before the ceiling caved in. According to the other firefighters, Trevor curled his body around yours and took the brunt of the falling debris."

"I have to go see him." I reach for my IV to pull it out, but Mo stops me.

"Wait until the doctors release you, and I'll take you to his room. He's only a few doors down."

"I don't want to wait." What doesn't she understand about that? "He saved my life, Mo. Not only did I put those kids' life in danger, I put his in danger too. I need to get to him and see for myself that he's okay and apologize and—"

"Whoa, Claire. Slow down. You didn't put anyone's life in danger. You got your class out, and you saved those boys."

I shake my head, but it doesn't deter her.

"Yes, you did. You were brave and—"

"Stop saying that," I cry. "I wasn't brave. Please, Mo. Please, take me to see him."

"Claire." She watches me cautiously, the same way my mother did minutes ago. "I don't know what's going through that head of yours, but you didn't put anyone's life in danger. That fire wasn't your fault, and if it weren't for you, who knows what would've happened to those boys. As for Trevor, fighting fires is what he does. It's his job."

"I understand that, but—" My words cut off with another sob. I need to keep my mouth shut. There's no way Mo or Mom will understand. *They* didn't hesitate. *They* don't owe my father the way I do.

"But what? What were you going to say?"

"Nothing," I whisper, fisting my hand against the blanket.

"I heard your mom talking to the doctor in the hallway. They're going to release you sometime tomorrow," she says, a spark of relief in her eyes. "Trevor has to stay a few more days, but as soon as you get released, I'll take you to his room, okay?"

I nod and blow my nose. The Kleenex in my hand is frayed

and tattered, much like my heart. "Please."

"I promise. You're going to get through this. And you can tell me anything. You know that, right? If you need to talk or vent—whatever, I'm here for you."

Dropping my forehead to her shoulder, I sniff. "I know."

Except I can't. I can't tell her like I can't tell Mom, because what would they think of me?

CHAPTER
Thirteen

Trevor

"Y ou're hovering." I glare at my mom, giving her the look that makes most men cower, but she's completely unaffected.

"I'm not hovering. You're my baby boy, and I just want to make sure you don't need anything. Are you comfortable?" Mom flits around my room, arranging and rearranging the various flowers and balloons that have trickled in over the last few days.

"Yes, I'm comfortable. I'm also full and tired, thanks to you."

"Better get used to it, bro," Rhett says, dropping onto a chair. He props an ankle on his knee and reclines. "When I was in the hospital, she did the same thing. Didn't stop until I got released, and then she still sent me daily texts to make sure I was feeling okay."

Mom scoffs and kisses my forehead. "One of these days, when you have your own children, you'll understand."

"Sorry, Ma. I imagine you'll have lots of grandchildren someday, but they probably won't come from me," I scoff.

"You just wait. You'll change your tune when you decide to

go after your girl," she says, picking up her purse.

"My girl? There is no girl, Mom."

She looks at me as though she's privy to some huge secret I know nothing about. I glance to Rhett for help, but he just shrugs.

"There's a girl, but your head and your heart have to be ready for her, and when they are, you'll see her," she says.

"You mean I'll find her."

"No, you'll see her. You're obviously not there yet, and when you are, you'll realize you don't have to look far because she's been right in front of you this whole time." With a final wave, Mom bustles out of the room.

"Did any of that make sense to you?"

Rhett shakes his head. "Not a word."

"Good. I thought maybe the pain meds screwed with my head."

"Speaking of pain meds, how are you feeling?" Rhett asks, standing up. Stuffing his hands in his pockets, he moves closer to my bed, looking at one of the bags hanging from the IV pole.

"I feel good. The headaches are gone, and my vision is back to normal. Doc says it was a concussion."

Rhett laughs, but it lacks any sort of humor. "Yeah, I know a little something about that. When are you breaking out of here?"

At the end of last summer, Rhett was flung off a bull and wound up in the hospital. A concussion and strained rotator cuff brought him back home to Heaven. He still has his house in Houston, but after reconnecting with Monroe, he's home a lot more.

"I'm hoping tomorrow. How's Claire doing?"

Rhett nods. "She's great. Getting released as we speak."

Thank God. I was worried about her. She was the first thing

I thought about when I came to in the hospital, and she's been on my mind ever since.

"Good. That's good."

"Is there anything you need? You're more than welcome to stay with Mo and me for a few days," Rhett offers.

"Now you sound like Mom."

He raises his hands. "It's just an offer."

"Which I appreciate. But I'm good. Doc says I'll need to take a week off work, and then I'll be back on the truck."

"That's good. Just don't push yourself. You need time to heal."

"Really? You want to lecture me on not pushing myself? Wasn't it you who woke up after three days in a coma asking when you could get back on the bull?"

"Touché." He laughs. "I guess I better get going. Can't leave Dad on the ranch for too long by himself."

Damn it. I forgot about the ranch. Dad is probably up to his eyeballs in work, and I imagine he's running himself into the ground.

"Tell Dad I'll be by as soon as they let me out."

"No worries, bro. The ranch is good. Coop and I have been keeping Dad in line and making sure the work is done. You take care of you."

"Good. Now get out of here and let me sleep." With my hands tucked behind my head, I relax against the pillows. "Turn off the light and shut the door on your way out."

Just to piss me off, he opens the blinds, bathing the room in bright rays of sunshine before he leaves.

"Fucker," I grumble, closing my eyes.

It's been nonstop since I was admitted. Not only has my family been in and out, but my crew has stopped by to check on me several times as well. I'm grateful that everyone cares, but it's hard enough to get rest in a hospital the way it is—too much monitoring and checking.

Taking a deep breath, I allow my brain to shut down—something I've taught myself to do over the years to keep from thinking about every fire, wreck, and victim I've ever encountered—not to mention guilt over my own shortcomings. I picture a black wall, focusing on it until my arms and legs become heavy, sleep creeping in around me, and then there's a soft knock on the door.

Jesus Christ.

I stare at the door, and when it doesn't open, I say *screw it* and close my eyes again. Everyone else simply walks in. If this person is dumb enough to knock and wait for me to answer, they're going to be standing there a while.

I conjure up the black wall again, ignoring another faint knock, and count backward from one hundred.

Ninety-nine.

Ninety-eight.

Ninety-seven.

CHAPTER
Fourteen

Trevor

"Trevor?"

The voice is so soft, I might've dreamed it, and then I hear it again.

"Trevor?"

Peeling my eyes open, I swallow and blink up at the nurse beside my bed. "You aren't Genevieve."

She points to the name badge on the left side of her chest. "Abby. I'm a student nurse. But if you'd rather have Genevieve, I can send her in," she whispers.

Genevieve is the charge nurse. She's also sixty-five, getting ready to retire, and told me I remind her of her son, which is why she sneaks junk food in on a daily basis for me. I'm tempted to tell her to bring Genevieve back, but Abby is a nice change of pace.

She has black hair, piercing gray eyes, and a smile that should make my dick twitch. *Should* being the operative word, because my dick doesn't do a damn thing. Traitorous appendage hasn't shown an inkling of interest toward anyone since it stood tall and proud the night I kissed Claire.

"I know your sister, Adley. We're in school together," she says softly while fiddling with the IV pump.

"I'm sorry."

She laughs and then covers her mouth. "Ooops," she whispers, her eyes darting to the side of me.

I smile. "Why are you sorry, and why are we whispering?"

She nods, and I follow her gaze. "I didn't want to wake her up."

There's a big blob of someone curled up on one of those horrid hospital chairs next to my bed. Whoever it is has snuggled up in a blanket, and when he or she shifts, I see a streak of wild, red hair.

Is that...*Claire?*

"How long has she been here?" I whisper, because now I don't want to wake her up either.

Abby shrugs. "I'm not sure, but you two have been sawing logs for a few hours. She looked cold, so I gave her a blanket."

"Thank you."

Abby shrugs. "No need to thank me. She's been through a lot. It was the least I could do."

She has been through a lot. More than you know.

Claire lets out a soft snore, and I can't help but smile. She's always so put together—dress clothes perfectly pressed, high heels, and her hair fixed in a way that makes me want to pull the little pins out and see how it looks cascading down her back. It's nice to see her out of her element for a change. Although I could do without the circumstances that brought us here.

"I'll leave you two alone."

"Thank you. Would you mind pulling the blinds shut on your way out?" I ask.

Claire needs to get some more rest. She's going to need it to heal, both physically and mentally.

Being trapped in a fire is exhausting to a person, even if there's no physical damage. There's something about being stuck in a burning building, surrounded by flames and smoke, wondering if you're going to make it out, that does a number on one's subconscious. Not to mention that Claire had her father's death in a fire to contemplate during those tense moments, which I'm sure made it a million times worse.

"Sure thing."

Tugging the blinds shut, Abby walks out and closes the door behind her. I'm grateful no one else is here and I have a few minutes to sit back and watch Claire.

Before the fire, I hadn't seen her for three weeks. Three weeks of wondering whether Mo had set her up on another date. Three weeks wondering if she was thinking about me half as much as I was thinking about her, and three weeks of doing my damnedest to avoid her because I knew if I saw her I'd cave—I'd beg her to forget everything I said, just for another chance of feeling her soft body against mine.

But if I did that, I'd have to come clean.

Claire shifts around in the seat, drawing her knees to her chest. Her face scrunches up, and she lets out a soft cry, mumbling something I can't quite understand. She rustles around again, and I reach out, resting my hand on her back. She settles under the weight of my touch, and something inside of me roars to life.

We've always had a connection—one I've forced myself to ignore—but it's hard not to touch her when she's this close. A couple of seconds later, my IV pump beeps, and Claire jolts awake, dislodging my hand.

Damn machine.

Her eyes dart around the room, as if she's trying to remember where she is, and when they land on mine, the first thing

I notice is how exhausted she looks. Dark circles tell me that besides the little nap she just had, she probably hasn't been sleeping.

"Hey," she says, scooting her chair closer to my bed.

"Hi."

We do that awkward staring thing for a few seconds, and then Claire clears her throat. "I knocked earlier, but you didn't answer, so I waited a few minutes and decided to let myself in."

Well, shit. Now I'm wishing I'd let her in. Maybe I could've spent the last couple of hours talking to her rather than sleeping.

"I was sleeping."

"I noticed." She smiles. "I'm surprised I fell asleep with all the snoring you were doing."

"Me?" I laugh, pointing a finger at myself. "You were the one snoring. If you were tired, you could've climbed in the bed with me. It would've been much more comfortable than that chair, and I certainly wouldn't have minded."

I shoot her a wink, and she rolls her eyes, and just like that, we're right back to our old selves.

"Good to know your injuries haven't hindered your personality."

"What injuries? A bump on the head isn't enough to keep me down," I say, holding my hands out to the side. "Now, why don't you tell me what really brought you by, because I highly doubt it was to take a nap."

"You're right." Claire reaches across the bed, resting her hand on my arm. A familiar jolt of electricity races across my skin. It's the same sensation I felt last time we touched. I thought it was a fluke, but I was wrong. I look at Claire, curious if she felt the same thing. Judging by the odd look she's giving her hand, I'm going to go with yes. She watches her fingers glide over my wrist and tangle with mine, and there we go, blurring those lines again.

Swallowing, she looks at me.

I could get lost in Claire's eyes—big, green, and always full of so much life. The long strands of her hair are piled on her head, and when she tucks a flyaway behind her ear, my eyes follow the movement. I can't stop staring. She seems just as taken by me, her gaze roaming across my face as if she's seeing me in an entirely new light.

Then she breaks the spell when she says, "You saved my life." *You saved my life.*

She might as well have tossed a bucket of ice water over my head. Every firefighter loves to hear those four words. Except me, from her, because this changes everything. I've always known Claire was off limits, and despite my wavering lately, this seals the deal. I don't date victims I've saved, and that's exactly what she is now. She isn't holding my hand out of affection toward me, but out of obligation. I pulled her from a burning building, and now she feels like she owes me something, though that couldn't be further from the truth. She doesn't owe me a damn thing.

"I had no idea it was you who came in for us until I woke up and Mo told me."

If it weren't for my last name spelled across the back of my coat, I'm not sure my own mother would recognize me in my turnouts. Add copious amounts of smoke, and it would be even harder.

"It's fine, Claire." I pull my hand away from hers.

She furrows her brow, looking down and then back up. "I'm so sorry, Trevor. I'm sorry you got hurt trying to save me. I don't know what I'd do if something had happened to you."

Her words frustrate me. "Don't." I shake my head. "I was doing my job, Claire, and you didn't have to come here and apologize for that."

I don't know what she was expecting me to say, but the pinched look on her face tells me it wasn't that. I've always hated when victims of a fire feel the need to apologize as if they've somehow inconvenienced me, and it's so much worse coming from Claire. Not only was I doing what I'm trained to do, but I could pull Claire from a hundred fires and still not make up for the pain I caused her and her family all those years ago.

My body stiffens at the memory of what I did. I should be the one apologizing to her, begging her to forgive me, not the other way around, and that makes me even more angry.

"I know I didn't have to, but I wanted to. It was foolish of me to run into a burning building, and I put you and Mikey in a tougher spot because of it. I'll never forgive myself for that."

I hate hearing her talk like this. I can see on her face that she's hurting. There are so many emotions racing through her eyes that she can barely contain them. I want to be the person to coax those feelings out and help her work through them, and I know she'd let me if I tried.

We're connected in a way most people will never understand, but it's a connection I'd prefer not to acknowledge—or to have at all.

"You're right. You shouldn't have gone back in. You could've gotten yourself killed." My words come out a bit harsher than I intend. I'm not trying to be an asshole, but I'm frustrated, and it needs to be said. Her dad was a firefighter. She knows better than to run into a burning building, no matter the circumstances.

"I wasn't thinking about myself."

"Clearly."

Her lips fall open, her eyes widening. "I'm sorry. I'm so sorry, Trevor. I'll pay for your hospital bills. I'll come to your house and take care of you until you get back on your feet, whatever you need—"

See, this is exactly what I was afraid would happen.

"Damn it, Claire, stop. Don't you get it? I don't want your apology. I don't want your money, and I sure as hell don't need you do anything for me. What I need is for you take care of yourself, and you can start by using your brain before making any more rash decisions."

Claire stands up, her chair scooting across the floor. She blinks, and I expect her to square her shoulders, call me out for being an asshole, and put me in my place. Instead, she cries.

If I were standing, the pain in her eyes would bring me to my knees. I hate that I'm the one who put it there, and if I ever see that look again, it'll be too soon. I want to beg her to forgive me for being angry. I want to tell her I'm not mad at her, I'm mad at myself because I want her and I can't have her and it kills me to look at her and not be able to touch her the way my body craves. But the choice is taken away from me when she spins on her heel.

"Claire, wait."

She doesn't. In three long strides, she's yanking the door open.

"Claire!" Damn it. "Claire, please, I'm sor—"

The door slams shut. I rip the covers off and swing my legs over the bed, intent on going after her, but a thought runs through my head, stopping me.

It's better this way.

Closing my eyes, I drop my head into my hands and try to convince myself she's better off without me. She doesn't need me to help her get through this; she has her mom and Mo and a slew of other friends who are probably waiting to help her pick up the pieces. As much as I hate that it won't be me, it's probably for the best. And I will *always* do what's best for Claire, even if it's at my own expense.

CHAPTER
Fifteen

Claire

"Get up."

The covers are ripped off my body, and I fly up in bed to find Mo glaring at me.

"What the hell?" I yank my covers out of her hands and pull them over my head—only to have them stripped away again.

Mo tosses my comforter on the floor and bops around my room, grabbing various articles of dirty clothing.

"I don't need you to do my laundry."

"I beg to differ," she says, dumping them all into the basket before hoisting it onto her hip.

She disappears, and a few seconds later I hear my washing machine turn on.

When she walks back into my room, I sit up in bed. "How did you even get in here?"

"I have a key."

"That was for emergencies only."

"This is an emergency."

"What? What is the damn emergency?" I yell, rubbing my hand across my chest to soothe the dull ache. It's been there since the fire, and I'm starting to wonder if it will ever go away.

"You," she admonishes, motioning toward me. "You're the emergency. You don't call me anymore, your texts are one word—and that pisses me off by the way, and you skipped our last girls' nights. Did I do something wrong? Did I say something to make you mad?"

"What? No, absolutely not."

"Then what's the problem? I know the fire was stressful for you, but everyone made it out. The kids are healthy, Trevor is back to his old self, but you...something's changed. You're different. It's like all of the smiles and laughter and joy have been sucked right out of you."

That's because they have. Everything in my life right now revolves around that fire. I even find myself categorizing things into *before the fire* and *after the fire*, which seems silly because she's right—we all made it out, and no one got hurt. It shouldn't bother me so much, except it does. I let my father and his legacy down. And that makes me wonder who I am anymore.

Before the fire, my life was pretty damn great. I was happy almost all the time—there wasn't a reason not to be. My job was rewarding, tutoring was fulfilling, and I couldn't wait to hang out with my friends and hear about their lives. It's like everything was full of bright colors, and then the fire came along and checked my reality, sucking away the rainbow. Now I'm in a black and white fog that I can't seem to work my way out of.

It's like I've lost Claire. I've always had a strong sense of who I am and what I stand for, but all of that shifted after the fire. I'm not the person I thought I was. I even returned Milo. How am I supposed to care for a dog when I'm clearly not able to make responsible choices, not to mention struggling to care for myself?

What would've happened to Milo if I'd been seriously injured or worse...

I shudder at the thought. It wasn't responsible to take her in.

But I'll never forget the shock on Mo's face when I showed up at Animal Haven.

"Oh, no, you don't," she said, refusing to take the dog.

"Trust me, she's better off," I told her. "Better it happens now before she gets any more attached to me."

"She's already very attached to you."

"She's still young. She'll forget."

Mo just stared at me like I'd grown a second head, and because I was in such a dark place, I simply set Milo down and walked away, ignoring her as she chased after me.

It's not something I'm proud of, but I didn't know what else to do.

The darkness has faded a bit since then, but it hasn't completely gone away. I just can't seem to let go of the guilt. It's eating at me. Though I didn't want to, I've tried to talk to both my mom and Mo about it. I've even talked to my friend Tess, but no one gets it. They tell me I don't need to feel the way I do, that my feelings are unwarranted, and I shouldn't carry that guilt around. But they don't understand that it isn't a choice. I'd structured my life, my choices, *myself* around making my father proud, and then I messed up. The shame is embedded inside of me, and while objectively I realize it's exaggerated, I can't let it go.

Our tutoring sessions were suspended for a week—and I did think about never, ever going back—but I'm forcing myself to move forward. I have to keep showing up for those kids. Maybe eventually I'll redeem myself. Anyway, for now, we're temporarily working out of the elementary school while Bright Start waits for its new building to become ready. Even though it's a different building on the opposite side of town, every time

I switch from my teaching role to my tutoring role and see my students' faces, I think about the fire and how I hesitated, and then how I forgot those boys.

The alarm went off, and rather than rushing the kids out like I should've done—like I was taught to do—I assumed it was a prank and asked them to sit down. That was mistake number one. And then came the twins. Their mom brought me cookies when tutoring resumed to thank me for running in after her boys. We both started crying—her because her kids could've died that day, and me because I forgot her boys were in the bathroom and didn't have the courage to tell her. If they'd died, it would've been my fault, and that's something I have to live with.

But that's not the worst of it. I have to drive past the firehouse to get to work every morning, and every time I pass, I'm hit with a fresh wave of guilt over Trevor's injuries. The way he looked at me and talked to me that day in the hospital room is all I think about. It's clear he was upset, and he has every right to be, but I was trying to make things right. I wanted to show my appreciation, but he didn't want any part of it.

And to add insult to injury, he doesn't seem at all affected or changed by the few minutes we spent alone together in that bathroom at Animal Haven. Foolishly, I thought the next chance he got, he'd pull me into his arms and tell me we never should've been apart and whatever this was brewing between us, we needed to figure it out.

That didn't happen, and I don't even know what to think about that. Probably it's for the best, but it doesn't feel that way. I don't know where I stand with my dating rules now, because dating is about the furthest thing from my mind.

Since walking out of his hospital room three weeks ago, my emotions have been running on an endless cycle, and I can't seem to process them. Mom has mentioned talking to a counselor. Maybe I need to consider that. She's also suggested I talk to Trevor about how I'm feeling, but there's no way I can do that. Not after our last conversation.

I haven't seen Trevor since that day in the hospital. I haven't seen much of anyone, actually, because I've secluded myself. I don't want people to see the shell of a woman I've become. I go to work, come home, and other than a weekly trip to Wal-Mart, there isn't much I do. Netflix has become my best friend. I see my mom and Mo about once a week—although they call me every day—and that's only because they force themselves into my home. Coop brought me pizza one night, and as soon I busted into tears, he was out the door.

Rhett showed up on my doorstep a week ago to try to convince me to take Milo back, said she wouldn't stop crying, but I shut the door in his face. Not my finest moment, but what did he expect was going to happen? After that day, I forbade Mo from mentioning Milo or sending me pictures of her—which she did often—and I threatened her within an inch of her life if anyone showed up on my doorstep again with the dog.

"I just really want my friend back," Mo says, pulling me out of my head.

I sigh. "I'm sorry. You're right. Things have changed. I'm in a funk, and I don't know how to dig myself out of it."

"Don't apologize. And you don't need to know how; that's what you have me for."

"Mo," I sigh. "I told you, I'm really not in the mood to—"

"Do you trust me, Claire?" she interrupts.

"Yes."

"And don't you want to get back to your normal life?"

"Of course, but it's not that easy."

"It is that easy. You just have to start living again. You have to remind yourself that you have things to live for, people in your life who love you and miss you."

"Mo…"

"And I'm going to help you."

Oh boy. "I'm afraid to ask."

She grins. "We're going to start by getting you a nice hot shower, and then we're going to Dirty Dicks. Coop promised to make you your favorite sandwich—"

"A turkey bacon club." My stomach growls and Mo laughs. Dirty Dicks has the best food, and it's been weeks since I ate there. "No tomato, extra mayo, a double order of fries, and a side of pickles."

"That's the one, and it's my treat."

"I don't know, Mo. It sounds good, and I'll admit that it would be nice to get out of the house, but I'm not sure I'm ready to see everyone."

"It's just me and you, babe. Coop is working, and Tess went to visit her family."

"Really? Tess doesn't talk about her family much. I wasn't even sure if she had anyone she was close to."

Mo frowns. "She's pretty tight lipped about them, that's for sure. I've tried getting her to open up a few times, but I don't get anywhere."

Maybe she's not ready to open up. "One of these days you'll get through to her."

"Maybe. But right now, I'm focused on you. Come on, it'll be just the two of us."

"Rhett?"

"He's helping his dad on the ranch."

"What about Trevor?"

"What about him?"

Mo smiles and waits for me. *Bitch.* I should've known she

wouldn't give up information that easily. I never told her what happened between Trevor and me, but she suspects something, and I think she's still holding out hope that I'll cave and give her details.

I take a deep breath and pick at the hem of my shirt. "How is he?"

Mo rests her hand on my arm. "He's good. Back to his old self, working a full schedule and helping out on the ranch."

"Good. That's good. I'm glad to hear that."

"He asks about you all the time."

I look up. "Really?" That's shocking.

Mo nods and sits on the bed next to me. "Really. He's always asking how you're doing and where you are. He made a comment the other night that he hasn't seen you since the fire. I think he misses you," she says, nudging me.

A real smile threatens my face, not one of those fake ones I've been plastering on. It's a foreign feeling, and I quickly push it away.

"He does not," I scoff.

"He does too. I could call him, get him to meet us for dinner, if you'd like."

"No." I answer a little too quickly, and Mo's brows shoot up.

"Come on," she coaxes. "I know you like him, and since he won't shut up about you, I'm guessing he likes you too. Maybe this is what you need, a good romp."

"A romp?"

"Yeah, you know, a one-night stand. Some sexy times between the sheets. I bet Trevor could pound you right out of your funk."

I bet he could too. Too bad he doesn't want that from me. "I doubt it."

"You forget that I'm sleeping with one of the Allen boys. If

Trevor is anything like Rhett, he's packing some serious heat," she says, waggling her eyebrows.

It's official. I hate her. And not because she's getting laid daily and I haven't been touched in well over a year, but because now she's got me thinking about how big Trevor's dick is and how great it would be to feel his thick, muscular body pressing me into the mattress. It's something I fantasized about many times before the fire.

"I'm not going to sleep with Trevor."

"Fine, then sleep with someone else. You need to brush those cobwebs off and get back on the horse. It's a great way to relieve stress, and you've got that in spades."

"I do not have cobwebs."

"Really? When was the last time you were with a man? And I mean a real man, not B.O.B."

It's takes a second to calculate back that far, and when I realize it's almost been two years, I decide to go on the defensive. "Are we seriously going to talk about this? I already feel like shit about myself and now you want to remind me that I'm practically a born-again virgin?"

Mo's smile falls. "I wasn't trying to make you feel like shit about yourself. I was just trying to lighten the mood and have fun."

Damn it. Now I've made her feel bad, and that wasn't my intention. "I'm sorry, Mo. You didn't make me feel like shit. I'm just not myself, and I'm not in the right frame of mind to have a conversation with anyone, let alone have sex with anyone. This is a bad idea."

I grab my comforter from the floor, crawl back into bed, and pull it over my head.

Mo immediately tears it off.

"Sorry, sister, you're not getting rid of me that easily. We're going out for dinner whether you like it or not, and we're going to have fun. I promise not to talk about Trevor and his giant penis or getting laid by a man."

"No."

"Claire…" She juts her bottom lip out and gives me puppy dog eyes. "Please," she says, grabbing my hands. "I miss you. I know you went through a lot and you're having a hard time working your way through it—although I don't understand why—but holing yourself up in your house isn't the answer. Just come with me, get some fresh air, say hi to a few people you haven't seen in a while, and maybe it'll help you clear your mind. Plus, there's only so much guy talk a girl can take, and I've hit my limit. I need my Claire back."

How am I supposed to say no to that? "I've missed you too."

"Does that mean you'll come?"

I sigh, sitting back up. "I guess. But you have to promise that if I want to go home, you won't fight me on it."

"I promise."

"I'm not kidding, Mo."

"I know." She squeals and pulls me to my feet. "Go get in the shower. I'll pick you out some clothes. Come on, I'm starving." She guides me to the bathroom, turns the knob to the shower, smiles, and then walks out.

I stand at the sink, looking at my reflection in the mirror. Lifting my lips, I try to force a smile, but it falls flat. I already know leaving the house tonight is a bad idea, but I've let so many people down, and I refuse to add Mo to that list.

CHAPTER
Sixteen

Claire

I t takes an hour to get me ready. I could've been done in twenty minutes, but Mo insisted on fixing my hair. I drew the line at makeup and heels, refusing to get dolled up just to go to Dirty Dicks. I'm in more of a ripped jean, concert T-shirt, and Chuck sort of mood, which isn't like me at all, and I'm not the only one to notice.

"Why is everyone staring at me?"

Mo and I take a table at the back of Dirty Dicks.

"Because they've never seen you in jeans," she says. "They also haven't seen you in a few weeks, and they've been worried about you."

I look up from the menu. "Why?"

"Really, you have to ask? Because you're one of them, and they care about you."

Sometimes I forgot how small this town is. "Oh."

My gaze drifts across the bar. She's right. I know everyone in here by name, and not only that, I can tell you who their significant others are and where they work, and if they have kids, I can tell you their names as well. They're all giving me curious looks.

My thoughts are interrupted when our waitress, Sarah, walks up.

"Hey, Claire. Good to see you. How've you been?"

I'm sick of people asking me that. I force a smile and look up at her. "I'm good, thank you."

She touches my arm. "Glad to have you back." She winks and turns to Mo. "Sean and I miss you. Things just aren't the same since you've been gone."

"It's only been a week. Coop told me he finally replaced me," Mo says.

Replaced her? What is she talking about?

"Yup. Her name is Willa, and she started last weekend. This is her first bartending job, but she's a quick learner. I think she'll fit in just fine."

"That's great."

Sarah pulls out her pen and pad. "So, what are you ladies having tonight?"

"Tell Coop Claire wants her usual, and I'll have a cheese-burger and fries."

"Got it." She scribbles everything down and then looks up. "Soda? Beer? Wine?"

"I'll have a Diet Coke," Mo says.

"Me too."

Sarah nods, stuffs the pad in her back pocket, and walks off.

Arms folded across my chest, I lean back in the booth and stare at Mo.

"What? Why are you looking at me like that?" she asks.

"You don't work here anymore? Why didn't you tell me?" I ask, feeling affronted. I don't know why I ask, though. I know the answer before it comes out of her mouth.

"Because you've had enough on your plate, and I've barely

seen you to tell you."

"We talk almost every day," I retort.

"No, I call to check on you, and you growl at me a few times and hang up. We haven't had a real conversation in a long time, and the few times you do say more than two words, I don't want to talk about me, I want to talk about you because I'm worried about you."

"Don't be. I'm going to be fine, Mo. I know I've been off, but that fire was scary and after what happened to my dad…I just need to work through some things in my head. But I'll be okay." As I say these words, I really, really hope they're true.

Her shoulders relax. "Promise?"

"I promise. This isn't much different than the rough patch you went through after your dad's stroke. And just because I'm working through things in my head doesn't mean you aren't my best friend. I still want to know what's going on in your life."

"I quit Dirty Dicks."

I laugh. "I can see that. But how?"

Mo was supposed to be a veterinarian. She was going to take over her father's practice. She was accepted into a program, but just a few months in, her father had a stroke. Mo's mother ran out on them a long time ago, so it was no surprise when Mo dropped out of school to come home and take care of her dad. Between taking over Animal Haven and managing her dad's medical bills—including paying caregivers, which happened to be my mom and aunt—Mo was sucked dry monetarily.

She started bartending on weekends to help make ends meet. She had her hands full until a few months back when her Dad moved in with my mom.

My mother devoted herself to Mo's dad. Taking care of him after his stroke kept her busy, something she needed after retirement, and it kept the bills paid. Phil uses a wheelchair, but other than some speech issues, he's completely with it, and over time they sort of fell in love.

I never expected my mom to meet another man. After my father's death, she was devastated. He was her first love—her only love—and she vowed no man would ever fill the void left in her life and in her heart.

There will forever be an empty spot at the head of our table on Thanksgiving. The Santa cap Dad wore on Christmas morning while doling out gifts is a reminder of how uneventful the holidays are without him. Birthdays mean a hug and a card instead of a bouquet of flowers and a trip around the living room in his arms. All the small things and moments most people take for granted are the things we miss the most.

The emptiness he left behind is part of the reason I vowed never to date a firefighter, let alone marry one. I want to keep my heart safe.

And to think I was ready to give that up for a shot with Trevor.

"I'm going back to school." Mo claps her hands, yanking me out of my thoughts, and I question whether or not I heard her right.

"What?"

"I'm going back to school," she repeats. "I start my first class in August."

"Mo, that's great." Reaching across the table, I grab her hand. "I'm so excited for you."

"Thank you. It all happened sort of fast." She gets a dreamy look in her eye, the same one she gets when Rhett walks into a room. "I couldn't do it without Rhett."

"Is he paying for it?"

She scrunches her nose. "No. He wants to, but I can't let him do that. But he is the one who encouraged it."

"I don't understand. You relied on that paycheck from bartending. How are things going to work out now?"

"Everything sort of fell into place after Dad moved in with your mom. I'm no longer paying for caregivers, and that frees up a lot of money. Plus, I've got Rhett, and now that he's connected to the shelter, donations have been pouring in. But I'm taking out a loan to pay for school."

"Must be nice dating a world-champion bull rider." I wink, and when Sarah drops our sodas off at the table, I pop the straw in my glass and take a sip.

"It has its perks, that's for damn sure."

She giggles, and we fall into easy conversation, talking and laughing like we've always done, and it feels good. For a brief moment, my sadness and insecurities fade away, making room for the bright ray of happiness I'm used to, and I feel like the old me again. The me who didn't have much of a care in the world.

That all comes to a screeching halt when I look up. Mrs. Marks is standing beside our table. She's a librarian at the local library, and we've known her most of our lives.

"Hi, Mrs. Marks, how are you?"

"Oh, I'm fine, dear. Saw you sitting over here and wanted to stop in and check on you. I haven't had a chance to talk to you since the fire."

I take a deep breath and reply, "I'm good. Thank you for asking."

"What you did was wonderful, Claire. Your daddy would be so proud of you."

Shifting around in my seat, I give her a tight smile, but I don't reply because she wouldn't like my answer. My father wouldn't be proud of me; he'd be disappointed, but those thoughts are better left in my head.

"You deserve some sort of metal. I'm going to make a

proposal to the town council, try to get them to put together an award ceremony."

"No." My eyes widen, and I shake my head. "No, I don't. Please don't do that, Mrs. Marks. It's completely unnecessary."

"Yes, you do," she insists. "You saved those boys' lives. It's the least the town can do to thank you for being such a devoted teacher."

"I didn't save them, ma'am. The firefighters did."

"Hmpf." She cuts a shriveled hand through the air, brushing me off. "You're a hero. Not many teachers would go back in for a student. You love those kids, and they love you."

"I may not agree with the hero part, but I appreciate the kind words. But no award ceremony, okay?"

"Okay, dear, if you're sure."

"I'm sure."

She smiles. "I better get out of here before the crowd gets too thick. I hate the name of this place, but the food is just so good." With a pat to my shoulder and following her husband's guiding hand, Mrs. Marks shuffles off.

Mo and I watch her cross the room, and then Mo looks at me. She opens her mouth but doesn't get a word out because Sarah approaches our table.

"Here's your food, ladies," she says, placing our plates on the table.

My mouth waters. "Tell Coop I said this looks amazing."

"Or you could tell him yourself."

Coop appears out of nowhere and kisses my cheek and then Mo's before pulling a chair up to our table.

Mo gives him a funny look. "What are you doing?"

"I'm joining you. Is that okay?" Without waiting for an answer, he turns to me. "Finally decided to join the land of the living, huh?"

"Something like that." Although I'm regretting it now.

"Just no crying, okay? That didn't work out so well for us last time."

"Coop." Mo nudges him in the side. "Get out of here. I thought you had to work tonight."

He winces, rubbing his ribs. "I said I had to work today. *Tonight,* I'm off."

"Well, you need to leave. We're having a girls' night."

Coop looks at me like I kicked his puppy—if he had a puppy—and I thaw just a little. "It's okay. He can stay."

"Thank you," says Coop.

"Are you sure, because I won't feel bad giving him the boot," says Mo at the same time.

Coop shoots her a dirty look, and I smile. I didn't realize how much I missed my friends until right now. "I'm sure. I'm not in the mood to hang out with a crowd, but one extra person doesn't hurt."

"So…now's the time I should probably mention that Rhett is on his way." Coop grimaces and waits for my reaction.

Mo looks at me apologetically, but she can't keep from smiling.

"And Adley and Trevor," he adds. "Oh, and Linc."

Grabbing my purse, I yank the strap over my shoulder and stand up, food be damned. It was bad enough to let Coop hang with us, but his siblings and Rhett's best friend? I think not. Coop's big hand on my shoulder stops me. He pushes me back into my seat and tugs my chair close to his. He wrangles my purse off my shoulder and out of my hands, then scoots my plate to me.

"Eat," he demands.

"I lost my appetite."

"Bullshit. You're practically drooling, and I slaved over a

hot stove to make you that food."

"It's a turkey club," I deadpan.

"And fries." He picks up a fry and shoves it in my mouth, causing Mo to laugh.

I glare at Mo, and her mouth snaps shut.

"Did you know about this?" I ask.

She shakes her head. "I swear, I thought it was just going to be us. If you want to go home, say the word and we'll leave."

"You're not going anywhere." Coop unwraps my silverware and hands me my knife and my side of mayo. "You're going to sit here and eat, and then we're going to get a beer and wait for everyone else to show up. And when they do, you're going to laugh and have fun—then and only then can you go home."

"I hate you."

"No, you don't. You love me. And when tonight is over, you'll thank me for making you stay."

I give him the side eye. "We'll see about that."

CHAPTER
Seventeen

Trevor

"Hey, Trevor."

Shayla Caruso catches me the second I walk through the bar and runs a red-tipped nail down the front of my shirt. "You just get off work?"

"Yup. Long-ass day and now I'm going to relax and knock a few back with my family."

Shayla's lips form the perfect smirk. Her eyelids droop as she leans in close. "I don't have any plans tonight, if you want to come over afterward."

I grab her wrist before she hits the buckle of my jeans. I've used Shayla more times than I can count. There's nothing like a warm, tight pussy to chase away the stress of a long day. I'm tempted to tell her to leave her front door unlocked, but when I glance toward the back of the room and see Claire sitting at the table with my family, the words die on my lips.

Today was rough. Two structure fires made for a busy morning, and then we were called out to a fatal five-car pile-up on the interstate. When Coop and Rhett called to see if I wanted to have drinks and hang out, my initial answer was no. All

I wanted was an ice-cold beer, a hot shower, and my bed. But those assholes bitched and moaned, and when Rhett told me Claire was going to be at Dirty Dicks with Mo, I caved.

I haven't seen Claire since she walked out of my hospital room, and seeing her now is the drink of cool water my charred soul needs. It's been hell, though I keep reminding myself that separation makes things easier for both of us.

Claire looks up, and my heart slams against my ribs. She holds my gaze for what feels like forever, and although her face is a blank mask, I can see the pain in her eyes—pain I'd hoped would've faded long before now.

Her eyes drop to Shayla's hand on my chest, and she turns away. I have no idea what's going through her head, but I want to run over there and tell her Shayla and I are nothing more than old friends. But that would be silly.

If I was smart, I'd grab Shayla's hand, drag her out of the bar, and let her spend the night riding my cock, ending my year-long drought. Maybe then I'd finally be able to forget about Claire. *Yeah, right.* Unfortunately, I'm a glutton for punishment, and I'd rather end up with a major case of blue balls after sitting next to Claire all night than spend it blowing my load into another meaningless woman.

"Sorry, not tonight." I drag Shayla's hand from my body and walk away before she has a chance to argue.

My family is far from quiet. Add Mo and Linc to the mix, and things get downright crazy. I can hear them laughing and carrying on from across the crowded bar—everyone except Claire. Arms folded tight across her chest, legs crossed, she's closed herself off, and it doesn't look like she's too keen on being here tonight.

She watches me walk across the room, and when she glances at the empty chair between her and Linc, her back stiffens.

Not wanting to make her any more uncomfortable than she already looks, I take the empty chair between Rhett and Linc. But if I'm not mistaken, a flash of disappointment crosses Claire's face.

"Where's my beer, asshole?" I ask, shoving Rhett's shoulder.

He raises his hand, flagging Sarah, and then motions to me. There's no need for her to come over; Sarah knows my poison, and within minutes, she places an ice-cold Bud Light in front of me.

"Thank you, sweetheart."

Sarah winks. "Anything for you, Trevor."

Coop tosses a napkin, hitting me in the nose. "Stop flirting with my employee."

"I wasn't flirting." I snag the napkin off the table and toss it back, aiming for his mixed drink. The napkin hits his mark, and all of the arms at the table go up in celebration. Well, all but Claire's and Coop's.

Nose scrunched, Coop pulls the napkin from his drink, tossing it on the table.

"How's it going, Linc?" I ask, reaching out a hand. "It's been a while."

Linc captures my hand for a quick shake. "Work. Same ol' shit, different day."

"Don't I know it." I make my way around the table, checking in on everyone's day, and when I get to Claire, I tip my hat. "Red."

She swallows. "Trevor."

"Good to see you out and about."

She tilts her head. The brilliant smile she normally wears is gone. "Yes, well, I didn't have much of a choice. Mo forced me to come, and Coop forced me to stay."

Coop hooks an arm around her shoulder and whispers

something in her ear, making her smile. I love my brothers. I've always been closer to Coop than the other two, but right now I want to kill him, and if he doesn't stop touching Claire, I might do just that.

Smart son of a bitch catches the warning in my eye and drops his arm, but not before giving me a curious look.

"So, what's up with you and Shayla?" Mo asks. "You two an item?"

"Nah." I slouch back in my seat, taking a drink of my beer. The cool liquid slides down my throat as I steal a glimpse of Claire over the end of my bottle. "Just friends."

"Really? 'Cause y'all looked like more than friends a second ago."

What the hell is she up to? "What do you care who I screw around with, Mo? Unless of course you've decided to ditch my brother and take the better, younger Allen brother for a ride."

"Get your own girl." Rhett punches me in the arm.

He's strong. I'm stronger. Which is why I laugh when he rubs his fist.

"Leave mine alone."

I hold up my hands. "I can't help it that ladies love me."

It's all fun and games. My brothers know I'd never touch their women, sloppy seconds or otherwise. I might have a reputation for liking my women fast and easy, but even I know where to draw the line.

"Excuse me." Claire pushes away from the table and stands up. Mo reaches around Coop and grabs her hand, stopping her before she can get away.

"Where are you going?"

"To the bathroom."

"Hold up. I'll go with you."

Claire shakes her head. "No need."

Mo looks around the table and then back to Claire. She lowers her voice, but we can still hear her. "Are you okay? Do you need me to take you home? I swear I didn't know everyone would be here."

Claire places her hand on Mo's shoulder. "I'm fine, Mo. Stay."

We watch Claire walk toward the bathroom. Mo waits until she rounds the corner and then grabs her purse and makes a move to stand up.

"Babe." Rhett puts his arm around Mo, pulling her back into her seat. "She said she's fine. Give her a minute."

"She's lying." Mo frowns. "And I feel bad. I told her it was just going to be us tonight, and then everyone else showed up, and—"

"She's fine." Rhett kisses Mo. "Maybe she just needs some fresh air."

Mo nods, and I'm left wondering what's going on. Rhett has mentioned that Claire's been sort of distant since the fire, but the way she's acting tonight makes it seem a lot worse than he let on. It's not like her to be this quiet and withdrawn.

"What's going on with Claire?" I ask.

"Nothing." Mo takes a drink of her beer, glancing back toward the bathroom.

"Bullshit. What was that all about?"

Rhett runs a hand through his shaggy hair. "I told you she's been struggling."

"Yeah, you said it in passing a few weeks ago and made it sound like it wasn't a big deal."

Rhett opens his mouth, but his words never come because the front door of Dirty Dicks flies open, bringing with it my baby sister, Adley, and a gust of warm air.

"I'm here, I'm here!" She waves, gliding across the floor.

I love my sister, but she is notoriously late, and it drives me insane.

"Punctuality is a virtue," I joke, earning a glare.

"So is empathy." Bending down, she kisses me on the cheek. "Cut me a break. It's my last semester, and I'm commuting back and forth to Houston for clinicals."

"They've got you driving that far for clinicals?"

Lincoln pulls out the empty chair between him and Claire. Adley drops her purse to the floor and sits down.

"Unfortunately, but it's necessary. Houston Memorial has the best pediatrics floor, and I'm learning a ton." Adley points to the empty chair beside her.

"Claire." Coop answers her silent question. "She's in the bathroom."

"Good. I'm glad she's here. I've been wanting to talk to her."

"You could always stay in my house," Rhett offers when Adley turns her attention back to the table. "Mo and I aren't there very often."

"Oh..." Adley's eyes dart around the table. "That's very generous, but I don't think it's necessary."

"We insist," Mo counters. "It's silly for you to drive an hour and a half before and after an eight-hour clinical rotation. And your brother's place isn't far from the hospital."

"I—" She looks around, avoiding eye contact with all of us except Mo. "I've got a friend who lives in the area. If I'm tired, I just stay there."

"Better not be a guy," Coop warns.

Lincoln sputters, choking on his beer, and Adley pounds on his back.

"You okay, buddy?" Rhett asks.

"Yeah. I'm good." Linc covers his mouth. "Just went down the wrong pipe, that's all."

"So what if it is a guy?" Adley argues, her hand lingering on Linc's back. "I'm a young, healthy female, and I have sexual needs just like you—"

"Shit," I hiss, covering my ears. Coop and Rhett scowl at our baby sister. "We don't want to hear about your needs, Adley."

"Okay." She holds her hands up. "Fine. I won't talk about my sexuality as long as you buffoons don't tell me who I can and cannot stay with."

"Deal." Coop drains the rest of his beer. "But if we find out it's some prick and he hurts you in any way, all bets are off."

"We'll kill him," Rhett adds.

I raise my beer to that, along with Rhett and Coop. We all look at Linc. He smiles and taps his bottle to ours, and we drink to protecting Adley's virtue from all men everywhere.

"Why are men so stupid?" Adley says, looking at Mo.

"No clue," she mumbles absently, her eyes drifting toward the bathroom.

The worried look on her face doesn't sit well with me. I stand up from the table, and Rhett stops me. "Where are you going?"

"To get another beer."

He gives me a knowing look. "You don't have to get up for that."

"I know I don't."

"You're going to check on Claire." It isn't a question because Rhett knows me all too well.

"You got a problem with that?"

He cocks a brow. "If I say yes?"

I turn away, giving him my back, and when I get a few feet from the table I hear him say, "Yeah, that's what I thought."

CHAPTER
Eighteen

Trevor

Fucking Rhett.

If I didn't know he was madly in love with Monroe, I'd think he has a thing for Claire. I know he's just looking out for her, but I'm his brother. What does he think I'm going to do? Hurt her? I saved her life, for God's sake.

I stride across the floor, shouldering my way through the crowd at the bar and shrugging off a few grabby hands along the way. There's a small line of women outside of the bathroom, and lucky for me, Shayla is at the front.

Her eyes shine with delight when I walk up. "How many women are in there?" I ask.

"Two, they went in together." She glances over my shoulder at the line behind her and whispers, "Come in with me, and I'll give you a sample of what you're missing out on tonight."

There's a reason the men around the firehouse call her Shameless Shayla. She'll do whatever, whenever, wherever, and she doesn't care who's watching or listening.

Just then the door opens, and two women who aren't Claire stumble out. "Hold that thought." I push the door open and walk into the ladies' restroom.

"Claire?" There are two stalls. Both appear to be empty, but I push the doors open for good measure and then slip back out.

Where did she go?

I scan the hallway, the bodies along the bar, all of the tables, and the pool room, and when I come up empty, I decide to check Coop's office—although I highly doubt she's there. When I don't find her there either, I walk back to my table.

"She's not in the bathroom," I say, looming over Mo.

Her eyes widen. "You went into the women's bathroom looking for Claire?"

I nod curtly.

"Do I want to know why?" she asks, pulling out her phone.

"Probably not."

Rhett frowns, so does Coop.

"Shit." Mo types out a quick message on her phone and tosses it in her purse. "She left."

The hair on the back of my neck stands up. "What do you mean she left? Why would she just up and leave?"

"Because she isn't herself. I shouldn't have pushed her to come out tonight. That damn fire messed with her head, and she hasn't been right since." She tosses a few bills on the table to cover her tab. Coop tosses the money back, and Mo rolls her eyes. "I've got to go after her."

"Maybe you should let Trevor go," Adley suggests.

"What?" I pull a face, looking at Adley and then Mo.

I expect Mo to cut the idea down, but she doesn't. Instead she sets her purse on the floor beside her seat and leans back.

"Why should I go talk to her?"

I'm pretty sure I'm the last person she wants to see right now, but I can't tell them that.

"Well, for one, you were there that evening, so you can

relate to what she went through. Maybe you can get her to open up and talk. Mo sure as hell hasn't been able to," Adley says, reaching for her purse. "And she has a thing for you, so…" She doesn't finish her sentence, just shrugs and looks down.

"You're full of shit. She doesn't have a thing for me."

Mo laughs, and then her face sobers. "You're joking, right?"

Hell yes, I'm joking. I know she has a thing for me. Or *had* a thing for me. But they don't know that, and unless I want to get into a bar brawl with my brothers, I have to play dumb.

"Come on, bro. You're not stupid. You have more hose honeys than I've got buckle bunnies—*oomph*." Rhett grunts when Mo elbows him in the chest.

"You've only got one buckle bunny, and that's me. And if you ever refer to me as a buckle bunny, I'll shove my Ariat up your ass," she warns.

Rhett grins as though she just challenged him rather than threatened. "Two can play at that game, sweetheart. Only it won't be a boot I'll be shoving up your ass."

"Oh, for fuck's sake. Are they like this all the time?" I ask the rest of the table.

Linc pops a fry into his mouth. "Pretty much. You'll get used to it after a while."

"No, you won't," Coop says. "But as much as I hate to admit it, I agree with Adley. You should go talk to her."

"Funny, because if I remember correctly, you and Rhett were the ones keeping this information about Claire from me in the first place." Not that it's any of my business—I lost that privilege—but I want it to be. "In fact, you've been acting all protective and shit over her for years."

Coop shrugs. "That's because we don't want you to hurt her."

"Hurt her? Why on Earth would I hurt her?"

"Because Claire is relationship material, and you're not," Coop says. "On top of that, you're our brother, and she's one of our best friends. If something happened between the two of you, we'd be forced to kick your ass and then choose sides."

"And we really don't want to have to kick your ass," Rhett adds.

"I'd never intentionally hurt Claire." No truer words have ever come from my mouth.

Coop nods. "You better not."

Mo smiles.

"Good," Rhett says. "Now go after her, and keep your dick in your pants."

"Or not. Just remember to talk first and then hanky panky." Mo's eyes widen when Rhett elbows her in the side. "What? Claire could use some action, and even though Trevor is a player, I don't think he's the worst choice for a one-nighter."

"I'm not a player."

"I don't think he's the worst choice either," Rhett says, ignoring me. "But that doesn't mean we should encourage them. He's my little brother, and she's your best friend, and you know damn well if one of them fucks the other over, it's going to be Trevor."

"I'm standing right here."

Adley pulls a nail file from her purse and looks up at me. "Save your breath. This is some sort of weird foreplay for Rhett and Mo. They bicker until they get all worked up, and then they'll have crazy monkey sex and work it out. It's really quite disgusting. Want my opinion?"

"Not really."

She shrugs. "I'll give it to you anyway. Claire likes you, and you like her. Something happened between you two, but I'm not sure what it is because she wouldn't tell me."

I open my mouth, wanting to ask Adley when she and Claire talked, but she continues.

"But that doesn't matter. What matters is that she's hurting, and maybe you can help, so you need to put whatever happened between you two aside and go after her."

Damn, she's good.

Putting Claire's feelings aside will be nearly impossible, because I'm not sure she still has said feelings. I wish things were different between us, and if we were different people in a different universe, they might be.

But that doesn't change the fact that what Adley is saying is true. I can relate to Claire, and if she'll forgive me for being an ass at the hospital, maybe I can get close enough to her to figure out what's going on and help her through it.

But then I have to walk away. I absolutely cannot get sucked into the vortex.

"Trevor?"

I blink and look at Mo. "Yeah?"

"You're wasting time."

"Right."

I rush out of Dirty Dicks, jump in my truck, and peel out of the parking lot. I take a left, knowing it's the quickest way to Claire's house, and not even half a mile down the road, I see the silhouette of a woman.

What the fuck? She walked?

Heaven isn't a dangerous town, but it's dark out, and this is a busy road, and *what was she thinking?* I know this isn't the best way to approach an upset woman, but I'm pissed. Pulling alongside Claire, I roll the window down.

"Get in the truck."

She startles at the sound of my voice. Hand covering her heart, she stops and takes a breath. "You scared me."

"The feeling is mutual. What are you doing walking down this road at night? It's dangerous."

She rolls her eyes. It's not a gesture I'm fond of, but somehow Claire makes it look sexy. "It's not dangerous."

"Bullshit. I barely saw you. You could've gotten hit—or worse yet, kidnapped."

Claire ignores me and keeps walking. "Go away, Trevor. I want to be alone."

I inch the truck along the road, checking my rearview mirror every few seconds to make sure no one is flying up on us.

"At least let me take you home."

"No."

Damn stubborn woman. I take my hat off and flip it around. "Get in the truck, Claire, or so help me God, I will chase you down and toss you in here myself. And make no mistake about it, if you push me that far, I will spank your ass."

She stops, her breath hitches, and when she looks at me, I can tell she's wondering if I would actually do that.

The heated look in her eye pulls the seductive words from my mouth before I have a chance to stop them. "You'd probably like that, though, wouldn't you, sweet Claire?"

"In your dreams."

Hell yeah, in my dreams. That's what I want to say, but I've got to get a grip on this wild feeling that runs through me when I'm around her.

"Damn it, Red, just get in the truck."

"Go home, Trevor."

Her voice is lifeless, and although I can't see her eyes because it's dark and now she won't look at me, I imagine they're the same.

Screw this.

Rolling up the window, I step on the gas and fly past her.

CHAPTER
Nineteen

Claire

Rocks go flying as Trevor revs his engine and takes off, leaving me on the side of the road.

I'm two miles from home, and Trevor was right, walking probably isn't the smartest idea.

My eyes burn with tears, but I have no idea why I'm crying. He's only doing what I asked.

Asshole. Don't men know to do the opposite of what we say?

Trevor's truck pulls to the right about fifty feet in front of me. His door flies open as he slides out, and I stop in my tracks. A cool breeze whips through the air, sending my hair in front of my face. I tuck the loose strands behind my ear and take a deep breath. Trevor makes no move, and he doesn't say a word.

I toss my hands out and let them fall to my side. "You gonna chase me?"

"You gonna run?"

Propping my hands on my hips, I bite my lip. "You gonna spank me?"

His lips twitch. "You want me to?"

I don't know what kind of game he's playing. Hell, I don't

know what kind of game I'm playing. All I know is that Trevor is way out of my league when it comes to stuff like this, and my heart and my head and every other organ in my body are not ready for the likes of him. Dropping my chin, I look at the ground for a moment and then bring my eyes to meet his.

"Why are you really here, Trevor? Why are you doing this?"

He takes a step forward. And then another and another, and the closer he gets, the more my body vibrates with energy, and I hate it. I hate that he has this control over me.

"Because you're stubborn as shit, and you ran out on your friends, and now everyone is worried about you."

"Does that include you? Are you worried about me?"

"I'm always worried about you."

"Hah." I let out a burst of laughter. "Really? Last time we talked, you seemed more angry and less worried."

He takes another step forward, putting himself all up in my personal space, and I don't have the strength or willpower to take a step back. In fact, I like him here. Too much. I'm bombarded with the fresh smell of cucumbers and soap as Trevor's scent wraps itself around me, stealing my thoughts along with my words.

"You want to know why I was angry in the hospital?" he asks.

I take a deep breath, but all I can do is nod.

"You tell me why you fled the bar like your ass was on fire, and I'll tell you what all my anger was about. Deal?"

"Fine," I say, not really sure what I'm agreeing to because my head is still swimming in all things Trevor. Suddenly I've got the intense urge to throw myself at him and just see how he'll respond, see if his body will react to mine the way I want it to.

Needing to get away from his intoxicating scent, I take off

walking, figuring he'll either toss me over his shoulder as promised and insert me into his truck, or he'll hop in his truck and follow me. He does neither. Instead, he falls in step beside me.

"You going to walk me all the way home, Trevor?"

"Not letting you walk home by yourself."

"It's a long walk."

"We've got a lot to talk about."

Talk.

Everyone wants me to talk, and I do. They all sit and listen, offering words of encouragement, but none of them *listens*—I mean really listens.

Maybe Trevor will be different.

I glance over at him. He's wearing jeans and a black henley that stretches tight across his chest. The sleeves are bunched around his elbows, and his ball cap is on backwards, making him look all sorts of badass.

Who am I kidding? He is a badass. A badass firefighter who smells delicious and has positioned himself between me and the road. Always the protector. But who's protecting him? Who listens to his stories at the end of the day and comforts him? Who understands Trevor Allen? So many questions I'd love to get answers to.

We reach Trevor's truck, and I stop.

"What are you doing?" he asks. "I thought we were going to walk."

I stuff my hands in my pockets and shrug. "I'm cold, and two miles is a long way."

He smiles, and it's a full, bright grin that shines a sliver of light through my dark world and offers me a ray of hope. I want to see it again, and more than that, I want to be the one to put it on his face.

With a hand at the small of my back, he guides me around

the front of his truck, opens the passenger door, and helps me climb inside.

He waits until I'm situated and buckled before getting in himself, and then he starts the truck, turns on the heat, and points the vent toward me.

"Since when did you become so chivalrous?"

"I'm not. You just seem to bring out the best in me."

I watch Trevor unabashedly as we merge onto the road. I watch the muscles of his forearms tighten and shift along with his thigh as he shifts gears, and that's when I realize that two miles isn't all that far—not when you're staring at a gorgeous man. Before I know it, Trevor pulls into my driveway and shuts his truck off.

I unbuckle, slide out, and walk to my front door. When I turn around, Trevor is still sitting in his truck. His gaze cuts straight through me, and it's as though I can feel what he's thinking. I can feel him trying to convince himself to get out of the truck; I just don't understand the struggle.

What I do know is that I don't want to force him to come in, and I certainly won't beg. Releasing his gaze, I turn toward the door, unlock it, and walk inside. I flick on the light and drop my purse on the end table next to the couch, and a minute later, I hear the door shut behind me.

Trevor's presence is all-consuming. I can feel his big, strong body move across the room before I ever turn to look at him.

"Would you like something to drink?" I ask.

"A water would be good."

My house has an open floor plan, but it isn't big, and I feel the weight of his stare on my back as I walk into the kitchen and grab a bottle of water from the fridge. I lean into it, allowing the cool air to seep around me in hopes that It'll calm my nerves, but all it does is make my nipples pucker tight beneath my shirt.

Shit.

"You okay in there?"

Trevor's smooth voice washes over me, making it all but impossible to gain any sort of control over my breasts.

"Yeah. I'm good." With my arms crossed awkwardly across my chest, I walk into the living room. Trevor is sitting on the end of the couch, tossing a yellow ball into the air.

Milo's yellow ball.

"Where'd you find that?" I ask.

"Found it stuffed between the seat cushions. Heard you returned her."

"It's easier this way. I'm never home."

"You're always home," he argues.

I hold out the bottle of water. "Is this what you want to talk about, a dog?"

He sets the ball down and grabs the water. "Not particularly." Twisting the top off, he takes a drink and sets it on the coffee table. He watches me for a second and then pulls the afghan off the back of the couch and tosses it to me.

"What's that for?"

"You look cold."

Oh. Right. "Thank you."

I pull the blanket to my chin, take a deep breath, and close my eyes. Now or never. Here goes nothing.

"When I close my eyes, I can smell the smoke, and it feels so real. At night I wake up coughing, and sometimes I wake up because I swear I can hear the boys screaming for me. Does that ever happen to you?"

"Every damn day."

I hear Trevor shift around on the couch, but I don't open my eyes. It feels safer here in the dark, my words bleeding from my mouth more freely than they have with anyone else.

"I made a rookie mistake—one I shouldn't have made, and I swear this is my punishment. When I close my eyes, I see the scared faces of my students. Those boys' screams echo through my head, the roar of the fire pulls me out of my sleep, and sometimes I find myself doing whatever I can to stay awake because the nightmares are too intense."

"What mistake, Claire?"

I peel my eyes open, wanting to look at him when I tell him what I did, hoping he'll take on my pain and bear some of the weight—maybe help me understand it or work through it, or whatever the hell it is people in these situations do.

"I hesitated."

CHAPTER
Twenty

Claire

Trevor is perched on the edge of the couch. His elbows rest on his knees, his hands dangling between his legs as he looks at me.

"What do you mean you hesitated?" he asks.

"I hesitated, putting not only my life at risk, but the lives of my students, and inadvertently you and Mikey's lives as well."

I swallow past the lump in my throat and tell Trevor everything that happened that day. I tell him about my goal of living up to my father's standards, then about wavering when the alarms went off. I tell him how I forgot the boys were in the bathroom and every little detail in between, and when I'm done, my heart is racing, my palms are sweaty, and tears are threatening to spill from my eyes.

"Claire." Trevor runs a hand along his jaw and shakes his head. "You did not make a mistake. You got your entire class out. You saved those boys' lives."

Damn it, that's exactly what I don't want to hear. I was stupid for thinking Trevor would look at this any differently than everyone else.

"You don't understand, Trevor, and I don't expect you to."

He flinches as though my words slapped him across the face. "Are you serious? I don't understand? Do you know how many times I've wondered if I've done the right thing? And I do this for a living, Claire. This is my job. Every single day, people depend on me to react quickly and make the right choice. Some days are great and I save a life, and other days I'm not so lucky. Do you know what that does to a man, wondering if something he did—a choice he made—could've been the deciding factor in someone's life? I live with that guilt on a daily basis, Claire. So yes, I get it. I understand what you're going through, probably better than anyone else ever will."

Shit. Now I feel like an ass because he's right. I can't imagine how stressful his job must be. "How do you do it? This one thing has my head so messed up I can barely function, let alone concentrate. How do you deal with it day in and day out, over and over and over again?"

"It's not easy," he admits. "Some days are better than others. I've learned that in order to be happy and not let those moments consume me, I've got to check them at the door."

"I don't even know what that means."

"I acknowledge what I'm feeling. I internalize it and accept it, and if it's a really bad day, I let myself ponder it, and I get rip-roaring drunk, and then I let it go. Because if I don't, it'll consume me, and that's the last thing I want."

"It's consuming me, Trevor. And you were right, it was stupid of me to go back into that building. I knew better—my dad taught me better than that. My whole life I've worked hard to make him proud, and I failed that night, Trevor. I failed him."

My nose burns. My chin quivers. I drop it to my chest to try to hide the tears.

Trevor pulls me into his arms and holds me. He doesn't

whisper words of encouragement or inspiration, he simply offers me comfort in his warm, strong embrace. I open the floodgates and let it all out. I cry harder than I've ever cried. I cry for the pain I still feel from the loss of my father. I cry for Mom and the years she's had to live without the love of her life. I cry for Milo and Mo and Rhett and Cooper. I cry because Trevor has to deal with this sort of thing every single day. I cry for Tara and Troy and Marcus and all of the kids in the building that day. But most of all, I cry for myself. I cry because I need to, because I have to purge this pain from my system so I can find some form of normalcy again.

Minutes pass, maybe hours—who the hell knows—but eventually the sobs slow and my tears dry. I pull back, but I can't look Trevor in the eye, because I'm afraid if I do I'll break all over again, and damn it, I'm tired of breaking.

So very tired of breaking, and tired of feeling all this guilt and shame.

"Claire, look at me." It's a gentle command.

I shake my head, my hair dropping in front of my face.

With a finger under my chin, Trevor lifts my head, and when our eyes connect, it's as though he's opened himself up to me, and I can see into his soul. It's as if the worst moment in my life, aside from my father's death, has bonded us in a way I'll never experience with another human being.

"Do you know what I saw that day when Mikey and I busted through the bathroom door?"

I shake my head, afraid to talk.

"You were hovering over those boys, protecting them, putting their needs above your own. You were strong and brave, and it's because of you that they made it out of there that day. I was so damn proud of you, Claire, and I know your dad would be as well, and I'm sorry if I let you believe otherwise."

A tear slips down my face. Trevor frames my jaw with his hands. Using his thumb, he brushes the tear away.

"Can you imagine how scared Troy and Marcus would've been without you? They sure as hell wouldn't have known to put a wet piece of cloth under the door to keep the smoke out, and what if they'd tried to run out of the building on their own? They could've gotten burned or killed by falling debris. I don't care what you say. You will never convince me that you made the situation worse."

His words soak into my soul, gripping it tight, forcing me to hear them, and I do. For the first time since the fire, I allow myself to believe that maybe, just maybe, I ultimately did the right thing. It's overwhelming, and emotion bubbles up my throat. I let out an unladylike cry.

Trevor tucks me against his chest. "You've got to let it go, baby. You've got to move past this."

I want to. God, how I want to. "I don't know if I can."

"Well, I do. I know you can, Claire, and I'm going to be here every step of the way. We'll do it together, okay?"

Pinching my lips together—a poor attempt at not crying again—I nod.

"Good. That's good. The first part of letting go is realizing that you're okay. You're alive and well and so are those boys, and the rest of the kids in your class."

"And you."

"And me." With his arms still wrapped around me, Trevor leans back, and my heart flutters when he smiles. "We're all okay. No one got killed or seriously injured. For now, I want you to focus on that. Focus on the lives that were saved instead of the what-ifs, because those what-ifs? They'll eat you alive."

"I've been what-if-ing myself to death."

Trevor laughs. "I know you have, and it stops tonight."

"Trevor?"

"Yeah?"

I lace my fingers with his, needing to feel his touch, hoping the warmth of his skin will continue to soothe me the way his words have. "Will you stay with me tonight? I'm tired of being alone."

His eyes cloud over, darkening for a split second, and then he draws me closer into his arms. "Whatever you need, Red."

"You. I just need you."

CHAPTER
Twenty-One

Trevor

Y*ou. I just need you.*
     When she said I didn't understand what she's going through, I should've spilled my guts and told her about the part I played in her father's death. If that experience alone doesn't show her I know what she's feeling, then I don't know what will. But I couldn't get the words out. She was already a complete mess, and I didn't want to make things worse. And I can't tell her now because now an entirely different set of words is rattling around in my head.

You. I just need you.

No one has ever said something like that to me with so much conviction and so much heart. In this moment, she's not a victim holding on to her hero; she's a friend holding on to a friend, a woman holding on to a man, and I believe her. No one has ever needed me like this, and it's left me more than a little speechless.

I lean back on the couch and bring Claire with me. She burrows her face against my chest as I reach over and pull the afghan across our bodies.

Her tears soak through my shirt, but I don't care. She can cry as much as she wants for as long as she needs, and I'll stay right here, acting as her human Kleenex. Threading my fingers through her hair, I stroke the strands, letting them fall before repeating the process. Eventually, Claire's cries soften, her breathing evens out, and when I look down and see her asleep on top of me, my heart flips over inside my chest.

I don't know how long I sit and watch her sleep, but eventually I must pass out because when I wake up, the darkness has given way to the light of a new day. Bright sunlight filters through the blinds, and even though my back is killing me, I've never been more comfortable, and it's because of the precious woman lying on me.

Sometime during the night, Claire must've moved. Her body is now cradled between my legs, her head resting in the crook of my neck, and the only thing that hasn't changed are her arms. They're still wrapped tight around my body as though she was afraid if she let go I'd disappear.

Not a chance in hell.

The afghan fell off the couch, but we didn't need it because our bodies pressed together created more than enough heat to keep us warm. Claire rustles around in her sleep and accidentally knees me in the balls.

"*Ooomph.*" I jerk on instinct, and Claire's head pops up.

She blinks heavily against the bright light. Her red hair is plastered to the side of her head, and I've never seen her look so beautiful.

"What's wrong?" She rustles around, adjusting herself against me, and my dick decides to sit up and take notice.

"You kneed me in the junk. *Again.*"

"Oh my God," she says, trying not to laugh.

She tries to lift herself up to look down, but I hold her in place—mostly because I'm not ready to let her go.

"That's twice now," I tell her. "I'm starting to think you have it out for me."

"I swear I don't."

"I could let you rub it and make it all better." It's probably wrong of me to flirt with her after everything she's been through, but I can't help myself. I don't want to help myself. Not anymore.

"Oh, I bet you'd like that wouldn't you?"

"A little too much, probably."

She laughs and buries her face in my chest, and I decide it's the best sound in the entire world. If I could, I would bottle it up and save it.

Eventually, she looks up. A shy smile pulls at the corner of her mouth. "Good morning."

"It's always a good morning when I wake up with a beautiful woman sprawled out across my chest."

Her smile widens, and I lied. This, right here. The way she looked moments ago doesn't hold a candle to how perfect she looks right now. Her eyes look lighter than they did last night, as if clouds have finally parted to make way for the sun.

"You shouldn't say those things to me."

"Why not?" I say, brushing the hair from the side of her cheek. "It's the truth."

"Because it makes me happy."

I draw in a slow breath, choosing my words wisely, because this might be the loophole—the brief moment in time when I have the opportunity to get us back on the right track. And by the right track I mean on the track of getting together.

If there's one thing I learned by staying with Claire last night, it's that waking up with her in my arms is the best damn feeling in the entire world, and I'm ready for it.

I'm ready to have this day in and day out.

And I want it with Claire.

I see now that letting her walk away that night in the bathroom at Animal Haven was a colossal mistake, one I refuse to make again. That doesn't mean things will be easy, or that they'll even work at all—I still have a massive secret that could rock us to our core—but I'm finally willing to take that chance if it means a shot at a future with Claire.

But first, I need to take things slow and figure out if she's ready to toss her rules aside for someone like me—for a firefighter and a rancher and a reformed player.

"Maybe I like making you happy."

She smiles, but as she watches me, that smile fades.

"What is it?" I ask, brushing my thumb along the apple of her cheek.

"I just don't know where we stand," she says, her eyes dropping to my chest before meeting mine again. "That night in the bathroom was…"

"Was what, Claire?"

"Perfect," she sighs. "And I know we agreed to walk away, and I know that us being together goes against my rules, but I haven't been able to stop thinking about you—about that kiss and the way your hands felt on my body. I finally decided to toss my rules out the window, but then the fire happened, and in the hospital room you seemed so angry at me. I just spiraled out of control after that and—"

I don't know what else to do to get her to stop rambling, so I kiss her.

Claire's eyes widen, but I coax her into submission with my lips, and within seconds her body is melting against mine.

"I wasn't angry, Claire, far from it," I whisper against her lips.

"Then what were you?"

"Scared, frustrated, sad, you name it. I'll never be able to tell you what it was like for me when I heard you were in that fire. I was trying desperately to keep my emotions in check, because I knew I had to get you out of there. I was frustrated that you put your life in danger by running back in, but I got it. I got it, Claire. I understood why you did it. Doesn't mean I liked it, because I don't know what I would've done if something had happened to you that day. I was scared—scared of the feelings I had for you, scared that you didn't feel the same way. And then I freaked out because I have a rule that I don't date victims, and suddenly you were a victim. That frustrated the hell out of me, and I lashed out."

She grins. "Us and our damn rules."

"I hate our rules."

"Me too. And I don't want to be your victim, Trevor, any more than you want to be my test dummy."

I smile. "You're not my victim. Far from it. I'm just sorry it took so long for us to get to this point. I shouldn't have kept you at arm's length for so many years, and I should've told you sooner that I think you're amazing and I want a chance to be with you. I'm sorry I got angry with you in the hospital. I didn't know how else to process everything. Lashing out at you was easier than facing all those emotions, and honestly, I wasn't sure if you were ready to hear everything I have to say."

"I probably wasn't. But I am now."

"I know, sweetheart, and we're going to talk about it, I promise. But it's going to have to wait because I've got to work today. Speaking of which, what time is it?"

Claire reaches for her phone on the coffee table. "Six o'clock."

"Shit." As much as I hate to do it, I extricate myself from

under Claire. "I've got to be at work in an hour, and I've still got to go home and shower."

"Sorry, I should've set an alarm."

"It's not your fault. We both got sucked up in our conversation last night. Speaking of which, how are you feeling this morning?"

She shrugs. "Lighter."

"That's a start. The feelings are still there, I'm sure. It'll take time to move on, but you'll get there, and I'm going to be with you every step of the way."

"Thank you for talking to me and staying with me. I really appreciate it."

Resting my hand on hers, I squeeze. "Anytime, Claire. I'm always here for you."

Claire looks at my hand on top of hers. "I slept better last night than I have in weeks."

"Me too."

"You know, you could always come back tonight, if you wanted."

Oh shit. This woman is going to be the death of me. "I can't. I'm on for a forty-eight-hour shift."

"Right," she sighs. "I forgot you work those crazy hours."

"But we'll talk soon, okay?"

She nods. I squeeze her hand one last time and stand up. Making sure my wallet is still tucked in my back pocket, pick up my hat, which somehow ended up on the floor, put it on, and grab my keys. My hand hits the knob, and Claire's voice stops me.

"Trevor?"

I turn around. Claire walks toward me. Her clothes are a wrinkly mess, her bare feet sticking out from her jeans, and I wonder when she ditched her socks. She stops in front of me and looks up. Sliding her hands up my chest, she wraps her arms around my neck and pulls me down for another kiss, and this time I let her take the lead.

She angles my face over hers in a way that pulls me in deep, and when she moans, I snap and drag her against me. We fall against the door as Claire practically climbs my body. We're a mess of arms and hands and tongues, and I'll be damned if she didn't just make leaving that much harder.

We're panting and breathless when she breaks the kiss. Her eyes are glossy. I'm sure mine are the same.

"I don't care what excuses you come up with over the next few days," she says. "You'll never convince me we shouldn't give this a try. Life is short. There's only one thing more precious than our time, and that's who we spend it with. And I'd really like to spend my time with you."

"Claire."

I can't believe I have to go to work when all I want to do is drag her back to her room and make sweet, sweet love to her. I want to worship her body and promise all of the shit I swore I'd never promise a woman.

Since that isn't an option, I tug her in for another kiss.

When I pull back, we're both panting for air.

With a coy smile, she reaches around me and pushes the front door open. "Don't want you to be late for work. Just wanted to give you something to think about while you're there."

You did a damn good job of that, sweetheart. Now I'm wondering how the hell I can tell her my secrets and keep her at the same time.

"This conversation isn't over," I say.

"That's what I'm counting on."

CHAPTER
Twenty-Two

Claire

"Mom, I've got to call you back, someone's at the door."

"Okay, sweetie, I'll talk to you later."

I disconnect the call, push my phone into my back pocket, and pull open the front door.

"Here." Mo shoves a tan ball of fur at me. "I can't take it anymore."

I take Milo before she falls to the floor. Her glassy eyes look up, and when she catches a whiff of me, her tongue darts out, swiping my upper lip.

"Gross," I say, pushing her nose away. "I don't know where that mouth has been." But Milo doesn't care, she keeps licking anything and everything she can get her slobbery little tongue on.

"I'm sorry, but I can't take her back. That dog is a hot mess," Mo says, holding her hands up.

"She is not," I say, stepping to the side so Mo can come in.

"All she's done since you dropped her off is cry. I even swiped one of your T-shirts to put in her pen; it's the only way

I get her to eat or sleep."

"Which T-shirt?"

"Your Bon Jovi one."

"I've been looking for that. When did you take it?"

"I don't know." She shrugs. "A week ago. Snagged it off your floor when you went to the bathroom, and I'm not sorry. She's a mess, Claire. She misses you."

I want to tell Mo it doesn't matter, that she needs to take Milo back, but damn it, I miss Milo too. It's been weeks, and I still find myself wanting to fill her food bowl every morning and take her on a walk every night, even though I always ended up carrying her. And as much as I hated the feel of her cold nose being shoved into my neck at the crack of dawn, I've missed that too.

"Fine. I'll keep her."

Mo's eyes widen. "Really?"

"Yes." I set Milo down, and she runs straight into the wall before turning around and heading in the opposite direction. "One of these days she's going to learn not to just take off running."

"You do know you can't bring her back again, right?"

I look at Mo. "I know."

"You're her person, Claire. That might not seem like much to us, but to them, it's everything."

"I know, Mo. I get it. I promise she has a forever home with me. I won't let her down again." I mean that with every fiber of my being.

"Thank God Trevor called this morning." Mo drops down on the couch and leans her head back on the cushion. "Because I was about to lose my mind with her incessant howling."

"Why did Trevor call you this morning?"

"To tell me he thought you'd turned a corner last night, and you woke up in a good mood, and if I was ever going to convince you to take the dog back, now was my chance."

"Did he now?" That conniving, wonderful, sexy man saw an opening and took it.

She nods. "Yeah. And you know, I wasn't surprised to hear you'd turned a corner last night. I figured if anyone could get through to you, it would be him. But I *was* surprised to hear him say you woke up in a good mood. How would he know that, Claire?"

I pause to collect my thoughts a moment. "He stayed the night."

"Like, slept on the couch because it was late and you talked all night and he didn't want to drive home, stay the night? Or because he pounded the funk out of you like I told you he would, stay the night?"

I roll my eyes. "There was no pounding. He stayed because I asked him to, and he slept on the couch." *With me on top of him.*

There's a wicked gleam in her eye. "Did something happen between you two?"

"We talked. A lot. He helped me work through some things, and he's right. I did turn a corner."

I wasn't lying this morning when I told Trevor I felt lighter. The guilt over my actions still simmers beneath the surface, but it's no longer boiling over, and that's a huge step for me.

"That's not what I meant."

"I know what you meant, and nothing happened."

"Damn." She pouts, patting Milo's head when she jumps up on the couch.

Milo stumbles across Mo's lap, landing face first in mine.

I scratch the top of her head, and then her belly when she flops over, but I look at Mo. "Thank you."

"For what?" Mo asks.

"Everything."

"I didn't do anything, Claire."

"Yes, you did. You didn't give up on me when I was struggling not to give up on myself. You called every day even though I was grumpy and short with you. You cooked for me and took care of this little girl while I got my head on straight."

"I did what any friend would do."

"No." I shake my head. "I've got other friends, Mo, and not one of them went as far as you. Thank you for that. And thank you for forcing me to get out of the house last night and for bringing Milo back this morning. You're a really great friend, and I'm lucky to have you."

Her eyes fill up with tears.

"Don't cry," I say, pulling her into my arms. Milo grunts between us, but doesn't bother to move.

"I can't help it. I've been really emotional the last few days. I think I'm getting ready to start my period."

"Period?" I laugh. "Nothing about shark week for you is a period. It's a damn exclamation point."

She's crying and laughing, and it feels good to be back to this place with her. "I missed you," she says.

"I'm going to be fine, Mo," I assure her. And this time I think I mean it. "It might take some time to get back to normal, but I promise I'm getting there."

She holds me tight in her arms for several minutes before pulling back. "Sean and Rhett are taking care of Animal Haven. Wanna hang out? We could watch a move or grab lunch."

"I'd love that."

CHAPTER
Twenty-Three

Trevor

"What's up, Allen?" Darius, or Big D as we like to call him, comes into the washroom at the firehouse and drops his gear next to the washing machine. "You using this?"

"I'm done." I smile and pat his back. "It's all yours."

"What's gotten into you?" he asks, shoving his turnouts into the washer. "I don't think I've seen you smile this much since the Cardinals won the World Series."

"Nothing's gotten into me. Just ready to be done with this shift." So I can go see Claire.

We texted off and on all day yesterday and made plans to meet up tomorrow night. My shift ends tonight, but I won't get home until late, and tomorrow I have to work at the ranch. But after that, she's all mine.

Still don't know what in the world I'm going to say to her, but I'll figure it out.

Big D bobs his head. "Don't I know it. My shift is over effective…" He looks at his watch. "Right now, and all I want to do is go home, take a hot shower, bang my wife, and sleep for a day."

I laugh. "What the hell are you hanging around here for? Go. I'll take care of your gear."

"I appreciate the offer, and any other day I'd take you up on that, but Todd and I have to go to the elementary school for community career day."

"On your day off?"

He shrugs. "No one else wanted to do it, and I can't let the kids down like that, man. They love us."

I glance over at Todd, who is in full gear, doing a check on truck 1090. I vaguely remember seeing a sign-up sheet on the bulletin board asking for volunteers for career day, but that's never been my thing, so I ignored it.

"You said it was at the elementary school?"

"Yeah," he answers. "First and second grade."

Thoughts meet brick wall.

I've never really believed in fate, but this has to be some sort of sign.

I turn to Big D. "I'll do it."

"Really? Because I don't mind."

"I know you don't, but your shift is over. You should get home to that gorgeous wife of yours."

"You're sure?"

I nod. "Absolutely. And don't worry about your gear; I'll finish it up for you."

"Thank you, Trevor. I'll owe you one."

No, thank you. "Anytime, Big D."

I watch him leave, and then I walk over to Todd. "I'm your wingman today. What do you need me to do?"

He tosses a clipboard on the front seat of the truck. "What happened to Darius?"

"I told him to head home. No sense in him going on his day off when there's a dozen others here to do the job."

"Sounds good to me. I don't care who goes, just as long as I'm not alone. Those kids can get a little rambunctious." He shuts the truck door. "I told the principal we'd come after first period, so we'll leave here at nine. We're doing first grade first, and then second grade."

"Sounds good." I look at the clock. One hour to kill.

And it's the slowest hour in the history of hours. All I do is think about Claire and her beautiful smile and bright green eyes, which are on full display when we finally go and she sees me pull up in the fire truck.

The kids are all lined up on the sidewalk, squirming around, faces full of smiles as they prepare to learn about being fire-fighters. But nothing compares to the look on Claire's face. The clouds that were in her eyes two nights ago are gone, and I'd like to think I had a little something to do with that.

"Hey, Red." I give her my best smile, and with one hand on her elbow, I lean in and kiss her cheek.

She squeaks, her eyes darting toward the kids on the side-walk, but they're paying no attention. She looks back at me, her smile growing by the second. "What are you doing here? Where's Darius?"

"Don't pretend you aren't happy to see me."

"Cocky much?"

"Admit it. You've been thinking about me just as much as I've been thinking about you."

"Have you thought about what I said before you left?"

"Among other things."

She tilts her head. "What other things?"

"The kiss you gave me. I've been thinking about that a lot." Claire's cheeks turn pink.

"Are you ready, Trevor?" Todd asks.

"Yeah, I'll be right there." I return my gaze to Claire. "Have you thought about the kiss, Claire?"

"Come on, bro," Todd hollers. "Let's get this show on the road."

With a mischievous grin, Claire places her hands on my chest and slowly pushes me away. "You better get to work, Mr. Allen. You've got a group of kids waiting on you."

"You're evil," I whisper, joining Todd on the sidewalk.

We spend the next hour talking to the kids about the fire truck, showing them how to explore and see what each thing does. The kids get the chance to climb inside, and we let them turn on the sirens and lights, and it's a lot more fun than I thought it would be.

After we've gone through our normal spiel, Todd and I have the kids sit back down on the grass. "We've still got plenty of time. Does anyone have any questions?" he asks.

Two little boys in the front row throw their hands up, and I smile to myself when I recognize them as Marcus and Troy. They probably don't recognize me, and I'm not sure how they've been handling the fire, so I don't plan to bring it up.

"What's your name?" I ask, pointing to the boy on the left. The boy on the right pouts while the other smiles proudly.

"Marcus."

"What's your question, Marcus?"

"Have you ever saved someone's life?"

Yeah, buddy. Yours. "I have."

"How many?" he fires back.

"I don't know. I don't keep track."

"More than ten?" his twin brother asks.

"Way more than ten."

They look at me approvingly, and Todd moves on to the next kid. "What's your name?" he asks a little girl in the back row.

She stands up. "Lilah."

"What's your question, Lilah?"

"My mom watches a firefighter show on TV."

Todd and I watch Lilah, waiting for her to get the questions, but she just stares at us.

"Cool," I say. "Did you have a question for us?"

She shakes her head and sits down.

Todd laughs and claps his hands together. "Trevor and I have time to show you one more thing before we finish up today. We can either practice our stop, drop, and roll, or we can show you the different ways to do a one-man carry. Raise your hand if you want to stop, drop, and roll."

All the kids keep their hands down, and Marcus blurts, "We stop, drop, and roll all the time."

"Okay then, one-man carries it is." Todd looks through the sea of kids. "Who would like to volunteer?" Twenty hands go up in the air, but when I spot Claire behind the kids, an idea pops into my head.

"How about we use your teacher?" I ask, making it sound exciting and cool.

The kids fall for it hook, line, and sinker.

Claire's eyes widen, and she shakes her head. "No. No, no, no. Use one of the kids."

"Come on, Ms. Daniels," a few of the kids taunt, and then they all break out in a chant:

Ms. Dan-iels.

Ms. Dan-iels.

Ms. Dan-iels.

I should've brought candy for these kids. Not only do I get to stare at their beautiful teacher, but because of them, now I get to touch her.

Finally giving in, Claire rolls her eyes and walks over to

Todd, but I grab her wrist and pull her toward me. "He'll talk. I'll demonstrate."

She grins. "Of course you will."

"The first hold is called a one-person lift. Place one arm under the victim's knee and the other around their back."

I step into Claire. "Good thing you didn't wear a skirt," I whisper.

Before she can respond, I bend down and scoop her up the same way a husband would carry his new bride. Claire wraps her arm around my neck. Her body is warm against mine. She feels so damn good, and today she smells like lavender.

"I've thought about the kiss a lot," she whispers, while smiling at her students.

"I knew it."

"I'm also not wearing any underwear," she adds.

My cock starts to grow thick in my pants, and I think of anything and everything I can to make it stop, because no way in hell can I get a raging hard-on in front of a group of first graders.

That little minx knew exactly what she was doing.

Bunnies.

Pink bunnies.

Kittens.

"This hold only works with a child or someone you can easily lift," Todd explains while I run through a list of cute little animals. "If someone is really big or overweight, we would have to find a different way to move them. The next hold is called a firefighter carry."

I set Claire back on her feet. She smooths her hands down the front of her blouse and takes a bow when the kids clap for her. She tries to step away, probably thinking I'll use a different volunteer for each hold, but I put a quick stop to that when I grab her arm and fling her over my shoulder. The kids all laugh, and Claire places her palms on my lower back for leverage as I parade her around the group so they can get a good look at how I'm carrying her.

"With this hold, the victim is carried over one shoulder. The rescuer's arm, on the side that the victim is being carried, is wrapped across their legs, and the rescuer grasps the victim's opposite arm. This technique is used for carrying a victim longer distances," Todd says.

"It's also used to carry a woman to bed and provides the perfect opportunity spank her ass if she's been bad," I whisper, so only Claire can hear.

I can't see her, but I hear her breath hitch.

"And it's a mighty fine ass," I add.

"If a victim is on the ground, this hold is difficult and will require a strong rescuer," Todd says, continuing to the next hold. "The last one-man carry we're going to show you today is the pack-strap carry."

I let Claire down. She turns away, pretending to be unaffected by me.

"In this hold, you'll see that Trevor is going to pull the victims arms over his shoulders from behind."

I follow Todd's direction. I step in front of Claire and bend at the knee. She lifts up on her toes, allowing me to hoist her up on my back.

"You'll notice that this is similar to a piggyback ride, but Ms. Daniels leaves her legs hanging rather than wrapping them around Trevor's waist. When injuries make the firefighter carry unsafe, this method can be used." Todd smiles. "That's it. Doesn't anyone have any questions?"

I lower Claire to her feet, and before she can turn away, I grab her wrist. "Did my words turn you on, Claire?"

"Why would you think that?" she says, adjusting her top.

"Because your nipples are hard. They were cutting into my back."

She spins us around so my back is facing the kids and then she steps in close, as though she's giving me a hug. Her fingers curl around my erection through my pants. She gives it a solid squeeze, followed by a pat, and then she winks. "And now so is your cock," she whispers.

Well played, Claire. Well played.

"That's it?" Marcus asks.

I turn around to face the kids and watch Claire take her spot by the tree.

She winks, and while my cock is definitely hard, there are other strange things happening in my body—a warmth radiating to my toes and a gallop in my heart that wasn't there before. I know without a doubt that I've got to come clean, and if she decides she hates me, I'll do whatever it takes to win her back, because I need this woman in my life.

"No, those are just one-man carries. There are two-and three-man carries, and we also use stretchers, ropes, straps, and chairs to move victims," I answer.

Todd looks at his watch and steps forward. "It looks like our time is up. Does anyone have a question they have to have answered before we move on to the next class?" The group of kids sit quietly, no one raising their hands, and Claire claps hers together.

"All right, class." She steps around the group and stands in front of Todd and me. "What do we say to these two firefighters for coming and talking to us today?"

"Thank you," they all say in unison.

"I want you all to stand up and form a single-file line behind Tara," she tells them.

The kids rise to their feet, and Claire turns to us. "Thank you so much for coming. We really appreciate it." She wraps Todd's hand between hers.

"It's our pleasure. We'll see you next year," he says.

She nods and watches Todd walk toward the fire truck before turning to me. "I take it you haven't come up with any excuses."

I shake my head. "Not one."

"Good." She smiles, and I notice her clear eyes once again.

"You look good…happy," I say.

"I have you to thank for that. And I have you to thank for calling Mo yesterday morning."

I was hoping I wasn't crossing any lines by calling Mo. Judging by the easy smile on Claire's face, I think it's safe to say I'm in the clear. "I take it you got your dog back."

"I did."

"That's good."

A bell rings. Claire's eyes dart to the school and then back to mine. "Will I see you tomorrow night?"

"Absolutely."

She turns to her class and starts them walking. I join Todd by the fire truck, but keep my eyes on her until she disappears into the school.

CHAPTER
Twenty-Four

Trevor

"You're here early."

I toss the shovel and tool bag in the bed of my truck. "We're ranchers. We always start early."

Dad looks at his watch and lifts his brow. "I do, but you're coming off a two-day shift, which means you usually sleep in."

"I figured you could use a little extra help with Rhett back in Houston."

And I didn't sleep worth shit last night, so I was up anyway.

I tossed and turned all last night, trying to find a way to tell Claire about my involvement in her dad's death and keep her interested in being with me at the same time. But no matter how it plays out in my head, it always ends the same way: with Claire hating me.

This is the reason I always kept my distance. I knew we would be explosive, and I knew that once I got a taste of her, I would only want more. Now I'm fucked because I either tell her the truth and risk her hating me, or I walk away first—and damn it, I can't do that, not again.

"Son."

I blink when Dad lays a hand on my shoulder.

"Are you okay? Is something bothering you?"

"No." I shut the tailgate and tug my shirt off, because just thinking of Claire has me hot and bothered.

"Ahhh. Now I get it."

"Get what?"

"Woman problems. Nothing to be ashamed of, boy. We've all got 'em."

I shake my head. "There are no woman problems, because there is no woman."

"Well," Dad says, nudging my arm. "Maybe that's your problem."

"You telling me I need to find a woman? Because I'll have you know that women love me."

"I know they do, son. You've got too many to pick from," he says. "And hell no. I wouldn't tell you to get a woman until you're one-hundred-percent ready, because women are a pain in the ass, and they'll drive you insane. They're completely worth it in the end, but it's the middle shit that'll make you lose your mind."

"And how does someone know he's made it through all the crazy shit? When does the headache become worth it?"

"When you've got the girl. When she smiles at you like you hung the moon and promises to love you forever, you'll know you made it."

"Sounds like a lot of work."

"It's not easy; that's for damn sure."

Dad and I climb into the truck and head for the barn.

"Was Mom a pain in the ass?"

"The worst. Your mother made me chase her for years before she finally agreed to go out with me."

I laugh because I can totally see my mom doing that. She's

stubborn to a fault. "And you've been together ever since."

"Hell no. We both made a lot of mistakes, and we broke up several times before we got it right."

"That doesn't sound like fun."

"Love rarely is, but it's a beautiful thing, and once you get a taste of it with the right person, you'll never get enough. You'll spend the rest of your life fighting for it."

I keep my eyes trained on the dirt road, afraid that if I look at him he'll see how much his words have resonated with me.

"Just take your time, son," he says, rolling down his window. "There's a girl out there for you. You've just got to find her."

I think I already have. "What if I've already found her, but I've kept something from her?"

Dad gives me a curious look, but asks only one question. "Whatever you've kept from her, will it hurt her?"

"Maybe."

Dad nods. "You have to be honest. Lay it all on the line and let the chips fall where they may. You can't control fate, son. If she's meant to be yours, you've got nothing to worry about. But no secrets. You can't build a solid foundation on lies. You need trust for that."

"Thanks, Dad."

"Anytime, son." He claps a hand on my shoulder. "Now, let's get to work."

Today I need to work my ass off. Maybe if I concentrate on the things I need to get done, I won't think about how soft Claire's lips are and how her breasts felt pressed against my back yesterday. And I certainly won't think about how badly I want to touch her again.

Yeah right.

CHAPTER
Twenty-Five

Trevor

After a grueling ten hours in the field, I pop the top on a cold beer and walk out to my parents' patio. Settling on a lounge chair, I look out across the ranch. It's been in our family for years. There was a time I wanted nothing to do with it, had no desire to take over one day. But somewhere along the way, that's all changed. The thought of taking over and raising a family in the house I grew up in has become a distant dream—although I'm afraid I'll have to fight Rhett for it.

I love firefighting, but I have a feeling that one of these days—maybe when I have kids—I'll want to come home at night rather than working the long-ass days I do now. The life of a rancher isn't easy, but it's not twenty-four-or forty-eight-hours shifts either.

My dad worked his ass off when we were growing up, but he was home every night for dinner, and he never missed a sporting event or school concert.

Closing my eyes, I rest my head against the cushion, imagining how different life would be if I came home every night to a warm meal and two spunky kids running around. Claire would greet me at the door with a kiss, we would spend the evening playing with our children, and then I'd lay her down and worship her body for hours—

"Sleepin' on the job or what?" Rhett says, kicking the side of my chair.

I open my eyes. "Hardly. But it's nice of you to finally show up after all the work is done."

"I would've been here if I could've." He sighs, dropping into the chair next to mine. "I'll tell you what, bro…" He blows out a harsh breath. "I'll never understand this."

I kick my legs over the side of my chair and sit up. "Understand what?"

"How dreams can shift and change so rapidly." Rhett runs a hand over his face. "I used to live for bull riding. The PBR was all I thought about. After a day like today, I would've hit the bar with my buddies and had a few beers and a hot meal before calling it a night. Instead, I skipped it all and drove my ass home—even though I've got to drive back in the morning—just so I could sleep in the same bed as Mo. She's all I think about. What's she doing? Does she have enough help at Animal Haven? Did she remember to pack a lunch?" He looks up. "Because she forgets it half the time and will go without eating if I'm not there to remind her."

"This must be the insane part Dad was talking about."

"Huh?"

I shake my head. "Nothing. Keep going."

"I'm counting down the months until my season and endorsement contracts are up so I can walk away from it all."

"Wow. That's huge. When you and Mo got back together, you mentioned giving it all up, but I wasn't sure you meant it."

"I meant every word. I want to be here, helping you and Dad on the ranch and helping her run Animal Haven. I don't want to rely on you for that shit—it's my responsibility. I don't want to be away from her anymore."

"Then don't be, brother. But if you're dying to see Mo, why did you stop here first?"

"I'm going to ask her to marry me," Rhett blurts.

"Well, I'll be damned." I reach out and give my brother a half hug, clapping him on the back. "Congratulations. Maybe you're past the insane part after all. Maybe you've made it to the end."

"You okay?"

"Yeah, why?"

"Because you aren't making a bit of sense."

"It's nothing. Just something Dad and I were talking about earlier. This calls for a celebration. You want a beer?"

"I'd love one."

I leave Rhett stewing over his impending proposal as I walk inside and grab him a beer. The poor sap probably needs it.

"When are you going to pop the question?" I ask, handing him a bottle.

Rhett cups his hand over the cap and twists it off. "No clue. Sometime soon. I'm just waiting for the right moment."

"You've already got the ring?"

He nods, his eyes growing wide as he takes a swig. "That's why I'm here. Mom's hiding it for me. Those damn things are expensive."

"I'll take your word for it."

"How did Dad do today?" he asks, reclining in his seat.

I see-saw my hand in the air. "He did okay. Moving slower than normal."

"Yeah, that's what I thought last time I worked with him."

My father—Sawyer Allen—is a brute of a man. Tall, broad, and made for life on a ranch, but that life has worn him down.

He's not old by any means, but he's not a spring chicken either, and Rhett and I have been worried for a while that one of these days he'll end up hurting himself. The man doesn't know when to stop, and he constantly works himself into the ground. This is despite the fact that he has a handful of farmworkers he trusts to help with day-to-day tasks. On top of them, he has Rhett and me, who spend our days off—from sunup to sundown—doing whatever work needs to be done.

"You know as well as I do that he'll never stop working."

"I know," I sigh.

There's a pause. Both of us look out across the land, watching the cattle graze.

"You sure nothing else is on your mind?" Rhett asks.

I shrug and look over at him. "Just thinking."

"'Bout what?"

"Nothing much. Just life in general."

Rhett sits up. "Come on, man. I just spilled my guts. I'm your brother. You can tell me anything. You get some woman knocked up?"

I frown. "Not even close."

For months, I've felt unsettled. First it was the women and my lack of desire for a one-night stand. And then it was coming home to an empty house. That snowballed into watching other couples, wondering if I deserved that sort of commitment from a woman. But it was kissing Claire in the bathroom at Animal Haven that drove me to the edge, and waking up with her two days ago tipped me over. Wrapped in her arms, I felt worthy and surrounded by a sense of peace I haven't felt for a damn long time.

I'm not sure if telling Rhett is the right thing, but he's recently taken the plunge into the relationship pool, so I figure why the hell not? Wiping my hands on my jeans, I go for it.

"I'm thinking maybe it's time I settle down."

Rhett laughs, but when he realizes I'm not, he sobers. "You're serious?"

"But now I know where you stand on the matter," I say, punching him in the arm. "Thanks, brother."

"I'm sorry, Trevor. It's just…you love women almost as much as they love you. And you've never even had a girlfriend."

I don't tell him I haven't been intimate with a woman in months. He'd have a field day with that. And over the years, I've found that sometimes it's easier to let people believe what they want to about you. It keeps the expectations to a minimum, doesn't leave as much room for disappointment if you fuck up—and I always fuck up.

"You're right." I take a swig of my beer. "I'd probably fail miserably."

Rhett drains his beer, stands up, and tosses the empty bottle in the trash. He walks back over and lays a hand on my shoulder.

"No, I'm not right. And no, you wouldn't. You're not the annoying little brother who followed me around for years. You've grown into a successful, hardworking man, and any woman would be lucky to have you by her side. If you're ready, I say go for it."

I nod once and smile. "Thank you. I appreciate that."

"Just don't go for it with Claire."

It takes a second for his words to sink in, and I furrow my brow. "Why not Claire?"

"Shit," he sighs, running his fingers through his hair. "It's Claire, isn't it?"

"Look, I know she could do a hell of a lot better than me, but—"

"Whoa." Rhett holds his hands up. "It's not because she could do better than you. You're one of the best men I know.

She'd be damn lucky to be with you."

"Then what?"

"I told you at the bar; it's because she's one of my best friends, and you're my brother. I will choose you, always, but if you break her heart, I'll have to kick your ass, and I'll risk losing her in the process, and I don't want it to come to that."

"And I told you I would never intentionally hurt her."

Rhett takes a deep breath in, and when he blows it out he says, "I know you wouldn't. But love is unpredictable and messy." He sighs. "Just be good to her, okay? Don't make me hunt you down." He gives me a pointed look before he turns away.

"Rhett?"

"Yeah?" He stops and looks over his shoulder.

"Do me a favor and don't mention this to Mo. It's all still new, and nothing is official, and—"

"Your secret is safe with me. But fair warning, *those* two tell each other everything. And I mean *everything*."

Maybe not everything. Because if Mo knew half of what's gone on between me and Claire, she'd be all up in my business. "Thanks for the heads up."

I'm the last thing a girl like Claire needs. She's all sweet and good, and I'm tainted—tainted by my past and by the profession I've chosen, which is way outside what she typically seems prepared to handle. But despite all of my efforts, I can't stay away from her.

Now I need to know if she can forgive me for the mistake my twelve-year-old self made so we can sort this out together.

There's only one way to find out.

CHAPTER
Twenty-Six

Trevor

Taking a deep breath, I knock on Claire's front door. It's late, but I know she's up because the light in her living room is on. She's probably waiting on me, and now I feel like an ass for not getting here sooner. The porch light flips on, and a second later she opens the door. Milo darts out, stumbling between my feet, and I pick her up.

"You lost something." I hand Claire her dog.

"Thank you."

She smiles as she holds the door open, and all I can think of is that damn fantasy of coming home to her after a long day on the ranch.

"Come in."

I step over the threshold and hear her shut the door and lock it behind me.

"How was your day?" she asks, quietly.

"Rough."

Turning around, I take Claire in. Her back is against the door, Milo squirming in her arms. She's wearing a pair of silky shorts and a matching purple tank top that leaves very little to the imagination. Her nipples are puckered, threatening to break through the thin material, and I want to lift her top up and suck a tight peak into my mouth.

She takes a step forward, drawing my eyes up. "What happened?" she asks, setting the pup down. Milo scurries off, leaving me alone with her owner.

I grab Claire's hand. "Couldn't stop thinking about you."

"Oh," she says. "That must've been awful."

I tug her forward until her body falls against mine. "Wasn't sure I was going to make it through the day."

"Maybe I can make it up to you." Pushing up on her toes, Claire presses her lips to my mouth, and I let her because I need this connection. I need to ensure I get one final kiss before I say what I've come to say.

Her soft mouth molds against mine, but when she pushes her tongue against the seam of my lips, I stop her, afraid that if we take it any further, I'll chicken out.

"Can we talk first?"

"As long as you haven't changed your mind or come up with an excuse for why this won't work."

I hate the uncertainty in her voice. "I haven't, but *you* might after you hear what I have to say."

"Okay," she says cautiously. "I'm listening."

Every worst-case scenario runs through my head. I take a deep breath and motion for the couch. "You might want to sit down for this."

She swallows hard. "I'm good."

"Please, Claire, sit."

"You're scaring me, Trevor," she says, lowering herself to the couch.

"I, uh...wow." I rub my hands together. "This is a lot harder than I thought it would be—"

"Listen, if this is some weird it's-not-you-it's-me thing you're trying to figure out how to say, then just forget about it." Claire pushes up from the couch, but I catch her before she makes it far.

"No. I swear it's not like that. Please, sit back down."

She eyes me warily but returns to her seat. "Come on, Trevor, just tell me already."

"I'm the reason your dad is dead," I blurt. My entire body trembles as adrenaline pumps through my veins, and my arms and legs go numb as I wait for her to say something.

Claire's mouth opens, and a cold knot forms in my stomach.

"What?" she asks, shaking her head. "I…I don't understand."

I take a step toward her, but she doesn't move. She's staring at me like I just spoke in a foreign language.

"The fire your dad responded to the day he was killed? It broke out around twelve o'clock that afternoon, during my lunch period." I say, lowering myself to the couch beside her, making sure I keep enough distance between us.

I've relived that day more times than I can count, but I've never talked about it out loud to another person. "I was twelve and in a bad place—rebellious, crazy hormones, and mad at the world. I snuck out to the bleachers during lunch to smoke. It was freezing outside, and I kept lighting cigarettes, one right after the other, and the next thing I knew, the fire alarms at the school were going off. At first, I thought it was the bell, so I snuffed out my cigarette. By the time I made it across the football field, kids were spilling out of the school, tripping over each other, crying and screaming, and that's when I knew it was something more. And then the fire department showed up, and all hell broke loose. Your dad was the first one on the scene."

Claire's eyes are swimming in tears. She was in high school at the time, so she wasn't there during the fire, but I'm sure she's heard how horrific it was that day.

"He didn't waver, Claire. He ran into that building without abandon, dragging kids out. They eventually contained the fire, but there was one kid unaccounted for, and that kid was me."

My fingers are numb, my palms growing increasingly sweaty with each word, and I wipe them down the front of my jeans. "Your dad went in after me, but I was already outside."

Claire starts shaking her head, but I keep talking, needing to get it all about before she says anything else.

"God, Claire, I was already outside. I knew they sent him in to find me, and I could've spoken up, but I was scared. I was a coward. And I'll never forgive myself, because your dad went into that building one last time because of me, and he never came back out." The words get clogged in my throat, and I cover my face with my hands.

Claire inches closer, resting her hand on my back. "Trevor," she whispers, repeating my name a second time when I don't look up. "Trevor, that's not how it happened."

"Yes, it is," I say, pushing up from the couch to pace. "I saw it all play out from the bleachers. I heard them tell your dad to go back in. I should've hollered and jumped, run up to the chief—anything—but all I could think was that I didn't want to get caught. I didn't want my parents to find out I was smoking, so I stayed hidden. At some point during the chaos, I snuck into a crowd of kids and pretended I'd been there the whole time."

Stopping in front of Claire, I watch her, waiting for her to lash out and tear into me. I think I need it. I need her to tell me I'm a coward and she'll never forgive me for what I did. What I don't need is for her to stare at me like she is now: speechless, with more love and heartache in her eyes than I've ever seen reflected back at me.

"Say something," I whisper, falling to my knees in front of

her. "Tell me you hate me. Tell me I'm a coward, something."

She doesn't. Claire shakes her head as tears fall down her face, and I don't bother wiping them away because I don't deserve that privilege. I don't deserve to touch her. And now that my feelings have bubbled to the surface, I can't seem to keep them from boiling over.

"I was a coward, Claire, and I'm sorry. I don't expect you to forgive me. I would never ask that of you, but I want you to know I would give anything to go back to that day and change things. I'd give up my life if I could take it back." My voice cracks on the last word, and I can't keep it in any longer. My bottom lip trembles, and tears flow down my cheeks. I wipe them away, but they keep coming.

"I should've told you sooner. I should've come clean and—" I choke back a sob. "I'm so sorry. These words are pointless. They don't bring back your father, but I don't know what else to say. Tell me what to say, Claire. Tell me what to do." Dropping my chin to my chest, I swallow past the giant lump in my throat. "I'm sorry, Claire. I'm sorry."

"Stop, Trevor." Cupping my jaw in her soft hands, she lifts my face. "Please, stop saying that. Remember when you told me I wasn't allowed to apologize to you for pulling me out of that fire?"

I nod, unsure if I can form words without losing my shit.

"This is the same thing. You didn't kill my father, Trevor. He died doing what he loved. He died doing what he was trained to do. But he *did not* die because of you. The building collapsed, trapping him, but that wasn't your fault."

Did she not hear a word I said? "But I was out of the building, Claire." Pulling her hands from my face, I scoot back. She's not thinking clearly, and once she realizes what I'm telling her, she'll hate me.

"Yes, you were, and I'm so glad, because if you'd been in the building that day, something might've happened to you, and I can't imagine a world where you don't exist, Trevor."

"You're not listening to me."

"You're not listening to *me*." Her voice demands every bit of my attention. "He didn't go back in because he thought there was someone still in there."

"But I heard them. I heard the men talking..."

"I wasn't there, Trevor, so I don't know what you heard, but I've read the report, and I've talked to my dad's crew who were with him that day, and I promise you he did not go back into that building because of you."

I don't understand. "Then why?"

"Did you know my dad was an arson investigator?"

"No, I didn't."

She nods. "He was. The report says the final sweep of the building was all clear, and the structure was deemed safe. My dad went back into the school to begin his investigation."

This is all too much. I stand up, pushing my fingers into my hair while I pace the room. Tears burn my eyes, but I look up at the ceiling and squeeze them shut. For thirteen years I've carried this around with me. I've lost sleep over it, and I've let it eat at me. To find out everything I thought to be true is something entirely different—that's a little overwhelming.

"Then why do I remember hearing them say they were missing a kid?"

Claire shakes her head. "I don't know. The reports didn't say anything about a missing kid. That day was hectic. There were children and adults crying and screaming, and people running all over. Who knows what you heard. And you were only twelve at the time, Trevor. It's possible you misunderstood the situation, or maybe over the years that memory has been skewed."

"Maybe, but I…"

I don't know what to say. For years I've hated myself for that. It's the reason I've kept Claire at arm's length. It's also the reason I've kept a protective eye on her from afar—almost like it was my duty to watch out for her and somehow repay my debt.

"It wasn't your fault, Trevor, and I hate that you've lived with this for so long. I barely survived living with my guilt for a few weeks, and you've been battling it for over a decade."

I never told a soul—not my best friends, siblings, or even my parents. I was too ashamed. For years it consumed me, and as I struggled to become the man I am today, there were many nights I lost myself in the bottle or the arms of a willing woman. Other days I was able to cope, but no matter what, it was always there.

When I was eighteen, my career choice slammed into me with enough force to rock my life off its axis. I had a nightmare—the same one I'd been having for years. I was crouched behind the bushes, watching the firefighters fight the flames, but instead of the scene unfolding, a hand grabbed the back of my shirt and yanked me to my feet.

"Don't just sit there," a man yelled, tossing me toward the group of firefighters. "Get off your ass and help us."

That man was Claire's dad.

And that dream changed my life forever.

It wasn't until I completed my training and became a fulltime firefighter that I really learned the risks you have to be prepared to take every time you run into a burning building. But I promised himself I'd always be ready to take them, to pay forward the sacrifice Claire's dad made for me.

The guilt lessened after that, but it never quite went away, and now I'm not sure how I'm supposed to let go of something

I've carried around with me for so long.

"You have me," Claire whispers.

I blink, completely unaware that I said that out loud.

"It's not going to get better overnight—isn't that what you told me? So let me help you. Let's release your hold on that guilt, and day by day, we'll let it go."

Her words soothe my soul in a way nothing and no one ever has, and little by little, I feel the burden lifting from my shoulders.

CHAPTER
Twenty-Seven

Claire

My heart aches for Trevor. I wish more than anything that I would've found out about his secret sooner so I could've eased his mind. No one should carry a burden like that around. I just hope he can move past it, and maybe, if I'm lucky, he'll move past it with me.

Trevor pushes up from the floor and comes to sit next to me on the couch. Reclining, he rests his head against the back cushion and closes his eyes. A tear leaks out of the side of his eye, dripping down his temple. I brush it away. My thumb lingers against his skin, and he wraps his hand around my wrist. He brings my fingers to his lips and holds them there while the silence seeps in around us.

"Talk to me, Trevor. What are you thinking about?"

He opens his eyes and slowly lowers my hand from his face, resting it on his chest.

"I'm wondering what I did to deserve someone like you in my life. I'm thinking about how terrified I was that night I found out you'd run back into the building to save those kids. It reminded me so much of what your father did, and I didn't know how I was going to survive if I couldn't get to you. Come here, Claire."

Trevor opens his arms, and I waste no time crawling into his lap. With my head tucked under his chin and body nestled in the crook of his arm, Trevor holds me. Placing his lips atop my head, he kisses me and whispers, "I don't know what I would've done if something had happened to you."

Hooking an arm around his chest, I burrow as close as I can without physically mounting him. "You saved my life."

"I did what any good firefighter would do."

I contemplate his words, and while he's right, I also believe there was more at play that evening. I've always believed in fate, and Trevor was meant to be the one to save me.

I'm always here for you, Claire Bear. No matter where you are, I'm always here. I've come to understand my dad's desire for me to be safe a bit differently over the last few days. I've thought a lot about what Trevor told me about his job, and while I know I need to be smart and make responsible choices, I think it's okay to need help sometimes as well.

A smile touches my lips—maybe it was my dad who put Trevor there with me in that fire.

"You may be right, but not just any firefighter ran in after me," I tell Trevor. "You did. And not only did you get those boys out, you threw yourself on top of me when the ceiling caved in. I don't know how I'm ever going to repay you for that."

"We've already discussed this. You don't owe me anything. I'd do it again, over and over if it meant saving your life. You need to know that."

I lift my head to look up at him. "Because of my father? Because you feel like you owe me something?"

I hate the words even before they pass through my lips, but I have to ask him. I need to know—need to make sure that whatever is happening between us isn't because of the guilt he's been carrying around.

He shakes his head. "No." Threading his fingers through my hair, Trevor holds the back of my head. "Because of you."

❦

Trevor

Dropping my forehead to hers, I breathe Claire in. Her lavender scent surrounds me, infiltrates my veins, and brings peace in a way I never thought possible.

"What do you mean 'because of me'?"

Taking a deep breath, I give myself permission to be happy and take chances, and I tell Claire all of the crazy things that have gone through my head over the years.

"Because I have loved you for as long as I can remember."

I wait for dread to fill me, but it doesn't come. Instead I feel lighter than I ever have, and I realize it doesn't matter whether Claire feels the same way about me. What matters is that she knows how I feel. I love Claire Daniels. Her happiness means more to me than anything else, and I would walk through a thousand fires if it meant seeing her smile.

"What?" she gasps.

"You showed up at the rock quarry in a purple bikini, but it wasn't the swimsuit that stole my heart for the first time; it was your laughter and your kindness. Do you remember what you did for me that day?"

Tears fall down her face as she nods, but Claire makes no attempt to talk. That's okay, I can talk for both of us.

"A group of boys stole my clothes and shoes. I was stuck there, wet and cold, and you gave me your towel, stomped over to those boys, and demanded they give me my stuff back. That day you captured more than my attention. A year later, you, Mo, Rhett, Coop, and a bunch of your friends went four-wheeling at the ranch. I wanted to be just like my brothers, so I hopped on Beau's ATV and followed you guys. I thought I was hot shit because my brothers allowed me to tag along, but I didn't realize they were plotting against me. We stopped at old man Maynard's creek, and the girl who was riding double with Coop hopped on my four-wheeler, and everyone took off. They stranded me there, miles away from home, and what did you do?"

Claire squeezes her eyes shut, pushing out a fresh wave of tears, and shakes her head. "Trevor."

"Tell me, Claire. Tell me what you did."

She leans forward, pressing her lips against mine. The salty taste of her tears on my lips is almost too much. I hate that she's crying, but I know they're tears of joy, because she knows what's coming.

Opening her eyes, she whispers, "I made Noah stop, and then I got off his four-wheeler and walked home with you."

I smile, remembering how tall I felt walking home next to Claire, even though she was way out of my league. Not only was she four years older, but every boy in our school was drooling over her—myself included.

"To you it was something simple; you didn't want to leave me out there by myself. But to me, it meant so much more. You ditched your friends and walked three miles with me back to my house, only to get grounded for missing curfew."

She laughs and lifts a shoulder. "It was nothing."

"It was everything. That day you stole another chunk of my pre-teen heart and gained every bit of my respect. There's more. Can I keep going?"

Claire nods and cuddles her body closer to mine, which is a

good thing because I'm not sure I could let her go.

"A year after that, your father died. Mom got us all dressed up to attend the funeral, and I was terrified. It was the first one I'd ever been to, and on top of that, I blamed myself for his death. But Mom insisted I go. She even gave me a rose to place on top of the casket. When I got to the back of the funeral home, I lost it. I started bawling like a baby. Right there in a room full of people, I crumpled to the floor, and the only thing I remember from that moment is you wrapping me in your arms. You sat on the floor next to me and hugged me, and we cried together. You had just lost your father, and *you* were comforting *me*, completely oblivious to the guilt I harbored. I needed that hug more than anything. I may have been just shy of thirteen when I walked out of the funeral home that night, but I made a silent vow to always protect you, to never do anything to hurt you. But I also vowed I would always keep my distance, because I realized something else that night…"

Claire sucks in breath and holds it.

I smile.

"Breathe, Claire. Only good things for us from now on, baby, okay?"

She does as I ask and lets out the breath she was holding. "Please. Keep going."

"At the lowest point in my life, in a ball on the floor of a funeral home, wrapped in your arms, I gave you every last piece of my heart, knowing I'd never see it again."

Claire doesn't take time to ponder my words. No, my girl is coming right at me, ready to tell me how she feels.

"And whether I realized it or not, my heart accepted your gift and held onto it until I was ready to open myself up," she tells me. "And when that time came, it led me straight to you. I see it now; there's a reason I haven't been able to settle down, despite all my rules and precautions. And that reason is you. I was waiting for you, Trevor."

Warmth unfurls in my gut, spreading throughout my body as I lay it all on the line. "I know you have a rule about dating firefighters and ranchers, and I know I don't deserve you, Claire, but if you can break those rules, I promise to love you more than anyone else ever could. I promise to protect you and put you and your happiness above anything else, if you'll take a chance on me."

Claire's smile lights up every dark corner of my soul, and I can see the answer in her eyes before she voices it.

"There's no one else I'd rather break the rules with than you, Trevor Allen. But are you sure you're up for dating an older woman?"

"It's four years, Red, and age is just a number. I wouldn't care if you were ten years older than me. It wouldn't change how I feel about you, so whatever hang-up you have about our age difference, I'm going to politely ask you to get over it."

"I think I can do that."

"Good." I slip my fingers up the back of her shirt, stroking them along her spine, and she sighs.

"So, we're really going to do this?" she asks.

"We are really going to do this," I confirm.

Claire's pupils dilate. She blinks slowly, and I watch her eyes cloud over. "I need you to touch me, Trevor. I want you to make love to me, please."

She squeals when I lift her up.

"Nothing else I'd rather do."

CHAPTER
Twenty-Eight

Trevor

I kick open Claire's bedroom door, and Milo tries to dart inside, but I'm not having that. I lift my foot, blocking her entry while I balance Claire in my arms as we squeeze through the door.

Milo whimpers, and Claire juts out her bottom lip. "Awww...poor baby."

"Give me five minutes, and you won't even remember she exists."

Claire looks up at me with heavy eyes as I lower her to the bed, and when I pick up her foot, she closes them. She looks so incredibly sexy with her wild red hair fanned out on the pillow.

I push my thumb to the ball of her foot, massaging in an up and outward motion. "Open your eyes, Red. We've waited too long for this, and I want you here with me." Lowering my head, I kiss the inside of her ankle, and Claire's eyes pop open.

"There she is." I smile. Claire does not. "What's wrong? If you've changed your mind or you're not ready for this, just say the word."

"No." She shakes her head. "It's not that at all."

"Then what is it?"

"I hate my feet…and you're touching them."

I laugh. "I'm kissing my way up your leg, and you're thinking about how much you hate your feet?"

"Don't laugh. It's one of my many insecurities. I have a freakishly long second toe, and right now it's all up in your face."

I keep my eyes on hers, loving how expressive they are. "I read in an article that said having a long second toe is normal."

"You did not. You're just saying that to make me feel better."

"Did too. I'll find the article and forward it to you." I lower her foot to the bed and pick up the other one.

A smile threatens the corner of her mouth, but she holds it back. "Why are you doing that?"

"Doing what? Giving you a massage, or trying to convince you that your feet aren't gross?"

"Both." She shrugs. "You could just devour me. I don't need all the extra stuff."

There are a hundred different answers I could give her, but I decide to go with the truth, because that's what a girl like Claire deserves.

"Maybe I want all the extra stuff. Maybe I want to take it slow because all I've thought about today is touching you. I've thought about this moment for years, and I want to do it right. I want to worship every inch of your body. As for your toes, nothing about you is gross—far from it. In fact, I think you're the most beautiful woman I've ever seen, and I wouldn't change a single thing about you—including your freakishly long second toe."

She narrows her eyes. "You don't have a weird foot fetish, do you?"

I smile. "Not at all. I've never touched a woman's foot until yours tonight."

"Really?"

I nod, moving my hands up her calf. "There are a lot of things I've never done with a woman that I find myself wanting to do with you."

"Like what?"

"Different conversation for a different day, sweetheart, because right now all I can concentrate on is kissing every inch of this creamy skin."

I trail my lips up her calf, and when I make it to the soft spot behind her knee, Claire shudders.

"I have lots and lots of skin."

"Then I better get started."

I gently push my thumbs into the sides of her calf, moving them in slow circles. With a firm grip, I slide my hands over her knee, and the farther up her thigh I get, the more labored her breathing becomes.

"This could take all night," she moans as I knead the delicate skin.

"I've got nowhere to be."

I spend the next five minutes torturing her, massaging her. She watches my every move while I watch her, enamored with the breathy little moans coming out of her mouth.

Cupping my hands around her thigh, I slide them up her leg, this time pushing higher until I sneak below the hem of her shorts. I brush my thumb against her inner thigh and watch as Claire's breath hitches.

Her chest is heaving, and if my cock gets any harder, it's going to explode. Claire's knees fall open, and while I want nothing more than to rip her panties off and sink myself into her tight, warm heat, she deserves so much more.

I've closed my eyes, trying to slow myself down, when I feel her hand on mine.

I look up, my eyes meeting hers. She blinks and looks down at our hands on her inner thigh, and ever so slowly she guides my hand, pushing it until my fingers meet the edge of her underwear.

No words are needed. Everything she wants from me is written across her face. She's screaming at me to give her what she wants.

Please, Trevor. Touch me.

Claire

I can't believe I'm doing this, practically begging a man to touch me.

Oh, wait. Yes, I can, because that man is Trevor, and his magical hands are eliciting all sorts of sensations, and while I love the massage, I simply can't wait another second to feel his hands on other parts of my body.

Pulling my bottom lip into my mouth, I look down at him. One second he's watching me, as though he's warring with himself about what to do, and the next he's reaching for my shorts, pulling them down my legs with my panties, and tossing them to the side.

"Open." He shoulders his way between my legs, hooks his arms under my thighs, and buries his face against me.

"Shit." I moan, pushing my fingers into the short strands of his silky hair, holding him to me.

Wrapping his lips around my clit, Trevor sucks the tight ball of nerves into his mouth, and my hips buck against his face. Each swipe of his tongue pushes me closer and closer to the edge.

"You taste so damn good, Claire." His words, spoken against

my flesh, send vibrations through my body, and I grind myself against him.

The sight of Trevor's big body between my thighs, his mouth on me, is almost too much, but I force myself to watch because I don't want to miss a single second of what happens between us tonight.

Trevor pushes two fingers deep inside of me, curling them at just the right angle. Every nerve ending fires at once, and I dig my heels into the mattress, holding on to his head for dear life.

"That's it," he coaxes. "So damn sexy. You taste like heaven." He ends his verbal ministrations with a flick of his tongue against my clit, and that combination sends me hurtling into orgasmic bliss. I come, loud and long, and when the final tremor ripples through me, Trevor lifts his head from between my legs.

His smile is arrogant and sexy.

My eyes drift shut, and I know there's a lazy, sated grin gracing my lips as Trevor climbs up my body, leaving the sweetest little kisses along the way. His lips graze my inner thighs, my belly, the swells of my breasts, my neck, and when he reaches my mouth, he kisses me there too.

"You moan a lot when my face is between your legs."

"Mmm…" I hum, loving the feel of his five o'clock shadow against my jaw.

"Makes me wonder what other noises I could get you to make."

I grin up at him, open my eyes, and press myself against his erection. "There's only one way to find out."

Trevor's smile falls. "I don't have a condom."

Trevor Allen doesn't have a condom? Now that's something I thought I'd never hear. "Really?"

"I didn't come here tonight to sleep with you, Claire. I came here to talk." He sounds a little put off, and I feel bad because I didn't mean to upset him.

I cup his face in my hands and bring his mouth to mine. The kiss is sweet and simple, an apology of sorts. "I'm sorry. I shouldn't have said that. It's just…" *Crap.* I grimace. "I'm aware of the lifestyle you live and—"

Trevor's body goes rigid atop mine. "And what lifestyle is that?"

"I don't know…" I shrug, struggling to find a good way to explain it without offending him, which I've already done. "Women flock to you. Every time I see you at Dirty Dicks, you've got someone new hanging on your arm. You don't do relationships, and I've never seen you with the same girl twice. What am I supposed to think?"

A stark pain flashes in his eyes. "Geez, Claire. I'm not a manwhore."

Guilt slices through my chest. He tries to pull back, but I don't let him. "I know you're not. I know that. I'm sorry, okay? I shouldn't have assumed you'd have a condom with you. That wasn't fair of me. Please," I beg, running my fingers over his back. "Forgive me. I can barely think around you, let alone talk."

Trevor takes a deep breath and blows it out. "I haven't been with a woman in months. Probably close to a year if I were keeping track."

Wow. I had no idea. But now that I think about it, I've seen him at the bar with women, but I haven't actually seen him leave with anyone in a long time.

"Why?"

He shrugs. "Guess I'm ready for something more than meaningless sex…and I was waiting for the right girl."

My heart stutters to a stop inside my chest before

kick-starting into high gear. "And me...am I the right girl?"

Trevor's eyes soften. With a thoughtful smile, he rubs his thumb along my lower lip. "Claire." He whispers my name so delicately, like he could break it. "You're the only girl."

"Trevor." Curling my hand around his neck, I pull his forehead to mine. "I don't know what to say. No one has ever said anything like that to me before."

"You don't have to say anything, just let me love you."

I reach for the nightstand beside my bed, but it's too far away. "There's a condom in the top drawer."

"Yeah?"

I nod.

CHAPTER
Twenty-Nine

Claire

Trevor scoots off the bed, removes his clothes, and slides the condom over his cock. I sit up, and when he reaches for the hem of my shirt, I lift my arms, and he peels it off. The flimsy material lands somewhere on the floor.

Grinning, he leans down and kisses me. I can taste myself on his lips, and it turns me on. His tongue sweeps into my mouth with long, delicious strokes, and when he pulls back, his eyes are dark.

"Can you lay back for me, sweetheart?"

With one fist pressed into the mattress so he can hold himself up, Trevor moves his free hand between my thighs. His fingers push between my folds. I gasp, arching my back as he pushes them deep inside.

"Claire," he says, lowering his mouth to mine. He trails his lips across my cheek, stopping at my ear. "Please lay back. I need to get inside of you, baby, and I can't do it in this position."

With his hand between my legs, I lay back against the bed, and Trevor follows me down. He hovers over me and rubs his cock along my slit.

"You're so beautiful."

I lift my hips, groaning when he pulls his fingers out. Trevor props himself up on his elbows and looks down at me. The light from the moon filters through the window, bathing him in a dull glow as he brushes the hair from my face.

"I love you, Claire."

I run my fingers over his cheek and push them into his hair. Curling my fingers around his head, I pull his face close to mine until our breath is mingling. "I love you, too, Trevor."

He rocks his hips, grinding himself against me. I raise my hips, meeting his. The friction is almost too much, but not quite enough, and I swear he's going to kill me.

Death by anticipation.

"Please, Trevor."

Lifting his hips, he positions himself at my entrance, and I let my knees fall apart.

"That's it, Claire. Open up for me, sweetheart." In one gentle stroke, he sinks inside of me. Bracing his arms on either side of my head, he pulls out and pushes back in.

"Damn, you feel good."

"Oh..." Nothing has ever felt this amazing, and I'm not just talking about the way he fills me. It's his muscular body pushing mine against the mattress, the feel of his heart beating against my chest. It's the look of longing in his eyes.

It's the way he loves me.

"You're so tight, Claire. I don't know how long I'm going to last."

His hips are moving, dragging his throbbing cock in and out of my body. I rock my hips, meeting him thrust for thrust.

Trevor pushes his hand between our sweaty bodies. His thumb finds my clit, swollen and tender, and rubs in tight circles, with just the right amount of pressure. Within seconds he has me teetering on the edge of my second orgasm.

"Oh, Trevor." Pressure builds between my thighs, unfurling a heat low in my belly. My nails bite into his skin as his thrusts bring me closer and closer to the edge. Every muscle in my body contracts. I try to hold it in and savor it, but the feeling is too intense, and my body explodes. Heat blooms in my belly and spreads through my veins. My body trembles beneath Trevor's, and I wrap my arms around his back and hold him to me.

Gripping my ass, Trevor lifts my hips and slams into me one final time. A guttural moan pulls from somewhere deep in his chest, and when both of our bodies stop trembling, he kisses me gently.

"I would say that was worth the wait, wouldn't you?" he says, rolling off of me. He removes his condom, tosses it in the trash, and crawls back into bed beside me.

I settle myself in the crook of his arm and lay my head against his chest. Everything about this feels natural and right, and I can't believe we spent so many years apart when we could've had this. "I wish we'd done it sooner."

He laughs, pulling me tighter against his chest. "You and me both."

This is about the time things usually start to get awkward with a guy. One of us is trying to figure out a way to make a run for it, but with Trevor it's different. We both seem content to lay here in each other's arms.

I drag my finger over his nipple, swirling it around. "Say it again," I whisper.

Trevor's callused fingertips run the length of my spine. "Say what again?"

"What you said earlier." I want to hear those three words so bad.

"You're so tight?"

Laughing, I slap at his chest. "No, not that. Before that."

"Damn, you feel good?"

I shake my head, grinning because what we were doing did feel damn good. Better than good. It felt great and perfect, and it was everything I'd hoped it would be and more.

So much more.

Trevor hooks his arms underneath mine and pulls me on top of him. "That's it. Open up for me, sweetheart," he whispers against my ear.

"Come on," I whine. "You know what I'm talking about."

I can tell by the shit-eating grin on his face that he knows exactly what I'm asking for, but he's playing hard to get.

"Babe, we just had mind-blowing sex, and all I can think about are your pussy and tits and that perfect mouth of yours, so I'm going to need you to be a little more specific."

I decide to switch tactics. Straddling his hips, I reach across the bed for another condom. Trevor doesn't say a word when I grab his cock and roll the condom on. Lifting myself up, I guide him to my entrance. I rub the head along my slit and then lower myself until I'm fully seated. He's deeper in this position than he was earlier. I can feel his erection hitting my cervix, and for some reason, I find that satisfying.

Running his hands up my thighs, Trevor wraps them around my hips and guides me over him in slow, rhythmic circles.

Splaying my fingers across his chest, I look down. My hair falls forward, acting as a curtain around us. Lowering my body to his, I kiss him gently once, twice, and a third time.

"I love you, Trevor Allen," I say.

Trevor palms the back of my head, tangling his fingers in my hair to keep me from moving. "I love you, too, Claire Daniels. More than you'll ever know.

CHAPTER
Thirty

Claire

The smell of bacon pulls me awake. I stretch my arms above my head and roll toward the other side of my bed. The sheets are still warm from Trevor's body, and I press my face into the pillow he used and close my eyes as I remember all of the delicious things he did to me last night. My muscles are sore, along with the other parts of my body, and for the first time in as long as I can remember, I'm not looking forward to going to work. I'd like to stay here with Trevor and his magic fingers and his tongue and his mouth and his hard body, and everything. I just want everything.

Smiling like a goofball, I scoot to the side of the bed and sit up. I need to get my lazy ass into the shower, but my bones feel like jelly, and the smell of breakfast cooking in the other room is too enticing. I pick up Trevor's shirt and slip it over my head. Shoving my feet into a pair of slippers, I trudge into the bathroom and brush my teeth. Then I run a comb through my hair in a poor attempt to tame my wild locks, because the last thing I want to do is scare Trevor after our first night together.

I'm rounding the corner of the hallway when I hear him talking.

"Do you like bacon? Here, try a piece."

I freeze, wondering who in the world he could be talking to. Peeking my head around the corner, I smile at the sight in front of me. Trevor is standing in front of the stove in nothing but his boxer briefs with Milo perched in one arm.

Dear Lord, he looks sexy holding my dog. He looks even sexier cooking in my kitchen. Add the two together and *ovary explosion*. Propping my hip against the wall, I cross one leg over the other and watch him move. Every few minutes, he feeds Milo a bite, and she's more than happy to take whatever he's offering.

Trevor shifts Milo higher onto his chest. Her little chin rests on his shoulder, and if I didn't know she was blind, I'd swear she was looking at me and saying, *Back off, he's mine.*

"Are you going to stand there and watch or what?"

Smiling, I step into the kitchen. "How did you know I was watching you?"

Trevor turns around and puts Milo on the floor. She jumps around at his feet, trying to get him to pick her back up, and I don't feel at all sorry when I nudge her out of the way so I can step into his arms.

"I've always been able to tell when you walk into a room."

"Oh yeah?"

Trevor lowers his mouth to my neck and places a soft kiss below my ear. "Call it lover's intuition."

I tilt my head to the side, making room for him. "We haven't always been lovers."

I feel Trevor smile against my skin. "Tell my dick that."

Laughing, I push him away and walk toward the stove. "What's for breakfast?"

"Bacon and eggs. I hope you don't mind scrambled."

"Not at all. It smells amazing." I grab some plates and put them on the table. Trevor's already got two cups of steaming coffee waiting for us. "I didn't know you could cook."

He puts a generous helping of eggs and bacon on each plate and pulls a chair out for me. He doesn't sit until I sit, and I find myself smiling because my dad used to do that for my mom.

"I love to cook."

"Did your mom teach you?" I ask, shoving a bite into my mouth.

"Nope." He bites off a chunk of bacon. "I learned at the firehouse. We take turns cooking meals. I'm usually in charge of dinner, but I can whip up just about anything. How about you? Do you cook?"

I snort. "If by cook you mean heat up a frozen meal or park myself at my mom's dinner table, then yes, I cook all the time."

Trevor laughs, but doesn't seem concerned about my lack of culinary skills. "So you pretty much survive on frozen dinners and leftovers."

"That sounds about right. And every once in a while Coop will feel sorry for me and bring over food."

Trevor's hand stills midair, and then he slowly puts the bite into his mouth.

"What was that?" I ask.

"What was what?"

"You just got a funny look on your face."

He swallows his bite and shakes his head. "It was nothing."

I set my fork down and reach for his hand. "Tell me. If we're going to make this work, we have to be able to talk to each other."

"It's silly." He links his fingers with mine, and when I just stare at him he sighs. "Fine. I was just thinking that my brothers know you better than I do, and that bothers me."

Warmth seeps through my veins, making my toes tingle. I push up from my chair. Trevor scoots his back, allowing me to settle in his lap.

"Your brothers know all the surface stuff. They know I can't cook. They know I've never ridden a horse, that I hate hot dogs, and that appletinis are my favorite drink. They *don't know* that bacon and eggs are my favorite breakfast—"

"You're just saying that," he interjects.

I shake my head. "I most certainly am not. They also don't know that I despise my feet."

"Or that you snore."

"I don't snore."

"You do. And it's cute," Trevor says, kissing the tip of my nose.

"My point is that they only know the basic stuff. They don't know the deeper stuff, the things I keep hidden from the rest of the world."

"I want to know those things."

I run my fingers down the side of his face. "I feel the same way about you."

Trevor kisses me long and deep, and by the time we part, the bacon is cold and Milo has managed to find her way onto my lap, trying desperately to get to Trevor's face. I pick her up and set her back on the floor. She whines for a second and then prances away.

"I really want to tell you I love you again," I say, looking at Trevor.

"So why don't you?"

"Last night was emotional for both of us, and I wasn't sure if you said it because we were in the heat of the moment, or if you meant it, and then I was wondering if it's too soon—"

Trevor puts a finger to my lips. "You think too much."

"I've been told."

"Yes, last night was emotional, and yes, I said those things in the heat of the moment, but it doesn't make my words any less true. I told you I love you because I do. I've known you my entire life. There are pictures of you in our family albums, Claire. My love for you started out organically, and it has grown over the years into something much deeper. It is rooted in these spectacular memories I have of you, and it's growing by the second."

He runs his fingers through my hair and continues. "When I say I love you, it's not to get you into bed. It's because I mean it. I love your smile and the way your eyes light up when you laugh. I love your fiery red hair and how you've always got a strand of it wrapped around your finger. I love the way you scrunch your nose when you're thinking and how you talk with your hands. I love how loyal you are to your friends and how you talk to Milo like she's a human being. But most of all, I love how you make me feel. You make me want to be a better man, Claire."

"Trevor—"

He cuts off my words with a deep kiss. "I don't want you to say anything. You don't need to return the sentiment. I just want you to know that when I tell you I love you, I mean it, and if you love me, then please, tell me, and if you're not ready to say those words again, that's okay too. I'm in this for the long haul."

The long haul.

Thoughts of Trevor's occupation leak into my head, and I remember all the nights my mom sat up waiting for Dad to get home from a fire call. It would be easy to let my insecurities get the best of me. I could withdraw and push Trevor away and tell myself I'm better off without him, but I already know that's not true. Instead of letting my fears get the best of me, I choose to bask in the beautiful feelings Trevor brings out in me.

"I love you, too, Trevor."

He kisses me again. His fingers slide under my shirt and up my back as he holds me to him, and then he shocks the hell out of me when he grips me by the hips and lifts me from his lap.

"Hey," I whine. "I wasn't done with you." I try to climb back into his lap, but he stands up.

"No." He takes a step back. "If I keep touching you, I won't be able to stop, and you have to get ready for work."

"What are you going to do today?"

"Dad is working with a new bull rider, so I've got ranch duty."

"I didn't know your dad trained bull riders."

"Who do you think taught Rhett?"

"I knew he taught Rhett, but I didn't know he still worked with newbies."

Trevor shrugs. "He doesn't do it often. Usually just if it's someone he knows or a family member. It's not something he advertises."

"Will I see you when you get done?" I ask, sauntering toward him. Trevor eyes me but doesn't try to get away when I reach for him.

"You have tutoring tonight, right?" he asks.

I nod. "Yes, but I'll be done early and home by six."

"Then I'll pick you up at six thirty."

I tilt my head and grin. "Pick me up? For what?"

"For our first official date."

"Where are we going?"

"It's a surprise."

"I don't like surprises. I'm more of an instant gratification kind of girl."

Trevor laughs and pushes my roaming hands away. "Sorry, sweetheart. I love surprises, so get used to it."

"Can you give me a hint?" I ask.

He thinks about it for a second and then says, "No."

"What should I wear?"

"Something casual."

"Casual like jeans and a T-shirt or casual like stretchy eating pants?"

Trevor laughs. "You could wear a garbage bag and I'd still find you insanely attractive. Wear whatever you're most comfortable in. Now, go get ready for work."

CHAPTER
Thirty-One

Trevor

"This is not at all what I expected when you said you were taking me on a date tonight," Claire says as we stroll along the pier.

The air is filled with laughter and music and the delicious smell of fried food. Lights on the Ferris wheel twinkle in the sky as it circles around, and I take Claire's hand.

"Yeah? What did you expect?"

She shrugs and smiles at me. "I don't know. Most men usually take me to a fancy restaurant where they can wine and dine me."

"I'm not most men."

"I know you're not. And this is perfect." She pushes up on her toes and in the middle of the sidewalk with people milling about, Claire kisses me for all the world to see. "I've always loved coming here," she says, turning around to take it all in.

Stepping up behind her, I set my chin on her shoulder. "Where should we start? Food? Games? Rides?"

"Hmmm." She taps a finger to her lips. "How about food."

"Carnival food it is."

"But not just any carnival food. I want a funnel cake and a lemon shake-up and cotton candy."

"Sugar high, here we come." I kiss Claire's cheek, grab her hand again, and guide her to the closest vendor.

"One funnel cake, a lemon shake-up, and a tub of cotton candy, please."

The worker smiles and collects my cash. "The funnel cake will be just a minute," he says, handing me the tub of cotton candy and the lemon shake-up, which I hand to Claire. "Claire Daniels, is that you?"

Claire nudges me out of the way so she can look into the vending cart. Her eyes widen, and if I can tell by the look on her face that if she could throw herself at the man serving us, she would.

"Jerry, it's so good to see you! How've you been? I had no idea you were working down here."

The older man shrugs and hands her the funnel cake. "I'm good. I started working here a few months back. I'm only here a couple of nights a week, but It gets me out of the house."

A woman and her son step up behind us.

"It was so good to see you," Claire says. "Please, tell Joanne I said hello."

"I will." He waves at us through the window as we walk away.

I lead Claire to a picnic table off to the side, and we sit down. She digs into the funnel cake with abandon. I spend several minutes just watching her eat. Most women I've taken out wouldn't have dreamed of ordering a funnel cake and cotton candy. They probably would've searched for a salad or just starved rather than put that much sugar into their bodies. But that's one of the things I enjoy about Claire—she doesn't care. She is who she is, loves the things she loves, and she doesn't apologize for it.

"This is amazing," she mumbles around a bite. "I should've tipped Jerry."

"How do you know him?"

"Who, Jerry?"

I nod and steal a bite of her fried dough.

"He was on the fire department with my dad years ago. He and his wife, Joanne, used to come over and play cards."

"They don't come over anymore?"

Claire swallows her food and shrugs. "Not really. After Daddy died, everyone came over all the time to check on us, but as the days turned into months, that faded. Everything just sort of changed after his death."

"I'm sorry. I didn't mean to kill the mood. I was just curious."

She peels off another chunk of dessert. "Don't be sorry. I like talking about my dad. No one ever brings him up because they're afraid it'll upset me, but it does the opposite. It's fun to remember those times with him."

"Well, I'll have to bring him up more often."

She smiles. "I hope you do."

"Did you know he's the reason I became a firefighter?"

Claire's eyes widen as she washes her food down with her drink. "I had no idea."

"Watching him that day—running in and out of the building, worried about nothing other than getting those kids to safety—was truly inspiring. For years after I had dreams about the fire, about how heroic your father was. At first, they started as nightmares, but as I got older, they transformed into something more. During one dream in particular, your father yanked me out of the bushes and told me to help out. That seemed like a pretty good idea to me, so I guess that dream changed my life."

Claire gets a little teary, and while I wanted her to know

about the influence her father had on my career, I also want to keep our date light and fun.

"He would be proud to know that," she says.

"Thank you."

"My dad would've loved you, Trevor."

When she finishes off her funnel cake, Claire dumps the paper plate in the trash.

"Come here."

She leans over the table. "Why are you laughing at me?"

"Because you have powdered sugar all over your face." I use the napkin to wipe a smudge off. "No idea how you got it on your forehead."

"I talk with my hands, remember?" She opens her mouth and points to the corner. "You missed a spot."

Tossing the napkin to the table, I draw her face toward mine and kiss away the white residue.

"Mmm… Sweet," I say. "I'm not sure your dad would appreciate the thoughts running through my head right now."

Claire laughs. "You're probably right."

I stand up, hold my hand out, and pull her to her feet. "Are you ready for the cotton candy?" I ask, holding out the tub.

"Oh no. I'm saving that for later."

I tuck the tub under my arm and reach for her shake-up. "Can I have a drink?"

She hands it to me. I take a big sip, and when she reaches for it, I spin around so she can't get it.

"Hey, give me that."

She keeps reaching, but I keep moving. By the time she manages to grab her drink, we've bumped into three different people, and we're both laughing uncontrollably.

"I'm so sorry," she says to a little old lady.

The woman gives us a look and keeps walking.

Eyes wide, Claire turns to me. "I can't believe you made me plow into an old lady."

"I didn't make you do it."

She narrows her eyes. "Uh-huh. Next time we're getting you your own."

I stop next to the ping-pong toss. "You're thinking about next time?"

Pressing her lips together, Claire fights a grin and nods. "Are you?"

"I'm thinking about the next hundred times."

A slow smile spreads across her face just as a young boy walks by.

"Hi, Ms. Daniels."

"Hi, Troy," she says, but Troy doesn't stop.

"Can't talk, Ms. Daniels. I gotta get a stuffed unicorn."

"Stuffed unicorn?" I mouth.

Claire shrugs, and we turn and watch him step up to High Striker. He hands the carnie a dollar bill, takes the mallet from her hands, and swings with all his might. The rubber end connects with the base, sending a puck into the air, but it falls short of hitting the bell at the top.

"Oooh, so close," Claire whispers.

Troy tries three more times and fails.

"Here, hold this," I say.

Claire takes the cotton candy. "What are you doing?"

"I'm going to show this kid how it's done."

"Step on up," the carnie goads. "Do you think you have the strength to ring the bell?"

I dig out my wallet, hand her the money, and take the mallet from Troy. He frowns and takes a step back. With my feet shoulder-width apart, I lift the mallet and bring it down as hard as I can. The small puck launches up the track and slams against the bell at the top.

Bells and whistles sound and lights flash. Claire jumps up and down, cheering for me as I swing the mallet two more times, each time hitting the bell.

"Congratulations," the carnie says, motioning toward the prize tank. "You can choose any of the prizes in this barrel."

I sift through the barrel until I come across a stuffed unicorn. It's purple with lots of glitter and a braided mane. No idea why the kid wants it, but whatever.

"Wow, that was so cool," Troy says, approaching me. "I wish I could do that. Hey, you're the firefighter who came to my school the other day, aren't you?"

"I am." I bend down until we're at eye level, and then I hand him the unicorn. "Is this what you were trying to get?"

"Yeah, cool. You're giving this to me? Don't you want to give it to Ms. Daniels? I saw you holding her hand earlier."

I look over my shoulder. Claire is smiling down at us. "Nah," I say, turning back toward Troy. "I think she's good. You should keep it."

"Well," he says sheepishly, "I was actually going to give it to Maria."

"Who's Maria?"

"A girl in my class. She loves unicorns."

"Then give it to her."

Troy smiles. "Can I tell her I won it?"

"Sure, buddy." I stand up and ruffle his hair.

"Thanks." Troy runs off, and Claire wraps her arms around my shoulders.

"That was the sexiest thing I've ever seen."

"Really?" I say, spinning around in her arms.

"Oh yeah. Super sexy."

"You're not upset that some chick named Maria is going to

get the unicorn I won? Come on, Claire, a little jealousy would be nice," I tease.

She laughs and kisses me. "I'm totally jealous. Prove your manliness to me and win me another prize."

"Excuse me," a woman behind us says.

I let go of Claire to turn around and see who it is, but I've never seen the woman in my life.

"Claire? I didn't realize that was you." The woman pulls Claire in for a hug, but Claire remains stiff in the woman's arms. "I've been meaning to stop by the classroom after school. The boys and I got you a little gift, but I keep forgetting to drop it off."

Claire pulls out of the woman's embrace. "You didn't have to get me anything, Amy."

"But I want to." The woman looks between me and Claire. "You saved my boys' lives. It's the least I could do."

Oh shit. This must be Troy and Marcus' mom. I know Claire has felt so much guilt about this woman's boys. Everything between us has happened so fast, I haven't had a chance to follow up with her about that night we talked and how she's doing.

Amy smiles and turns to me. "I just wanted to thank you for giving my son that unicorn. He's been trying for the last hour to win it, and I don't think I've ever seen him this excited."

I wrap an arm around Claire's waist and pull her against my side. She relaxes in my arms. "You're welcome. I heard he's going to give it to Maria."

Amy rolls her eyes and laughs. "They grow up so fast, don't they? Well, thank you again, and I'll see you around, Claire."

Claire waves, and Amy turns away, only making it a few steps before her twin boys bombard her.

"You know, it's never too late to talk to her."

Tucking a strand of hair behind her ear, Claire looks up at

me. "What would I say?"

"Whatever's weighing on your heart." Claire opens her mouth, but I stop her. "And don't tell me nothing is weighing on your heart, because I can see it, Claire. I told you, your feelings about that night—the guilt—are not something that will just go away. But I firmly believe that if you talk to her about it and get it off your chest, it'll help you down that road to recovery."

Claire takes a deep breath and blows it out. She turns and searches the crowd for Amy, who has moved a few more feet away and is standing at the ring toss.

"Road to recovery makes it sound like I'm battling something dark."

"But you were."

"Yes." She nods. "But after talking with you, I've been able to move past a lot of it."

"But not all?"

She shakes her head. "No, not all."

"Go, Claire." I give her a little nudge, and she stumbles forward. I expect her to turn around and tell me all of the reasons why she needs to put this off, but she doesn't.

Nope, my girl is strong and determined, and even though she looks like she's going to vomit, she walks right up to Amy and taps her on the shoulder.

I stand back, hands in my pockets, a smile on my face, and so much love in my heart for this woman. She's facing her fears head on, and I couldn't be prouder of her.

CHAPTER
Thirty-Two

Claire

I shake my hands and fingers out as though I'm about to play some sort of instrument when all I'm trying to do is regain feeling. My legs are tingling as they carry me toward Amy, and while I'm physically sick at the thought of talking to her about that night, I know it's something I have to do.

The last several days have been masked by Trevor and the time I've spent thinking of him. But at night when I lay my head on the pillow, sometimes I still see Troy and Marcus's scared little faces.

I step up behind Amy and take a deep breath. When I blow it out, I tap her on the shoulder. "Amy?"

She spins around, smiling. "Hey, Claire."

"Can we talk for a second?"

She looks back at her boys, who are trying to land a red ring around the tip of a bottle in hopes of winning a goldfish.

"Sure," she says. "I have a feeling they'll be working on this one for a long time."

Together we amble off to the side, where she can still keep a close eye on the boys, but we're not in the thick of things.

"What did you want to talk to me about?" Her face falls. "Don't tell me one of the boys got in trouble again. I swear I threw that whoopee cushion in the trash."

I laugh. "No, nothing like that. It's, uh…" The words get stuck in my throat, and I'm seconds away from telling her it's nothing when I catch a glimpse of Trevor out of the corner of my eye. He gives me a reassuring smile and nod, and just like that, my fear wanes enough for me to get out what I have to say. "It's about the fire."

"What about it? Did they figure out what happened?"

"Yes, actually, it was electrical, but that's not what I wanted to tell you."

"Okay." She watches me and waits and waits a little more, and then she places her hand on my arm. "Claire, are you okay?"

Tears are clogging my nose and pooling in my eyes, and I'm seconds from losing it. I shake my head, hoping to keep from crying. Swallowing past the giant lump in my throat, I look Amy in the eye.

"I forgot your boys were in the bathroom."

"What do you mean?" she says.

"I let the boys go to the bathroom—"

She nods. "They told me they were in there a lot longer than they should've been."

"They were, but I knew they had a tendency to play in there, so I was keeping an eye on the clock. I got to helping another kid with something, and next thing I knew, the alarms were going off and everyone was rushing out of the room and the building. It was pure chaos. I ushered all of the kids outside, and that's when I realized I'd forgotten the boys. They were still in the bathroom."

The dam breaks. Tears fall down my face. I do my best to brush them away, but there are way too many, and eventually I give up.

"I forgot about your boys." My voice cracks, and Amy pulls me into her arms.

I wrap my arms around her. "I should've grabbed them on our way out. If I would've done that, they never would've been in that situation. It's my fault they were stuck there alone and scared, and I'll never forgive myself."

"No." Amy pulls back, her face pinched. "Oh my gosh, Claire, I can't believe that's the way you see it."

She's not a blubbering mess like I am, but tears are building in her eyes.

"I can't imagine how scary it was for you in that moment. I'm sure you were running on pure adrenaline, and you did what I would expect any teacher to do: you reacted. You got your kids to safety, and when you realized my boys were missing, you ran right back into that building to get them."

"If I would've remembered they were in there, I could've gotten them out right away."

"But what would've happened to the rest of your class? Do I hate that my boys were in that bathroom alone and scared? Yes. Do I wish they'd been in class instead of playing around in the bathroom for so long? Yes. But nothing you say will convince me that you acted the wrong way that day. I hate to think what would've happened to the rest of your class if you'd stopped on the way out for my boys. That fire was spreading fast, and you all could've ended up trapped in there."

The more she talks, the harder I cry. I probably look like a mess standing at the pier bawling, but I don't care because Trevor was right. It feels good to get this off my chest. And it feels good to have her forgiveness.

Amy reaches in her purse and grabs a couple of Kleenexes. "Is this why you didn't want to take the cookies we made for you?"

I take the Kleenex and wipe my face. "I just felt so guilty, and the fact that you took the time to do something thoughtful didn't feel right to me."

"I took the time to make you cookies. You ran back into a burning building to save my kids." Her lips are in a thin line, her chin quivering. "Those boys are my life, Claire. They are the reason I get up every morning. Every single thing I do, I do for them, and had it not been for you…" She swallows and dabs her eyes. "If it weren't for you, they might not be here, and I hate to think about that because I don't know what I would do. You gave me my life back that day, Claire, and nothing you can say is going to make me think differently, so just stop. Stop feeling guilty, and stop looking at what you could've done. Concentrate on what you did do." She laughs, but it lacks any sort of humor. "Crap. Now all my makeup is running."

I smile and wrap my arms around her again. Not because she's crying, but because I'm feeling so much relief that I can't not hold her.

"We're a mess," I whisper.

I'm not sure how long we stand there, but when we step back, all of our tears have dried, and there's a lightness in my chest I haven't felt for quite some time.

"Thank you," I say, softly.

"For what? I didn't do anything."

"For being so understanding. For letting me cry all over you. For raising two wonderful boys. For the cookies. Should I keep going?"

Amy's smile is wistful. "You're welcome, Claire. I just wish you would've talked to me about it sooner."

"Trust me, I do, too."

"Mom, I won!"

We turn to see Marcus running toward us with a plastic bag

in his hand. The bag is full of water, and there's a tiny goldfish inside.

"Great," Amy mumbles, plastering on a smile when Marcus gets to us. "That's so exciting, honey. What are we going to name him?"

"Nemo," he says, excitedly.

"You can't name him Nemo," Troy argues.

"Why not? He's my fish."

"They don't stop," Amy says as her boys fight over naming the fish. "It's like this twenty-four-seven. Bickering and fighting all day long."

"But you wouldn't have it any other way," I add.

She points at me. "You're right, I wouldn't. We better get going."

"That's right," I say, crouching down in front of the twins. "You have school tomorrow."

Marcus frowns, and Troy smiles. "I read two books after school today so I can take an accelerated reader test tomorrow."

"Show off," Marcus mumbles.

I laugh, noticing that the ache I normally get in my chest when I interact with the boys is gone. "I'll see you both tomorrow." I stand up and wave goodbye to Amy and the kids as they walk away.

CHAPTER
Thirty-Three

Claire

"There is nothing sexier than the smile on your face right now," Trevor whispers, wrapping his arms around me from behind. He's still holding my cotton candy and lemon shake-up, and I lean forward to take a sip.

"And I'm guessing by that smile that everything went better than you expected it to."

Placing my hands on top of his arms, I hold him to me. "It went great. She wasn't at all mad, and you were right; as I was talking to her about it, I felt like I was letting it go. I think it's always going to bother me, but I definitely feel lighter about the situation."

"I'm so proud of you."

Turning in Trevor's arms, I smile up at him. "I'm proud of me too. We should celebrate. What do you want to do next?"

"I figured you'd want to get home at a decent time since I kept you up late last night and you have to work tomorrow."

"I'm not tired, and this is the best first date I've ever had. I don't want it to end."

"Okay..." Trevor looks over my shoulder and grins. "How about we dance?"

"I love to dance."

"That's why I suggested it." He pulls away and motions to somewhere behind me.

I turn around and sure enough, there's a stage across the way. Equipment is set up, and a band is taking its place in front of a small crowd. A sign perched on the corner of the stage reads *Dancing: FREE Karaoke: $1 per song.*

"Let's do it."

Trevor tucks the cotton candy under his arm so he can take my hand. "I'll dance, but you're not getting me on that stage to sing."

For over an hour, we watch people climb onstage. Some sing perfectly, some off key, and others can't sing to save their lives, but it doesn't matter how they sound because Trevor and I are having the time of our lives. We've danced and laughed and when the middle-aged woman in a crop top and far too much makeup steps off the stage, we collapse onto a bench.

"That was fun," I say, blowing my hair out of my face. "I didn't know you could dance."

"There's a lot about me you don't know."

"Isn't it weird that we've known each other our whole lives, but there's still so much we don't know about the other?"

"Tell me something about yourself that I don't know," Trevor says. "Wait, tell me something no one else knows."

"Like a secret?"

"A secret, a hidden talent, a fear, anything. I want a piece of you that no one else is privy to."

"Okay." I look around, trying to come up with something I can tell him, when my eyes land on the microphone.

Singing was a thing between me and Dad—something I

cherished and loved. He would twirl me around the house, and we would belt out tunes while Mom cooked dinner. Most people don't even know I can sing, or that I love to sing. I haven't so much as a hummed a tune in front of another person since my father's death—not even Mom or Mo—but I find myself wanting to sing for Trevor.

"Wait here."

I leave him sitting on the bench. I walk up to the young girl sitting at a table beside the stage, hand her my dollar bill, and give her my song request. The band members wave me on stage, and that's when the panic sets in.

My heart is pounding, my palms sweating, and there's a good chance my entire funnel cake will end up on the floor at my feet.

"You okay, darlin'?" the guitarist asks.

"Just feeling a little uneasy," I say, looking out at the small crowd. Most of them aren't even paying attention, but Trevor is, and his smile is about as wide as it can get.

"You don't have to sing. We'll even give you your dollar back."

I smile up at the man. "No, I want to."

He nods. "Just relax and have fun. That's what this is all about."

"What if I mess up?"

He chuckles, his belly bouncing in the process. "No one's gonna care."

"That doesn't make me feel better."

The man covers the microphone with his hand and leans in close. He smells of Old Spice and cigars, and a wave of nostalgia washes over me. "You did hear the last woman sing, right? You can't be any worse than her."

I shouldn't laugh, but I do.

"You ready?"

I nod. He hands me the microphone, and I take a deep breath. Trevor wanted to learn something about me that no one else knew, and this is about as big as it gets.

The band beings to play. I listen to the opening chords, and when I hear the familiar tune, I lift the microphone and begin to sing. The melody flows through me as I close my eyes and sing the old country ballad. It's about a man who loses the woman of his dreams and battles his way through addiction to get her back. It was one of my dad's favorites, and when I find myself alone or in the shower, it's this song that finds its way to my lips.

My legs are shaking, but my voice doesn't waver. I pour every ounce of energy I have into the lyrics, and when the song ends and I hear thunderous applause, I force myself to look up. There are only about twenty people surrounding the stage, but they're all standing up and clapping, including Trevor.

"You killed it," the guitarist says, taking the microphone from me. "You up for singing another one?"

"Not tonight." I grin. "But you'll see me again soon."

"I hope so."

I bounce off stage, and Trevor is at the bottom of the steps waiting for me. He pulls me into his arms and kisses me. "I had no idea you could sing like that."

"It's nothing."

"It's not nothing. Your voice is beautiful. Have you been singing your whole life?" he says, guiding me back to our bench.

"My dad used to sing. Some of my fondest memories are of us dancing around the house. We'd both be singing as he twirled me from room to room. Johnny Cash, Michael Jackson, Whitney Houston, Snoop Dog—our playlist was endless."

"Snoop Dog?"

"Oh yeah." I nod. "My dad could spit out a mean beat."

"Do you want to do it again?" he asks, nodding toward the stage. "I'd love to hear you sing something else."

"Definitely, but not tonight. I think once was enough considering I've never sung in public before. Why are you smiling at me like that?"

"Because you amaze me. Everything about you amazes me." He blinks. "Come on, Tiny Singer, let's get you home."

Trevor and I talk and laugh the entire way to my place, which doesn't take long, and when he pulls into my driveway, he puts his truck in park. "Don't move."

He jumps out, jogs around the front, and opens my door. With my hand in his, he helps me out and walks me to the front door.

"Do you do that with all the girls?"

"I told you before, it's just you."

Grinning, I pull my keys out of my pocket. "Would you like to come in?"

Trevor takes my hand when I reach for the doorknob. "Not tonight," he says, pulling me in for a kiss.

"Really?" I sigh. "Because tonight was perfect, and I thought we'd end it with a replay of last night." I fist my hands in the front of his shirt.

"Tonight was perfect, and last night…" He shakes his head and smiles wryly. "Last night was phenomenal. But I've never done this before," he says, motioning between us. "And you're taking a chance on me, so I really want to do this the right way."

Ugh…can he get any more perfect?

"And by the right way, you mean you're going to end the date with a chaste kiss, and you'll call me in a few days to set up our next one?"

"Hell no." Trevor curls his fingers around the back of my

neck. Using his thumbs, he tilts my face up. His lips linger above mine. "We're going to end with a heated kiss that I hope will leave you thinking about me all night long and well into the morning, and then I'm going to pick you up again tomorrow night for another date."

"Another date?"

"I'm prepared to woo you, Red. That means lots of dates. I'm talking dinner, dancing, movies, walks on the beach... If it's something new couples do, we're going to do it."

Giddiness bubbles up inside of me. "No one has ever wooed me before."

"No?" he whispers, lowering his head.

I shake my head, my eyes dropping to his sinfully full lips.

"Well, hold on tight, sweetheart, because I'm about to woo the hell out of you."

CHAPTER
Thirty-Four

Claire

When Trevor said he was going to do things right, he wasn't kidding. Every night for the last week and half, he's done something special. The night after our trip to the pier, he took me to my favorite restaurant, Giovanni's, and the night after that we ended up an hour away at a mom-and-pop diner where we ate our weight in home-made chicken-n-dumplings and apple pie.

The next few nights he had to work, and that wasn't easy for me. I worried about him, wondering what types of calls he was getting and if he was okay, but Trevor made sure to let me know I was on his mind. Not only did he text me regularly, he had a gorgeous bouquet of wildflowers sent to my house on Saturday night, and on Monday night, half an hour after I came home from Animal Haven, he had a pizza delivered from Sal's Pizzeria with a note attached: *You mentioned going straight from work to Animal Haven, and I wanted to make sure you got something to eat. I hope you like pepperoni.*

I legit curled up on my couch with the box of pizza and cried as I sent him a text.

Sal's is my favorite.

His reply was immediate. ***I know.***

I don't remember telling him, and we haven't eaten there in the short time we've been together. ***How did you know?***

I manage to eat an entire slice while I wait for him to answer.

The summer of your senior year, Coop let me tag along with you guys to the movies, and afterward we had Sal's. You said it was your favorite.

You remember that?

I remember everything.

I swallowed my bite and stared at my phone in awe. ***Trevor?***

There was a short pause, and then his reply came through. ***Yeah?***

Thank you.

You're welcome, Red.

Trevor had the next few days off, and rather than spending them with our friends like we'd normally do, we chose to stay in and lay low. I skipped girls' night, he skipped drinks with his brothers, and instead we curled up on my couch and watched movies. Trevor cooked, and we used the time to just relax and get to know each other. It's not that we want to keep our relationship from everyone, we just want to revel in the newness for as long as we can.

Tuesday he helped his dad on the ranch, and after work I helped Mo at Animal Haven. Then that night he and I ordered Chinese and binge-watched the Fast and the Furious movies. I fell asleep after the third one, and I have no idea when Trevor fell asleep.

I woke up the next morning to a steaming cup of coffee, a warm cinnamon roll from the local bakery, and a note: *Had to go help Dad. Have a great day at work. I'll stop by this evening on my way home.*

Trevor is proving to be a man of his word. Either that, or he's as smitten with me as I am him, because he did stop by that evening—after I was done tutoring—as promised. I had lasagna in the oven, and he had a movie, and the evening couldn't have ended on a more perfect note.

Okay, that's a lie.

It could've ended with us between the sheets. Trevor and I have found ourselves in many heated situations over the last few days, but each time he's stopped things before we got too far.

"We've already slept together," I argued.

Wednesday night, Trevor had me so worked up, my body was ready to explode if he didn't touch me. It was bad. Bad enough that I was prepared to strip down and beg if I had to.

"Anticipation is one of the greatest aphrodisiacs," he reasoned. "We've spent the last week getting to know each other on a different level. Imagine how intense it's going to be when I get you back under me."

"There's no need to wait. I'm ready to get under you now," I said, dragging him down the hall.

But Trevor had other plans. Instead, he laid me out on the couch and gave me three of the best orgasms I've ever had. He walked away that night with a smug smile on his handsome face, and I was way too sated to chase after him.

But tonight—tonight is going to end much differently.

I pull up his number on my phone. He's worked a forty-eight-hour shift and is scheduled to get off tonight. He's planned to come over afterward.

I hit the green button, and he answers on the third ring. "I was just thinking about you."

"You were?" I ask, thumbing through my closet. I'm looking for something that will make Trevor swallow his tongue.

"Have you eaten? I was thinking I'd run by Dirty Dicks when I get off and grab us some dinner."

"Well, there's been a slight change of plans. Mo asked me to meet her for drinks, and I felt bad telling her no because I've been brushing her off for the last week."

"That actually works perfectly," he says, yawning through the phone. "It's been a long couple of days, and I'm exhausted. I'll just head home and catch up on some sleep."

Well, shit. That's not what I was hoping for. "Rhett and Coop are going to be up there. I thought maybe you'd want to join us."

There's a pause. I pull a blouse and a skirt from the closet and shut the door.

"Are we...you know...telling everyone now? Because I can't be around you and not touch you."

Bingo! That's what I was looking for. "I'm ready to tell everyone if you are. They're going to find out eventually anyway. We can't hide it forever."

"I don't want to hide it," he says. "I just wasn't sure if you were ready, and we haven't talked about it before now."

"I'm ready."

"Okay. I'll go home after work and get cleaned up, and then I'll meet you there."

"I'll see you there."

I hang up the phone and do a happy dance around the room. I'm a little too excited about putting my plan in motion and accidentally step on Milo. She yelps, and I pick her up.

"I'm sorry," I coo, setting her on the bed while I change. "I just got excited."

Milo turns in three circles on the middle of my bed before plopping down. My hair and makeup are already done, and it only takes a second to slip into a fresh outfit.

I slide my heels on, look at myself in the full-length mirror, and smooth my hands down the front of my skirt. "Perfect."

Milo barks, clearly agreeing with me.

"You be good tonight," I say, bending down to give her a kiss. She licks incessantly at the air, every few swipes hitting the side of my face. "If I come home to find something destroyed, you'll be spending tomorrow in your kennel."

Ten minutes later, I'm climbing into Mo's car.

"You look hot," she says, giving me a onceover. "What's the special occasion?"

"Nothing." I shrug. "Just felt like dressing up. You never know when Mr. Perfect might walk into your life, and I need to be prepared, right?"

She flips on her turn signal and sighs. "I'm glad to hear you say that, because I sort of invited someone to meet us at Dirty Dicks tonight."

"You didn't."

"I did." Mo gives me a nervous glance. "Don't be mad."

"I'm not mad; I'm furious. You promised no more blind dates."

"It's not a date. It's just someone I know, and he doesn't have a ton of friends in the area, so I figured it would be nice to invite him to hang out with us."

"And by us you mean me?"

"No." She shakes her head and then scrunches her shoulders. "Okay, maybe, yes."

"No, Mo."

"I don't see what the big deal is. You just said you never know when Mr. Perfect might walk through the door, and Everett is as close to perfect as you're going to get."

"Everett."

She looks at me and smiles. "He's tall, handsome, and super

nice. Oh, and he's a doctor so he falls within your occupational guidelines, and he's a foster dad to two of my rescue dogs."

I want to tell her that my rules are not being very well enforced right now, and my version of perfect is tall, handsome, and super nice, but also a firefighter and a rancher and every time he walks into a room I get butterflies.

"I'm not going on a date with Everett. I'm not going to sit by him or talk to him or flirt with him—"

"You don't have to be mean."

"I'm not going to be mean, but I'm also not going to encourage something that *will not* happen."

"Okay, fine." She takes a hand off the wheel, holding it up. "But I have a feeling you're going to change your mind once you see him."

"And I have a feeling you're going to be eating your words later tonight," I mumble.

"What was that?"

"Nothing. Just drive. The sooner I get an appletini the better."

CHAPTER
Thirty-Five

Trevor

"You're going to laugh about this," Rhett says, catching me as soon as I walk through the doors of Dirty Dicks.

"I'm going to laugh about what?"

He shoves a beer in my hand and spins me around. I take a drink, wondering what is so amusing when I see it—or rather who. The whole gang is sitting at a round table. Cooper, Mo, Adley, Lincoln—and Tess even made it out tonight. And then there's Claire. A smile stretches across my face until I see the man sitting next to her lean in close.

"I'm going to go out on a limb here and guess that by the look on your face, you've staked a claim on Claire since the last time we talked," Rhett says.

"I have. Who is that guy?"

"That's what makes this so funny. You see, this is what happens when you keep things from Mo. My lovely girlfriend has taken it upon herself to parade another single, successful man in front of Claire." I open my mouth, but Rhett continues. "Lucky for you, I had a clue as to what was going on, and I managed to keep the doctor away from your woman. But you should know that the second I got up, he moved over to my seat."

Lifting my beer, I drain the rest in three large gulps. I've never had a girlfriend before—or a woman I've claimed as my own—so I'm not sure what the proper etiquette is for getting upset about this sort of thing. But when I look at Claire with her arms folded tight over her chest and her legs crossed, it's clear that she's about as far away from this doctor as she can be.

"I'm not worried. And it's going to be fun to play with her and Mo."

"Shit. Do you have to bring Mo into this?"

"She tried to set my woman up with another man. I thought you told me she was putting an end to this shit."

Rhett shakes his head and runs a hand through his hair. "She said she was, but I've got about as much control over her as I do over you."

"That's not much."

"My point exactly. Just go gentle on her, okay? I'd really like to get lucky tonight, and when she finds out I knew about you and Claire before her, she's going to flip a lid."

"You didn't know about Claire and me," I say, pulling my eyes away from Claire.

Rhett rolls his eyes. "Close enough. So, how are things going anyway?"

"Great. She's perfect, bro."

"I'm glad to hear you say that. And I'm sorry if I ever led you to believe you weren't good enough for her."

I clap my brother on the shoulder. It's on the tip of my tongue to give him shit about growing a vagina and going soft on me since he's hooked up with Mo, but I decide against it. "Water under the bridge. Now, let's go make things awkward."

"Oh boy."

Rhett falls in step beside me as we walk across the room. I stop a few times along the way to say hello to some of the regulars, and when I finally make it to the table, Claire is watching me. She looks nervous, which I find cute as hell, and I can practically hear her eyes screaming at me.

I swear to God I didn't sit next to this guy!

Please, don't be mad.

I'm not attracted to him; it's you I want.

Why are you sitting next to him? Why aren't you making him move so you can sit next to me?

What the hell are you up to, Trevor Allen?

She narrows her eyes when I sit down next to the doctor, who has taken it upon himself to scoot as close to Claire as he can.

"Who are you?" I ask.

The guy turns to me, holds his hand out, and smiles. "Everett Smith."

I shake the dude's hand, giving it a nice firm squeeze. "Trevor Allen."

When he lets go, he rubs his fingers. "You help out at Animal Haven. Mo has told me a lot about you."

"And how do you know Mo?"

"Oh…" He smiles and looks at Mo. "I'm new to town. I've been here for about three months, took a job at the hospital."

"You're a doctor."

"I am, emergency medicine. Mo tells me you're a full-time firefighter."

"That's right."

"She also tells me you work with Rhett on your father's ranch and help her out at Animal Haven. That's actually how we met—I've started volunteering for her."

"He's fostering a couple of strays," Mo interjects.

Rhett leans back in his chair, one arm draped around Mo's shoulders as he watches the interaction.

"That's great. And your wife, she doesn't mind animals, I take it?"

Rhett rolls his eyes.

"I'm not married," Everett says, glancing around the table. His eyes linger on Claire a little longer than I'd like, but he doesn't try to touch her. She is the most beautiful woman in the room, so I'll give him a pass.

"Well, Everett, welcome to Heaven. It's a great place to live, and I'm sure you'll love it."

"Thank you." He smiles. "I have a feeling I'm going to love it too."

"You know, Claire just adopted her first dog."

Claire glares at me. Mo beams.

"You did?" he asks, angling himself toward her. "Tell me about him." Her eyes meet mine over his shoulder, promising retribution as she answers.

"Well, um, he is actually a she. Her name is Milo, and she's a blind Pomeranian."

"Mo told me about her," Everett says, touching Claire's arm.

My blood boils, and I'm seconds away from going caveman on his ass until he removes his hand.

"I've got Murphy and Rascal."

"Wow, two. I'm sure your job is demanding. I don't know how you find the time."

"It is, but..."

I try to pay attention to what they're saying, I swear I do, but I'm too distracted by looking at Claire. Her red hair falls in loose waves over her shoulder. She's got a chunk of it twirling around her finger. The movement is as hypnotizing as the swells of her breasts playing peekaboo along the neckline of her blouse. Every time she laughs they sneak out, teasing me, reminding me what a lucky bastard I am. The hem of her skirt has risen up just enough to expose the silky skin of her thighs— thighs that felt damn good wrapped around my head.

Just thinking of what I did to her that night makes my mouth water and my cock swell. Swallowing hard, I look around, wondering if anyone caught me eye-fucking Claire. I think I'm in the clear until my eyes meet hers. She's got her lip pulled between her teeth, and a quick glance down shows her thighs squeezed together about as tight as they can get.

Cocking a brow, I look up. She grins.

Releasing her lip, she pushes away from the table. "Hey, Coop, do you have any ibuprofen in your office?"

"Wait, I've got some Tylenol," Tess says, reaching for her purse.

"No, I don't like Tylenol. I need ibuprofen."

Tess gives Claire a strange look, but doesn't argue.

"You got a headache or something?" Coop asks.

Claire's eyes meet mine. "I've definitely got an ache, and I need to get it taken care of before it gets worse."

"Third drawer on the left," he says. "The door should be unlocked."

I watch Claire stride across the floor, her hips swaying from side to side, causing her ass to bounce, and that's my cue.

Slapping my hands on my table, I scoot my chair back and stand up.

"Where are you going?" Rhett asks.

"To the bathroom. Wanna join me?"

He gives me a you're-full-of-shit look, but I walk away before he has a chance to blow my cover. When I round the corner, I see Claire leaning against the wall. She pushes away and walks toward me.

"What was all that back there?" she asks.

"What was what?" I say, nudging her into Coop's office.

"You, pretending to get to know Everett and asking him if he's married."

I shut the door and lock it. "I was just trying to get to know the guy."

"No, you weren't," she says.

"You're right. I don't give a shit about what's his face." I press her against the door. "But I was jealous as fuck watching you two talk, and when he touched your arm, I about ripped his hand off."

"Oh, God." Claire moans when I push my thigh between her legs. "You could've stopped it," she pants.

The silence stretches, causing our heavy breaths to echo in the small space.

"I could've." I skim my lips down her neck, over her collarbone, and along the swells of her breasts. All I can think about is how grateful I am that we're finally alone.

Claire reaches for my pants, but I've got other plans.

She's so damn sexy. Her chest is heaving, pushing her breasts closer and closer to my face. Her cheeks are flushed, and I can feel the heat from her pussy on my thigh.

"Why didn't you?" she breathes.

I lift Claire's blouse, dip my finger into the top of her bra and pull down. Her breasts spill into my hands, her nipples puckering into tight peaks when I blow on them.

"What do you want me to do, Red?"

"I want you to tell me why you didn't get between Everett and me."

"Not exactly the answer I was looking for." I pull a tight bud into my mouth. I suck hard, and Claire drops her head against the door.

"Trevor." She tunnels her fingers into my hair and holds me against her body.

With one hand cupping her breast, I move the other to her outer thigh. Raw, sexual energy pulses through the air as I skim my fingers along her silky skin, dipping them below the hem of her skirt and up the inside of her thigh.

"Open." I nudge Claire's legs until they're shoulder-width apart, and then I move to the other breast. I suck her nipple into my mouth just as I scoot her panties to the side and plunge two fingers into her pussy.

With each swipe of my tongue against her sensitive skin and each dip of my fingers, I push Claire closer to the edge. She squirms and thrashes in my arms as I attack the tight ball of nerves buried inside of her.

My cock is throbbing, begging for release, but I hold out, knowing what I have in store will be more than worth the wait.

"Please, Trevor." Claire cups her breasts, holding them for me so I can feast on them and freeing up my other hand.

I release her breast with a wet pop and move back to the other side. "You're so beautiful, Claire. I'll never get enough of you."

That's all it takes. Claire's body convulses. She screams out my name, and I don't care if the entire bar can hear her, because nothing is as sexy as watching her come undone. I kiss my way up her neck, my fingers still sliding in and out of her, and she rides out the wave of her orgasm. She finally collapses against the door and blinks up at me, her eyes heavy and sated.

"Remember when I said anticipation is one of the strongest aphrodisiacs?"

She nods as I straighten out her clothes.

"Well, so is jealousy."

Claire's eyes smolder with a look so raw it leaves me stunned.

I slam my lips against hers. My tongue dives deep, exploring every inch of her mouth. Her hands are everywhere, and when she gets to the button of my pants, I stop her yet again. Circling my fingers around her wrists, I pull back.

"Not yet."

"What do you mean, not yet?"

Brushing my fingers along her cheek, I smile.

"Trevor."

It takes every ounce of strength I have to keep myself from shoving my pants down to my ankles and burying myself in her tight, warm body. With a ragged breath, I reach around Claire and push the door open.

CHAPTER
Thirty-Six

Claire

I'm going to kill him.

Running a hand over my hair, I take a second to catch my breath and right my clothes, which Trevor mostly already did. My clit is still throbbing, and no matter how I adjust my bra and shirt, I can still see my nipples protruding.

Fuck it, I think to myself. *This can be his punishment.*

My nipples poking out for all the world to see is his damn punishment.

With my shoulders squared and my head held high, I march out into the bar as if I didn't just have an orgasm to end all orgasms.

"What took you so long?" Mo asks.

The only seat open is the one I vacated earlier, between Mo and Everett. Trevor is tucked in cozy between Everett and Tess, and maybe if I'm lucky I can get her to switch seats with me.

"Tess?"

"Yeah?"

"Want to switch seats? You can get to know Everett."

"Oh, uh…" She looks about as uncomfortable as I feel, and

Trevor answers for her.

"We were actually just thinking about playing a round of darts. You guys up for a few games?" he asks the table as a whole.

"I love throwing darts," Everett says, a little too enthusiastically. "Claire, you can be on my team."

"Perfect," I mumble.

Everyone stands up and walks to the back room. I watch Rhett pull Trevor off to the side. They exchange some words, and when Rhett gives me a sympathetic look, I narrow my eyes.

Does he know about Trevor and me?

"You ready, partner?" Everett says, handing me a set of darts.

"Born ready."

I lean against the wall while Tess sets up the board, and when Everett positions himself next to me, I glance at Trevor. He smiles and walks toward us, propping himself on the other side of me. I scoot as close to him as I can.

He laughs and wraps an arm around my shoulders. It's not something he would've done before we got together, but our group has always been close knit, and the gesture goes mostly unnoticed.

I say mostly, because Everett gives us a curious glance. "Are you good at darts?" he asks me.

"She's okay." Trevor looks around me at Everett. "Don't expect her to hit the bullseye every time."

I elbow Trevor in the side and he laughs, rubbing his ribs. "I'm just kidding," he whispers, kissing me on the cheek.

Tess turns around. "Trevor, you're up first."

"Let's do this."

The rest of our crew shoots pool while Trevor and Tess beat us at darts. And they keep beating us over and over and over again.

"I'm tired of this game," I say, tossing my darts on the table.

"Come on, we're having fun," Trevor goads. "One more."

"You said one more four games ago, and you're having fun because you've won every time."

"Hell yeah." Tess holds her hand up, and Trevor gives her a high five. I roll my eyes and he hooks his arm around my neck, pulling me against his body.

"Don't be a sore loser."

"I'm not." I try to push Trevor away, but he's not having it. His grip tightens, and I eventually give up because his touch does things to me that no man's touch should be able to do to a woman.

"Sorry, Claire. I'm not very good at darts," Everett says.

"That's okay."

"We could try our hand at pool," he suggests.

"I'm not very good at pool."

"I can help you."

I picture myself bent over the table with Everett trying to help me align a shot. I cringe. Trevor must be thinking the exact same thing, because his body goes stiff against mine and his eyes narrow.

He wanted to get me with anticipation. Maybe it's time I get him with a little jealousy.

"Perfect." Grabbing Trevor's fingers, I remove his arms from my shoulder. "You break," I say to Everett.

My body brushes past Trevor's intimately when I reach around him for a stick on the wall.

Everett racks the balls, situating them on the table, and then rubs his stick with the blue chalk. "Ready?"

The game ensues. Everett sinks a solid and a stripe on the break, chooses to go with solids and lands a second ball before missing.

I've never been good at pool. Sure, I know the basics, but I've always sucked at lining up shots, which I'm going to use to my advantage. I walk around to the opposite side of the table, bend down low, and position the stick between my fingers.

"You trying to get this one?" Everett asks, pointing to the ball I'm aiming for.

"Yup. Why?"

"You're a little too far to the left." He's kneeling down, his eyes level with the ball, and when he looks up at me his eyes drop. I know he has a clear view down the front of my shirt.

"How's this?" I say, moving the stick a little to the side.

"Perfect. It's, uh, perfect," he stutters.

I glance at Trevor. He's standing tall, his arms folded across his chest, staring daggers at Everett. I almost feel bad. But then I remember the way he walked out of Coop's office and left me all hot and bothered.

I sink the ball, and Everett tosses his arms in the air. "You did it."

I shimmy past Trevor, doing a little happy dance that ensures my ass rubs against his crotch.

"Tease," he murmurs.

Shooting him a wink, I bend over the table for another shot.

"Nope. Too far to the left," Everett says.

I shift the stick.

"Nope. Too far to the right. You know what? Let me come help you."

"I've got it." Trevor doesn't even give Everett the chance to get close to me.

I've got the shot lined up, the stick between my fingers the way my daddy taught me. Trevor steps behind me, pressing his body against mine. He slides his arm alongside mine, his hand holding mine steady while he uses the other to line up the shot.

"Are you trying to make me jealous?" he whispers in my ear.

"It's an aphrodisiac, remember?"

"You're damn right it is, but I want to pound *you*, not his face, which is what's going to happen if he looks down the front of your shirt one more time."

In one smooth motion, Trevor guides the stick toward the cue ball. It bumps into the number ten ball, sending it into the corner pocket.

Setting my stick down, I laugh and turn around in Trevor's arms. Gripping the front of his shirt, I pull him toward me. "You're the one who started this game."

"And now I'm ending it."

Gripping my face in his hands, Trevor tilts his head and draws me in for a deep kiss. I don't hear much over the sound of my heart beating in my ears, but I manage to catch a gasp, probably from Mo, and then another gasp—Everett, I'm guessing. And then come the catcalls.

"I did not see this coming," Coop deadpans.

"I did," Adley chirps.

"About damn time. I was wondering how long it was going to take you," Rhett hollers.

"You knew about this?" Mo says.

Trevor smiles against my lips. He pulls back and rests his forehead against mine.

"Well…I didn't really know until tonight," Rhett explains.

"What do you mean you didn't really know? You kind of knew? How do you kind of know, and why didn't you tell me?" Mo argues.

"Shit, woman, give it a rest. Does it really matter how or when I found out? You're finding out now."

"Claire." Mo says my name, and I squeeze my eyes shut.

"Busted," Trevor whispers. He brushes his lips against mine, laces our fingers together, and faces our friends. "So, everyone, Claire and I are together. It's been brewing since Peanut had her baby and we spent the day together at Animal Haven."

Mo's eyes grow as wide as saucers. "What?"

"I said *brewing*," Trevor clarifies. "Calm down. Nothing happened until the night Claire ran out of the bar and you all sent me to go after her."

"I didn't run out," I say.

Trevor looks down at me. "You totally ran, but that's okay because I'm finding that I really love the chase."

"Awww." Adley cuddles in close to Lincoln. His hand sits low on her hip, but when he sees me looking at them, he quickly removes it, leaving me wondering if I haven't been the only one keeping a secret from the group.

"Were you ever going to tell me?" Mo says, sounding a little hurt.

I step away from Trevor. "Yes."

"When? It's not hard, Claire. In fact, it's really quite simple. Hey, Mo, I'm screwing around with Trevor."

"We're not screwing around," I say softly.

"You mean…" Her eyes light up. They bounce to Trevor and back to me.

"We're in a committed relationship," I answer.

"Trevor has never been in a committed relationship."

"Hey," he scoffs. "I resent that."

"Well, you haven't," she says.

Trevor wraps his arms around me from behind and kisses the side of my head. "There's a first time for everything, and I was just waiting on this girl."

"We were waiting on each other."

"Look," Adley says. "They're as disgustingly cute as Rhett

and Mo."

"If I ever get like that with a woman, knock me upside the head," Coop says.

Linc holds out his fist, and Coop bumps it. "I've got ya covered."

Trevor laughs at his brother, but I can't take my eyes off of Mo. She's just staring at us.

"Well, aren't you going to say something?"

She sighs and picks at the hem of her shirt. "I'm thrilled for you, but I'm a little disappointed I'm just now finding out."

I take a step toward her. "I'm sorry, Mo. Everything just happened so fast, and I wanted to give us a few minutes to settle down and get used to the idea of being together before we announced it to everyone."

"She's right, but we weren't trying to hide it," Trevor adds. "I took her to the pier and tons of people saw us together. I'm surprised you didn't find out about it sooner."

"Don't be mad," I say, hugging Mo.

She hugs me back. "I'm not mad."

"Thank God. Now I can tell you all the juicy details. How about tomorrow I bring pizza out to Animal Haven? We'll have lunch and spend the day together."

"I'd love that." She pulls me in for another hug and finally lets loose a squeal. "Oh my gosh, you're dating Trevor!"

"Excuse me."

Mo and I look at Everett. He seems a little unsure of himself. "Does this mean there's no chance of—"

Trevor takes a menacing step toward Everett, who snaps his mouth shut and takes a giant step back.

"Sorry, Everett," Mo says. "I didn't realize they were together."

"I see that."

"But I'm sure I can find someone else to set you up with."

"Or not," Rhett says, pulling her to his side. "Maybe we should put your matchmaking skills on the back burner for a little while."

"I have mad matchmaking skills."

"If we're all done here, Claire and I will be leaving," Trevor announces.

"We will? I sort of thought we'd stick around and play another game of pool."

"You thought wrong." Trevor tosses me over his shoulder in one of those fireman holds he demonstrated to my class. With his arm tight across the back of my thighs, he makes it so no one can look up my skirt.

"You can't leave already," Mo whines. "We have to celebrate."

"Trust me, that's exactly what we're going to do," Trevor says.

"Let's go, Trevor." I squirm on his shoulder. "The anticipation is killing me."

With a boisterous laugh and more than a few awkward stares, Trevor carries me out of Dirty Dicks.

CHAPTER
Thirty-Seven

Trevor

"My place is closer."

"I don't care where we go, just get there fast," Claire says, her lips roaming every inch of my neck. Her free hand lands on my erection, which is barely contained by my jeans, and I groan.

"Sweetheart, hang on. We're almost there."

"Don't tell me to hang on. You left me in Coop's office, remember?"

I laugh remembering the frazzled look on her face after I brought her to orgasm against Coop's office door. "Yes, but if you get your hands on me, I'm going to blow my load before we even get in the house."

"And that's a bad thing?"

"That's a very bad thing because I'd like to be in here when I get off," I say, moving my hand between her thighs. Claire is soaking wet, and she squirms in her seat when I brush my fingers along her panties.

"Oh God, you're killing me, Trevor. Just get there already."

"I love it when you're like this," I tell her, trying to

concentrate on the road.

"You're going to love it even more when I get you home."

"Counting on it."

When I hit the end of my lane, I pick up speed. I don't even bother pulling into the garage. I toss the truck in park, pull Claire across the seat, and climb out. Her legs wrap around my waist, her hands dive into my hair, and her mouth claims mine as I maneuver us up the front walk.

We stumble into the house a twisted mess of arms and legs and mouths. There's kissing and pulling and yanking and lots and lots of touching, and in a matter of seconds, my clothes are gone. My cock springs free, bobbing hot and hard between us as we tumble to the floor.

"May I?" she says, reaching for my erection.

"You don't ever have to ask." *But I can't even begin to tell you the things it does to me when you do.*

With languid movements, Claire scoots down my body and looks up at me. Wrapping her fingers around my cock, she guides me to her mouth. Her tongue darts out, licking the drop of precum off before she pulls the head into her mouth.

Placing my hand along the soft curve of her neck, I hold Claire steady as I slide into her mouth. Her tongue sweeps over the tip before pressing along the underside of my cock. She sucks me deep.

I brush her hair out of her face, fisting it at the back of her head so I can watch her pull and work my cock. Her mouth is hot and wet, and nothing has ever felt this good—except sinking into her tight, warm pussy, which I plan to do very soon.

"Claire, baby, you need to stop or I'm going to come in your mouth."

"That's the whole point of this," she says, licking her lips.

I grin. "Smartass."

"I want this. I want you to lose control."

"That's not going to take much," I say, guiding her head back to my cock.

She takes all of me in. Wrapping her hand around the base, she strokes as her tongue swirls around my shaft. Pressing her tongue toward the roof of her mouth, she sucks as she slowly pulls back, and I let out a guttural moan.

"Yes. God, yes. That's it, Red."

She takes me deeper, as though my words fuel her efforts. I squeeze my eyes shut when my cock hits the back of her throat. Claire's head bobs up and down. Her fingers slip between my legs and she cradles my balls, massaging them gently. I thrust, giving her more, and she moans. I can't hear it over the blood rushing through my ears, but I can feel the vibrations against my shaft.

"That's it, baby. Suck it hard." A sheen of sweat coats my skin. My hips move faster, my cock sliding in and out of her mouth. "You look so good with your lips wrapped around my cock."

Heat settles at the base of my spine. My balls tighten, drawing upward, and with a loud moan, I explode. My body jerks, but Claire doesn't stop. She keeps sucking, taking every last drop I give, and when my body goes lax beneath her, she licks the shaft clean. She kisses my belly, working her way up my body until she reaches my mouth.

"How is it that I ended up completely naked, and you still have all your clothes on?"

Claire smiles cheekily and puts her chin on my chest. "I guess I was just more determined than you were."

"I'll show you determined."

I flip us around so our positions are reversed and jump to my feet. I hoist Claire into my arms with ease and stride down the hall.

"You have a thing for holding me, don't you?"

"You fit perfectly in my arms," I tell her.

Kicking open my bedroom door, I walk in and lower Claire to her feet. I reach for her blouse, but she stops me. The weight of the moment and the emotion I'm feeling settle heavy in my chest.

"I need to be inside of you, Claire. Please."

"You will be." Pressing a hand to the center of my chest, she pushes until my legs hit the back of the bed, and I sit down.

With her eyes locked on mine, Claire peels off her shirt, tossing it to the floor. My mouth waters at the sight of her white lace bra. She licks her lips, her eyes dropping to my cock, which grows under the weight of her stare, and toes off her shoes. Her skirt is the next to go, falling in a pile on the floor.

Hooking a finger in the sides of her underwear, Claire slips them over her hips and kicks them to the side. "Eyes up here." Her command is gentle. I look up, and the vulnerability in her eyes matches the soft tone of her voice.

She flicks the front clasp of her bra. The flimsy material falls away, leaving me with the most breathtaking view in the entire world. Everything about Claire is beautiful. Her creamy skin, the soft curve of her hip, the seductive look in her emerald eyes. I swallow hard, my eyes bouncing around her body as I try to figure out which part of her I want to explore first.

"Scoot back, Trevor."

I lift a brow, but do as she asks. Reaching across the bed, I snag a condom from the nightstand and scoot back on the bed.

"Come here, Claire. Let me make love to you," I say, holding out my hand.

She laces her fingers with mine and crawls onto the bed. Straddling my hips, she puts both hands on my chest, pressing me back against the pillows.

"I thought you'd never ask," she says.

Taking the condom from my hand, she rips the foil, slides it over my shaft, and tosses the wrapper. With her hands still on my chest, she lifts her hips. I guide my cock to her entrance, and inch by inch, she welcomes me into her body.

"You feel incredible," I whisper, never taking my eyes off hers.

She tilts her head back. Her hair cascades down, tickling the tops of my thighs. I grip her hips, guiding her over my cock, slowly at first so I can savor the feel of her body on mine.

Nothing has ever felt anything like this, emotionally or physically. Our connection is so much more powerful than I gave it credit for.

Making love to Claire is like taking a dip in the quarry on a hot summer day, or curling up next to a fire on a frigid winter night. It's refreshing and comforting. It's like coming home.

Claire rolls her hips. She lifts up, only to drop back down, repeating the process several times. My grunts grow louder with each stroke as I slam my hips into her, pleasure just out of reach.

Squeezing a hand between our slick bodies, Claire finds her clit.

"Fuck," I moan. "That's hot, but this orgasm is mine, baby." I push her hand away, replacing it with my own. Pressing a thumb to her clit, I rub in tight circles.

"Oh God, Trevor."

My movements speed up, along with Claire's breathing. Her breasts bounce heavily in front of my face, and I capture a nipple with my lips, sucking it deep into my mouth. I flick it with my tongue, and Claire's pussy contracts around my cock.

I suck harder, rub faster, and Claire's body explodes.

"Trevor." The sound of my name on her lips pushes me over the edge, and my orgasm slaps into me with enough force to blur my vision.

She collapses on top of me while we catch our breath, and when I'm sure we're both going to survive, I wrap an arm around her waist and flip us over. Lowering myself to my elbows, I hold Claire's head in my hands.

I run my finger along her jaw, over her lips and smile. "Nothing has ever felt as good as it feels to make love to you." She swallows, her eyes growing increasingly glossy. "It's like you were made for me, Claire, and I don't want what just happened between us to ever end."

"It doesn't have to."

"That's what I'm hoping for." I kiss the tip of her nose and slide off of her.

I've got one hand tucked behind my head—because I feel like a king with Claire lying on my chest—and the other curved possessively around her hip.

"Trevor?"

"Hmmm?"

"Don't let me fall asleep," she murmurs.

"Why not? I'd love for you to stay. I could even give you the official tour."

"I'd like that." She blinks up at me, a sleepy smile on her face. "But Milo is at home alone."

"Rest, Claire. Don't worry about Milo. I'll take care of her."

CHAPTER
Thirty-Eight

Claire

One minute I'm having crazy, hot sex and the next I've got a cold, wet nose shoved into my cheek.

My eyes fly open, and I find myself face to face with Milo. Smiling, I reach for her. She grunts when I tuck her under my chest.

"Where did you come from?" I ask.

Trevor plops down on the bed. "You were snoring again."

"I don't snore."

"You do. Loudly." Milo climbs out of my arms and onto Trevor's lap. "I couldn't fall asleep, and I didn't want to wake you up because then you'd leave, so I snuck out and drove to your house to get Milo. I used the key on your key ring. I hope you don't mind."

"Not at all. Thank you for doing that."

"You're welcome."

"Where did she sleep?"

Trevor peers down at my fluffy pal, who is licking his abs. "On my chest." He pushes her face away, but Milo keeps licking. "Why does she lick this much? It can't be normal."

I giggle. "She likes you."

"It's not just me. She licks everyone and everything."

"I don't know. I just assumed it's her thing. She's a licker."

"Kinda like her mama," Trevor suggests.

My lips part. My cheeks grow hot as I think about the dirty things Trevor and I did last night, especially the things I did with my tongue. I drop my eyes to the comforter.

"Oh, come on. I've kissed every inch of your naked body. I've had my cock and other parts of my body inside of you, and you're embarrassed to think about sucking my dick?"

Heat spreads throughout my body, and if I looked in a mirror, my face would probably resemble a tomato. "Not embarrassed exactly... It's just not something I've ever openly talked about with a man."

Trevor sets Milo on the floor next to the bed and crawls toward me. He tugs on the sheet, leaving me naked as the day I was born. My nipples pucker under his heated gaze as he lowers himself on top of me.

"Good. Because I don't ever want you to be embarrassed about anything we do."

Milo barks. I can hear her running around the bed, probably trying to get the courage to jump up.

"Last night was...amazing." I run my fingers along Trevor's spine. He grinds his pelvis against mine, but his boxers are in the way, which is probably a good thing because Milo finally makes it onto the bed.

She barks excitedly, probably proud that she made that horrifying jump, only to be set back on the floor.

"Where were we?" Trevor says, cradling my head between his arms.

"I was just telling you how wonderful last night was. I've never experienced anything quite like it."

Trevor frowns. "You've had sex before."

"Yes, but that wasn't sex. That was…so much more."

"It's because we care for each other, Claire. We were making love. Every time I look at you, kiss you, or touch you, it's my body loving yours."

If hearts can hand themselves over to another human being, mine just threw itself at Trevor.

"I feel the same way. It was so intense. And not just what we were doing, but your words and—"

Trevor grins. "You like the dirty talk?"

"I do. It's never worked for me before, but with you, I expect it. I crave it."

"Because you're comfortable with me in a way you haven't been with anyone else." Trevor smiles down at me and runs his thumb along my lip. "It's called love," he says, kissing me.

"How do you know? You've never been in love."

"I just know. I can't explain it, but I can feel it. There is no other explanation. We've both been with other people, and neither one of us has felt this way before." Trevor lifts himself up so he can get a good look at me. "Why? Are you having second thoughts?"

"God, no." I shake my head and pull him back to me. "That's not it at all."

"Because it's okay if you are. It's okay if we need to take a step back. I told you I want to do things right with you, and I meant it. If we're moving too fast, say the word and we'll slow down."

I think about his words. While I agree that we have moved fast, I know in my heart that I love Trevor and I want the connection we have to keep growing.

"We're not moving too fast. I'm just trying to wrap my head around it all, and you seem to have a better understanding of it than I do," I admit.

"Claire, I'm as clueless as you are. I'm just telling you what's in here." Trevor puts my hand over his heart.

"I love what's in there," I say, rubbing my palm over his chest. "Who knew Trevor Allen would be such a romantic?"

"I'll show you romantic." He playfully attacks my neck, and I laugh, thrashing around when he tickles me.

Milo manages to make it back on the bed and is enthusiastic about joining whatever game we're playing. She jumps around us, barking at Trevor, and next thing I know she's rooting her nose between our faces.

"Awww…" I giggle. "She wants in on the lovin.'"

Trevor sits up and glares at Milo. "You're a little cockblocker. That's what you are." He ruffles Milo's fur and she barks, jumping around the bed. She gets too close to the edge and tumbles off before we can catch her.

"Whoa there." Trevor lifts her up and hands her to me. "Careful."

"Arf!"

I nuzzle my nose into her soft fur. "What she's trying to say is thank you."

Trevor looks at his watch and slides off the bed. "I better get going."

I reach for him but he takes a step back.

"Come back to bed."

"No." He grabs a pair of jeans from his drawer and pulls them on. "If I get back in that bed with you, neither one of us will get a damn thing done today."

"I don't have anything to do today."

"Wrong," he says, tugging a white T-shirt over his head. "You promised Mo you'd meet her at Animal Haven."

"Oh, right." I wrap the sheet around my chest and sit up.

"Will I see you later?"

"Of course." Trevor leans in and kisses me. "Stay as long as you'd like. Explore. I put a key to the house on your key ring. Lock up before you go."

I put a key to the house on your key ring.

I blink and then blink again.

He gave me a key to his house.

I fly out of bed, pull the sheet tight around my chest, and run down the hallway, skidding to a stop when I see Trevor with a hip propped against the island in his kitchen. He's grinning from ear to ear with his hat in one hand and a cup of coffee in the other.

"You're not going to freak out, are you?" he asks.

Am I? I take stock of my body. Pulse, *steady*. Palms, *dry*. Legs, *still*. I think I'm good.

I did have a minor freak-out, which is why I darted after him, but once I saw him again, the fear faded away.

I shake my head. In three strides, I'm in front of him. "No, I'm not going to freak out."

"Good." He sets his coffee down and reaches for me. "I wasn't sure how you'd handle that little bombshell. When I heard you come barreling down the hall, I figured you were seconds away from an anxiety attack."

"I don't have anxiety," I say, giving him a pointed look. "And it was a pretty big bombshell."

"It's just a key."

Really? Is he crazy? "Just a key? It is not just a key. You just gave me permission to enter your home at any time for any reason. Do you realize the magnitude of that? I could scrounge through all of your drawers and the deepest parts of your closet."

"Are you going to do that? Because I can already tell you there's nothing there."

"No, I'm not going to do that, but I could, and you're allow-ing it, which means you have nothing to hide and you trust me and—"

"You're freaking out."

"No." I swallow and take a tiny step back—not too far though, because *damn* he smells good. "It's just we've only been together…" I try to calculate the days in my head, but they all run together. "I don't know the number, but it hasn't been long."

"Do I have to keep reminding you that we've known each other for years? *Years*, Claire. I trust you as much as my own family. And I want you here. Milo too. I want you both here. I want to make love to you in my bed—and yours too from time to time—and I want to cook for you and curl up on the couch and watch movies with you."

Well, damn. That's super sweet.

"Are you crying?" he asks.

"No, I'm not crying." I sniff. "That was just really sweet."

"Are you sure you don't have anxiety?"

"Would you stop with the anxiety crap?"

"Okay. You think too much."

He's probably right about the anxiety, but I'll never tell him that. And I do think too much. I'm tired of thinking and over-analyzing every freaking thing in my life.

"Not about this." I push up on my toes and kiss Trevor. "I want all of those things you mentioned too."

"So we're good?"

I take a deep breath and nod. "Yeah, we're good."

"Can I give you a goodbye kiss now?"

"I'd like that."

Trevor grabs the sheet and yanks me in. The first brush of his lips is soft and tender, as if he's reiterating everything he just said to me. Then he settles in and the kiss deepens, hot and intense—the kind of kiss that would normally end with my clothes falling off. Oh, look, my clothes are already off. Perfect.

I release my hold on the sheet, but Trevor catches it before it falls to the ground. Wrapping it around my shoulders, he pulls it taut in front of me.

"You didn't do that on purpose, did you?"

"No, not at all," I say, feigning innocence. "It must've slipped while you were kissing me."

Trevor grabs his coffee and turns for the door. Then he looks over his shoulder. "You realize you're a terrible liar, right?"

"Yes, I know. Goodbye, Trevor."

CHAPTER
Thirty-Nine

Claire

The sun is shining, the birds are chirping, and there's a dull ache between my thighs. I'm not sure this day could get much better. After Trevor left this morning, I took a self-guided tour of his house. I'd seen it before, but always from the outside. I knew he'd remodeled the old farm house a few years back, but Rhett and Coop's descriptions didn't do it justice.

Trevor put a tremendous amount of time and probably money into the remodel. Granite countertops, state-of-the-art kitchen appliances, hardwood throughout, and a floor-to-ceiling stone fireplace are just a few of my favorite things. Oh, and the claw-foot tub in the master bath, which I may or may not have soaked in before I left earlier. I could've stayed longer, explored more, but Mo called, wondering when I was going to make it to the shelter.

An hour later, I pull into Animal Haven with a giant smile on my face. Mo is nowhere to be seen, although I know she's here because her truck is parked next to the barn.

I open the door, and Milo flies out of the car. It's not as fluid as most dogs make it look because she can't see shit, has no idea where the drop-off is, and plows face first in the ground. But that doesn't stop her. She picks herself up, shakes herself off, and starts wandering around.

My phone rings, and I fish it out of my purse and slide my finger across the screen when I see it's my mother calling.

"Hey, Ma," I answer.

"Claire Daniels, is there something you want to tell me?"

"Uh…" *Shit.* It's not her birthday. And I don't remember her asking me to do anything for her the last time I was over there. "I don't know…is there?"

"Trevor!" she shouts. "When were you going to tell me about Trevor?"

I get out of my car and shut the door. "How did you find out?"

"Mo," she says.

"Of course." I should've known.

"She mentioned it to her dad this morning on the phone, who mentioned it to me. Imagine my shock when Phil rolled into the room and told me my little girl, my only daughter, was dating Trevor Allen."

"Wow, Mom, you just had to stress the only daughter part, huh?"

"Well…"

"I'm sorry, okay. You're right. You should've heard it from me, but I wasn't trying to keep it from you, I just haven't had a chance to tell you."

"Or you knew what I'd say," she gently offers.

"What's that supposed to mean?"

"I just want to make sure you're, you know, walking into this with your eyes wide open."

I frown. "You don't think dating Trevor is a good idea?"

"No, that's not it at all. I think Trevor is a fine young man. It's just…sweetie, he's a firefighter, and you've always had your ru—"

"My rules. Yes, Mother, I know I've had my rules."

"I'm not trying to upset you, Claire. I just want to make sure you've thought about this. The last thing you want to do is rush into something you're not ready for."

My step falters. "Not ready for? You don't think I'm ready for a relationship?"

"That's not what I meant."

"That's what it sounded like."

"Claire—"

"I'm not rushing, okay? I know what you're thinking. You're worried because of what Trevor does for a living, but you shouldn't be, because I'm dealing with it. I'm dealing the only way I know how."

There's a silence that says *I'm going to need more than that.*

"Okay, yes, it's hard," I continue. "Some days are easier than others, but I'm working through the bad days—we're working through the bad days," I reassure her.

"Claire…" Her words trail off. I stop with a hand on my hip, watching Milo root around in the grass. She finds a spot she likes and lies down.

"What, Mom? Just say it."

"I love you, Claire, more than anything, and there is nothing I want more in this life than to see you happy. If Trevor makes you happy, I'm on board one hundred percent."

"Good."

"But—"

"I knew there was a but."

"—you've only been together a short time. There hasn't been a major catastrophe or something that's threatened his life.

How are you going to handle it when that happens? Because it will happen. Maybe not today or tomorrow or next year, but at some point—being a full-time firefighter—he's going to face some serious challenges."

"If I can get past the fire at Bright Start, I think I can handle something else."

"Except you weren't invested in him when that fire took place. Things are different now. You're invested. Your emotions are involved on a different level."

I hate her words because this is something I don't want to think about, let alone talk about. "Look, Mom, I appreciate the concern, but I'm fine, and I really can't talk about this right now. Mo is probably wondering where I'm at."

"Okay. I'm sorry if I upset you. That wasn't my intention."

I blow out a breath and look up at the fluffy clouds floating across the sky. "It's okay, Mom. I'm not upset."

"Bring Trevor by. I'd like to get to know him."

"I will."

"Okay, sweetie. I love you."

"Love you too, Mom."

She hangs up, and I stuff my phone in my back pocket. Well, that put a damper on my day.

"Milo. Come on, girl." She leaps to her feet and runs across the yard. "Over here," I say, guiding her with my voice.

I clip the leash on her, and together we walk through Animal Haven in search of Mo. We find her in the back, on her hands and knees scrubbing out the kennels. I put Milo in an empty cage so she can't get into anything she's not supposed to.

"Hey," Mo says, wiping an arm over her sweaty forehead. "It took you long enough to get here. Grab a hose."

Don't mind if do. "I've actually been here a little while, but I was stuck on the phone." I pick up the hose and turn the dial to full blast. "With my mother," I add.

Mo swallows, her eyes darting to the scrub brush in her hand. "Oh yeah?" she says, running it across the floor. "What did she want?"

I tap the spray nozzle against my palm and take a step toward her. "Oh, you know, just to talk."

"Good. That's good," she says, concentrating on the floor of the kennel as though she's performing brain surgery.

"Did you talk to your dad today?"

"Uh…yeah, actually, I did. But only for a minute this morning."

"And what did you two talk about?"

"Just the normal stuff. He asked about Animal Haven. That's really about it."

"Liar," I shout, squeezing the trigger. A heavy stream of water blasts Mo in the chest.

She falls backward, eyes wide. "What was that for?"

"You told your dad about Trevor and I."

"Trevor and me."

"Huh?"

"You said Trevor and I, it should've been Trevor and me."

I growl, and Mo throws her hands up.

"I don't need a grammar lesson from you right now."

"Okay. Sorry," she says.

"For correcting my English or blabbing to your dad?"

"Both?"

I blast her with another shot of water. Mo sputters, throwing her hands in front of her face.

Milo is going crazy in her cage, running in circles and barking incessantly, trying to figure out what the hell is going on.

"You deserve that," I say, lowering the hose. "You knew your dad would tell my mom. Did it occur to you that I hadn't told her?"

"I'm sorry, okay? I was just excited, and I tell my dad everything, and when he asked what I did last night, it just sort of came out. Then Rhett walked into the room and put his hands on me while I was talking, and I ended up rushing off the phone without telling my dad not to say anything."

"Let me get this straight. I had to endure a lecture from my mom about Trevor because you and your horny boyfriend couldn't keep your hands off each other?"

At least she has the decency to cringe. "Yes?"

I raise my nozzle, blasting her again, but this time Mo is ready for me. She lunges to the side, grabbing a second hose, and drenches me. We're both sputtering, trying to drown the other, and I'm sure from the outside we look like lunatics. But we're in the moment, and the only one here to judge us is Milo—and she's blind.

Mo tries to stand up but falls on her ass. The joke's on me, though, because her nozzle shoots upward, hitting me in the face, and I choke on my own laugh. She tries again to get up, but her rubber boots are no match for the slick concrete, and she falls again—only this time she lands in a pile of dog poo.

I gasp, releasing the trigger at the same time she does. Mo slowly lifts her free hand, which is now a disgusting shade of brown.

"Arf."

"Quiet, Milo." The yapping stops, and I scrunch up my nose and look at Mo. "That's a good color on you, matches your hair."

Her eyes narrow. "This is your fault, and now I'm going to have to work the rest of the day sopping wet and smelling like dog shit."

"Here, let me fix it." I flick the nozzle from stream to spray and aim it at her hand. "There, problem solved."

Mo shakes her head, flinging water from her face. She drops the hose and very carefully climbs to her feet.

"Truce?" I offer.

"Sure." The soles of her rubber boots squeak against the floor as she takes a step toward me. "We can call a truce."

"Good, because I really didn't mean to cause this big of a mess," I tell her. "I was just mad that your big mouth blabbed my life to your dad before I had a chance to tell Mom."

"Do you feel better?"

"I do, actually."

She takes another step forward, and that's when I notice her holding her other hand out to the side—the hand that had been gripping the hose. There's a streak of brown running down her arm. It must've gotten there when she fell.

"What are you doing, Mo?"

I take a step back as she closes in on me, and when she's about a foot away, she lunges, tackling me to the ground.

"Payback!" she yells, trying to rub her arm in my face.

I try to douse her with the hose, but we're too close together, and I end up drowning the both of us. Mo wrestles the hose from my hand, blasting me in the face. We're rolling around on the floor, both of us struggling for dominance, when a loud whistle pierces the air.

Mo and I freeze. She's on top of me, her hips pinning me to the floor. She looks up, and I tilt my head back. Trevor and Rhett are standing in the doorway, both of them grinning from ear to ear.

"What are you two doing?" Rhett asks.

Trevor walks the short distance to us and crouches down. He swipes a finger across my cheek, brings it to his nose, and recoils.

"Why do you have shit on your face?" he says, wiping his

finger on his work pants.

"Mo told her dad about us, and he told my mom, and then she called and gave me the third degree."

"And that's a problem?" he asks, looking at me tenderly.

"No, it's not a problem. I just wanted to be the one to tell her."

"Why didn't you?"

"Yeah, Claire, why didn't you?" Mo says, crossing her arms over her chest.

"You stay out of it," I say, pointing a finger at her before I look back up at Trevor. "Her grandclock is ticking, and I wanted to be sure you and I were, in fact, a *we* before I told her."

Trevor furrows his brow. "Grandclock?"

"Yeah, you know, when a mom wants to turn into a grandmother but her child isn't popping out kids so she hounds them every chance she gets," I explain.

"Oh. Oh, damn. Vivian does that with Rhett and me," Mo says.

"All the damn time," Rhett adds, grabbing two towels off the shelf.

He hands one to me and the other to Mo. She crawls off of me, and Trevor pulls me up to a sitting position.

"Speaking of my mother, she wanted to invite the two of you over for family dinner tonight," Rhett says. "Coop and Adley will be there."

"That's why we came by," Trevor says. "And to bring you lunch, which is in the refrigerator."

"Thank you. That was very thoughtful, and I would love to have dinner with your family. Tell Vivian I'll be there."

"Tell her we'll both be there," Mo adds.

Taking the towel from my hand, Trevor wipes the smudges off my face. "I would kiss you, but you stink."

I rip the towel from his hand, and Mo laughs.

"Why are you laughing?" Rhett goads. "You look worse than she does."

Mo gives Rhett a sugary sweet smile. "Are you going to be a nice boyfriend like your brother and come wipe me down?"

"Hell no. I know that look, and you're evil. If I get within reaching distance, I'll be in just as bad a shape as the two of you," he says, taking a step back. "And Trevor's right; shower before you come."

Trevor stands up. "Maybe twice."

"Yeah, yeah." I wave them away. "I'll ride out later with Mo and go home with you."

"Sounds good. Dinner is at five," Rhett says, dipping his hand in his pocket.

Trevor's gaze bounces between Mo and me. "You two okay here?"

I look at Mo slumped against the wall. She smiles, and I nod.

"Yeah, we're good."

With a smile on their faces, Rhett and Trevor walk out. A second later Trevor walks back in. "Where's Milo?"

I point to her old kennel. "Down there."

Trevor opens the gate and reaches for her. As soon as she catches a whiff of his scent, her little tush is wiggling like crazy. He scoops her up and heads for the door.

"Where are you taking her?"

"With us. You two have a mess to clean up here, and she can run around with Duke and Diesel at the ranch," he says, referring to Rhett's dogs.

"Don't let her get trampled by a horse."

Trevor stops and looks at the mess around us. "Trust me, she's safer at the ranch than she is here."

CHAPTER
Forty

Claire

M o waits for Trevor to leave again, and then she looks at me. "I'm sorry I told my dad about you and Trevor."

"No, you have nothing to be sorry for. It's my fault. I should've told my mom sooner. I'm sorry I drenched you with the hose."

"And I'm sorry I wiped poop on your face."

I look down at my soaking-wet clothes and the questionable stains I got from rolling around on the floor, and for some reason I bust up laughing.

Mo smiles, watching me, and after a few seconds she starts laughing too. Before I know it, we're a hysterical mess.

"Look at us," I pant, trying to catch my breath. "Two grown women having a water fight."

Mo wipes the tears from her face and sighs. "I haven't had this much fun in years."

"Me neither."

"I'm thinking I should piss you off every few months just so I can have a good laugh."

"I'm all down for the good laugh, but lets try to avoid the pissing-off part."

Mo nods and holds out her hand. I grab it and yank her in for a hug.

"I'll agree to that," she says.

"I guess we need to clean up this mess."

She looks at wet floor and nods. "I guess you're right. And I still have to do afternoon chores. I'll be lucky to make it to Vivian and Sawyer's on time."

"I'll stay here and help you. Together we'll get it done."

She lifts a brow. "Yeah?"

"Yeah."

"How about while we clean you give me the lowdown on you and Trevor? You know I've been dying to get the details."

"I can do that."

Mo and I spend the next hour cleaning up the mess we made, which was more extensive than I'd realized. Water easily drains on the floors because of the way the building was built, but we had water everywhere—the walls, the ceiling, the giant food trough. And that was unfortunate because the top layer of dog food was soggy, and we had to scoop it up and throw it out. And that doesn't include the poop smeared across the floor.

But by the time we got done, the kennels were spic and span, and Mo had heard my tale from the very first time Trevor and I kissed right here at Animal Haven to the dirty deed that went down last night. Of course I left out all of the intimate details—those are just for Trevor and me—but I am a girl, and I do like to indulge myself in a little girl talk from time to time.

"So Trevor's a dirty talker? Rhett's the same way."

My eyebrow juts up. "Really? I never would've guessed that."

"Oh yeah, he lives for it. It must be an Allen thing."

"Must be."

"Well, I'm happy for you."

"Thank you. I appreciate that. Now if I can just get my mom on board."

Mo purses her lips. "I'm sorry, Claire, but I've never known your mom to be anything but completely supportive of you and your decisions. I have a hard time believing she isn't on board. She's known the Allens her whole life, and she knows Trevor. Why wouldn't she be on board?"

"It's not Trevor she has a problem with, it's me."

"Explain."

"She thinks I'm still insecure after Daddy's death."

"Well, are you?"

"No." I frown and think about it a second. If I can't be honest with my best friend, who can I be honest with? "I don't know. I don't think so."

"Claire." Mo stops what she's doing and looks at me. "Safety and occupations and firefighters have been a huge source of anxiety for you since your dad passed away, and this is your first time dipping your toe back in the water, and you didn't really dip your toe—you dove right in."

"Because I'm tired of being so uptight and following my damn rules. I don't want to have those insecurities, Mo, and I really want this with Trevor. I love him."

"I truly believe that you love him, and I know you don't want to have those insecurities, but what happens if they rear their ugly heads and you change your mind?"

"I would never intentionally hurt Trevor."

"I know you wouldn't, but you might unintentionally hurt him if you're not careful. I know you don't want to hear what your mom has to say, but maybe she's right. Maybe you should take a step back and do some soul searching and make sure this is something you're one-hundred-percent ready for before you wade into the deep end."

"I think I'm already there."

"I think you are, too, but it's not too late for me to toss you a safety ring."

"Why are we talking in pool lingo?"

Mo laughs. "I have no idea. Maybe because we're both still soaking wet."

I smile and then sigh. "I don't agree with you and my mother entirely, but I see your point. Maybe I should talk to Trevor about this and get his take—although I don't want to spook him."

"He won't be spooked. From what Rhett told me last night after we got home, Trevor's already floating around the deep end in his raft—with a beer in one hand and an engagement ring in the other."

"Oh no," I laugh humorlessly, shaking my head. "We're far from that."

"I mean that you're it for him. He believes in you and in the two of you together that much." She reaches out to squeeze my hand. "I agree. Talk to him and give him fair warning that you're a flight risk. That way he can at least be prepared."

"I'm not a flight risk, but I'll talk to him tonight after dinner."

"Good. Now let's finish here so we can get cleaned up and make it to Vivian's on time. She's an amazing cook. I don't even know what she's making, and my mouth is already watering."

CHAPTER
Forty-One

Trevor

"Thanks for keeping an eye on Milo while I ran home and took a shower."

"No worries," Mom says, looking over her shoulder. "She's out back with Duke and Diesel."

That little fur ball loved hanging out with me today. Normally I'd look at a prissy little thing like her and think there'd be no way she'd last a minute on the ranch, but Milo is something. I had to keep a close eye on her because, well, she's blind, but I'll be damned if that little thing didn't use her nose and ears to get her everywhere she needed to be.

"It smells amazing in here. What are you making?"

"Garlic chicken and loaded mashed potatoes. It's Claire's favorite home-cooked meal."

"How do you know?" I ask, lifting the lid to one of the pans on the stove. There's a white cream sauce simmering inside, and it smell delicious. "What is this?"

"I know it's her favorite because I called her mother and asked. I made Mo's favorite the first time we had her over for dinner after she and Rhett started dating, and I wanted to do the same for Claire." Mom slaps my hand away and puts the lid back on the pan. "That's a provel garlic cheese sauce for the chicken."

"You called her mother?"

"Yes. And I even invited her and Phil to dinner. They're out on the patio having a glass of wine and keeping an eye on Milo."

Shit. I look down at my shirt and pants, wondering if I'm dressed up enough to meet Claire's mother. Okay, I'm not meeting her for the first time, but that's what it feels like.

"You look fine." Mom stands in front of me and runs her hands down the front of my shirt. "Sharon is going to love you almost as much as I love Claire."

"Almost?"

She smiles and shrugs. "I'm just glad you finally saw what's been right in front of you this whole time."

I squint, thinking back to that conversation Mom and I had in the hospital after the fire.

"There's a girl, but your head and your heart have to be ready for her, and when they are, you'll see her."

"You're obviously not there yet, and when you are, you'll realize you don't have to look far because she's been right in front of you this whole time."

"Wait. You knew about Claire?"

Mom pats my cheek. "I'm your mother, Trevor. I know everything. You think I didn't notice the way you looked at Claire every time she came over here? When she was around, you'd trip over your own feet. And she was the same way, but I think she fought it a little more than you did. I knew if you two would give each other a solid chance, you'd have a shot at real relationship."

"Do you think I'm relationship material? This is the first real one I've ever had."

"Sit down." Mom pulls out a chair, and when I sit down, she sits next to me. "It's not about being relationship material. It's about finding your other half—the one person who makes you smile and laugh, who's there for you when you're down and picks you back up. The person who makes you want to be better and do better. Your father is *my* person, and I know there's someone out there for each of my children."

I blink, a wave of memories washing over me.

Claire sticking up for me at the rock quarry.

Getting the nerve to ask her to dance at my freshman prom, and her saying yes.

Holding her in my arms as we swayed to the music, and the kiss she planted on my cheek when the song ended.

Teaching her how to drive the snowmobile when Rhett and Coop were too busy trying to impress other girls.

Carrying Claire down the hill after she hurt her ankle.

Battling her at Mario Brothers in the basement while my brothers and all their other friends played spin the bottle in the barn.

Kissing her that first time at Animal Haven.

And the second kiss we shared, and third and the fourth.

Touching her and making love to her for the first time.

Watching her come alive on that stage at the pier.

Curling up on the couch and watching movies.

God, the memories are endless and perfect and, "Claire is my person," I announce.

"I know she is, darling. I can see it in your eyes. Now you have to hold on to that, and no matter what, you don't let go. You fight for her no matter what the cost."

"Maybe Claire and I have made it through all the shit. Maybe this is our end," I say, recalling my conversation with Dad.

"Oh shit. You've already talked to your dad, haven't you?"

"Yeah, why?"

"Don't tell your dad I said this, but his theory on relationships and love is way off the mark. Next time you need relationship advice, you just come to your mama."

"Really? I don't think he's all that far off the mark. Everything he said made perfect sense."

"Okay." She sighs and grabs a rag from the table. "Don't tell him this either, or he'll never let me live it down. His theory isn't completely right, but it's not completely wrong either."

"What do you mean?"

"Your entire relationship will be the shit part your dad talks about, because relationships are work—hard work that doesn't end. It never, ever ends. You'll have good periods and bad periods, and there will be times you'll wonder if it's worth it, and you'll be tempted to throw in the towel. But if your love is pure and strong, you'll work through it."

"So then when do you hit the end that Dad talks about?"

"You don't. And it's not the end that's important anyway; it's all the stuff that comes before it. It's the memories and the laughter and the fights and—oh my gosh, Claire is here."

Mom flies out of her chair, leaving me to ponder everything she said. I think there's truth to both Mom and Dad's theories, and they both must know what they're talking about if they've made it this far, right?

"You better get to Mom before she tackles your girl."

I blink up at Coop. He's leaning against the counter with an easy smile and two beers. He hands me one. "Huh?"

"Mom," Adley says, walking into the kitchen. She nods toward the front door.

Sure enough, there's Mom, bouncing on her toes by the front door with her sights set on Claire.

"She did this same thing with Mo, and you have about thirty seconds to intercept her before it's all over," Rhett says, joining us.

"I've got this." Dad claps a hand on my shoulder as he walks by. He wraps an arm around Mom's shoulders and pulls her farther into the room.

"What are you doing?" She nudges Dad in the side, but he just laughs.

"Let the poor woman get out of her car."

"I just want to talk to her and welcome her into our home."

"And you can greet her with a handshake and friendly smile like most normal people would do."

"I'm not normal."

"We know that, sweetie." He kisses the side of her head, and all of us laugh. "Let's get the table set."

There's a soft knock on the door. I set my beer down and stride across the floor with purpose. Mo smiles up and brushes past me as she walks into the house.

"Hi."

I look at Claire, and the words fly right out of my mouth. She's wearing a blue sundress that hits just above her knees. Her hair is wrapped in a loose bun at the base of her neck, with red tendrils framing her face. All I can do is stare at her and wonder how in the world I got so damn lucky.

Her smile slowly fades, and she glances nervously at her dress.

"Oh God, it's too much, isn't it?"

"What?"

"The dress." She's got a horrified look on her face. "I knew I should've worn jeans like Mo." Spinning on her heel, Claire steps off the porch, but I catch her arm as she hits the grass.

"No," I say, swinging her around. She falls awkwardly against my chest, which is really quite perfect because I like having her in my arms. I cup her jaw and kiss her. "You look perfect."

Her shoulders relax. "Really? You're not just saying that? Because you were looking at me funny back there and—"

"There you go thinking again."

My lips on hers stop everything. Claire melts into me, her tongue pushing between my lips, and when we hear a catcall, she pulls back and holds her fingers to her lips. Her cheeks turn pink, and just like every other time, it turns me on.

Claire leans to the left, looking around me. Her eyes grow wide. "Your entire family just saw us making out."

"Not my entire family. Beau isn't here. And now's probably a good time to mention that your mom and Phil are on the patio."

"What?" she hisses.

"Hey, look at me." I smooth my hands down her arms, and she follows my command. "These people are our family. They love us and support us, and there's no reason to be nervous."

"I just really wanted to make a good impression on your parents, and now my mom is here, and you've got to make a good impression on her and—"

"Claire."

Her mouth snaps shut.

"My parents already love you. You have been here more times than either one of us could ever count. As for your mother, don't worry about it. I know I'm not," I lie. Hell yeah I'm worried about making a good impression on her mother. What man wouldn't be? Claire's father is gone, so I have one shot at this.

"You're right." She takes a deep breath, and I watch the heat drain from her cheeks. She straightens her back and squares her shoulders. "Let's do this."

We take a step toward the house and Milo barks. Claire stops in her tracks, her jaw dropping as Milo walks around from the back of the house.

"Oh my gosh, what is this?" she says, kneeling down, undoubtedly to look at the small rope I used to hook Milo's leash to Duke's.

"She kept running into things and stumbling, so I hooked her up to Duke and let him guide her around." The contraption Rhett and I came up with has enough slack to give each dog room to move. Essentially, it's no different that Milo being on a leash, only it's Duke who's walking her. "He's her eyes. Watch this. Duke, come here, buddy."

Duke might tower over Milo, but the second I hooked them together, he became hyperaware of her, walking more slowly and taking extra precautions to ensure her safety.

When Duke starts walking, so does Milo, and when he stops at my feet, she stops, too. "Sit." Both dogs sit. Milo's head is tilted in the air as though she's looking up at Duke, waiting for him to make his next move.

"Trevor," Claire breathes. "This is absolutely fantastic. I can't believe this. She's like a different dog. He's her navigation." She gives Milo a pat on the head and scratches Duke behind the ear. "I'm going to have to get another dog."

I squat down next to Claire. "I don't think she needs a guide all the time, but it would be nice when you take her places where she could get hurt—like Animal Haven, or if I bring her here."

Claire gives me a teasing look. "You mean you'd want to bring my prissy dog to the ranch more often?"

"She's not so bad," I say, petting the dogs. "She's got a huge personality that I'm sort of falling in love with. Kind of like her owner."

Claire leans toward me. "That was smooth, Mr. Allen, using my handicapped dog to get to me."

"Did it work?"

"Oh, it so worked."

CHAPTER
Forty-Two

Trevor

"Mrs. Allen, dinner was amazing," Claire says, leaning back in her chair. "I'm stuffed."

Mom scoffs. "You've been calling me Vivian for years, dear, no sense in changing it now."

Claire's smile is bright. "Okay. Vivian it is."

The dogs are all napping under the oak tree. I've got my arm along the back of Claire's chair, one foot propped up on my knee, a cold beer, my family, and a beautiful girl. I'm not sure life gets much better than this. I've felt unsettled most of my life—first as an angry, awkward teen, then as a guilt-ridden young adult. I wasn't sure I'd ever get to this place.

Claire reaches for my plate, stacking it on top of hers. "I'll do dishes."

"Oh, no, dear," Mom says. "The dishes can wait."

"Are you sure? I don't mind." Claire looks down at me and then back at my mom.

With a hand on Claire's hip, I draw her back into the chair. "Don't fight with her on this. You'll lose."

"He's right," Adley says, standing. "We prefer to enjoy each other's company while we can. Cleanup can come later."

She stacks everyone's dishes and carries them into the house. She comes out a few minutes later with a fresh set of plates and silverware, and a pie.

"Dessert anyone?"

"I'll take a s-s-slice," Mo's father says. His speech isn't the best since his stroke, but it's clearer every time I talk to him.

Claire's mom, Sharon, leans forward and cuts each of them a piece.

"You want one?" I whisper to Claire.

"I might explode, but I'm afraid if I say no I won't get to try it."

"I'll share a piece with you."

"Okay."

"Okay." I carve out a slice, grab two forks, and hand one to Claire. We both dig in as the conversation swirls around us. Everyone is laughing and carrying on, and Claire has just fed me the last bite when my phone vibrates and the fire tones go off.

We used to have to carry big clunky pagers when we were on call, but thanks to modern technology, there's an app for that.

I reach for my hip, pulling my cell off the clip, and stand up. My crew rotates with the others in case we're needed for a mutual aid call, and this is one of those times. Lifting the phone to my ear, I step away from the table to listen.

The three dogs have perked up at the loud tones and sit patiently, like the rest of my family.

We don't get second-and third-alarm fire calls very often, but every once in a while, they happen. My family is used to it, but Claire stands up and closes the distance between us. She stands at my side and listens as the dispatcher gives me the information I'm looking for.

"*Attention Heaven Fire Department, Heaven EMS, second-alarm fully involved structure fire at the corner of Route Forty and Berkshire Road in Dayton. There's a report of occupants inside. Dayton Fire Department is on scene and is requesting backup.*"

My phone vibrates again with an incoming call. I spin and walk quickly toward my truck with Claire hot on my heels. I answer on the next ring.

"What do you need, Chief?"

"Truck 1049, 1050, and 1051 are responding. Suit up and meet us there."

"On my way."

I end the call and unlock my truck.

"What's happening?" Claire asks. "Where are you going?"

"There's a fire in Dayton I have to respond to." I grab my bunker gear from the back of my truck. I kick off my shoes and toss them in the cab. Shoving my feet in my rubber boots, I pull my suit up, wrapping the straps over my shoulders and then shrug on my coat.

"But you're off today."

"I am, but I'm on call, and I've got to go."

Claire shakes her head. "What does that even mean? I didn't know you took call."

I cradle her face in my hands. "Claire, I will explain all of this to you, but I can't right now because I have to go. People are counting on me; my department is counting on me."

Her eyes cloud over, but she takes a step back. "Go."

I toss my helmet into the front seat, but instead of leaving, I reach for her. "I'll see you later tonight, okay? I love you, Claire."

I kiss her softly, climb into the driver's seat, and pull out of my parents' driveway onto the road. Dayton is a neighboring town about fifteen minutes from where I am. As I drive, I listen to dispatch giving updates, and my mind wanders back to Claire. My gut twists when I recall the uncertainty in her eyes as I left.

With that one look, I knew I'd failed her. This—firefighting, my occupation—has been Claire's biggest insecurity, and I should've prepared her for something like this.

It took a lot of courage for her to push her fears aside and give me—us—a chance, and the last thing I need is for her to get spooked and withdraw. I don't care how late it is, when I get home tonight, I'm going to sit down with her, and we're going to have a serious talk. I'm not going to hold anything back. I'm going to explain what it is that I do, what part I play when I arrive on scene, and what she can expect from different calls. I want her to have every piece of information she needs to move forward with me with a clear mind.

Which is what I need to have as I pull up on scene. I can see smoke billowing into the air from several blocks away. The closer I get, the thicker it gets, and I pull over on a side street, not wanting to get too close. I flip on my hazards, grab my helmet, and get out of my truck. I walk straight toward the fiery mess, meeting several of my crew members along the way. Fire trucks are lined up along the road, some hooked up to fire hydrants, others not. People are screaming and crying, and there are officers and emergency personnel doing their best to keep the growing crowd back while attending to the injured.

Chief waves us over and fills us in. "There were fifty to one hundred people inside when the fire broke out. Twenty-seven have been accounted for."

"Fifty to one hundred?" Mikey asks. "Which is it? That's big gap."

"No one really knows. The warehouse is abandoned, and

young kids from around the area come here for parties. The building is divided into five different sections, and while the majority of occupants were in two of the sections, it's unclear how many occupied the other areas. Mikey, Trevor, Casey, get your packs on. You're going in."

I've never given much thought to running into a burning building, but tonight I can't help but think of Claire. For the first time, I have a reason to come out. I have a reason to fight and get home at the end of the night.

Not that my family wasn't a good enough reason—they would be devastated if something happened to me—but Claire is different. She's my life. My future. My reason to get in, do my job, and get out. But even though she weighs heavily on my mind, there's only one answer I can give Chief. The same answer as Mikey and Casey.

"Yes, sir."

CHAPTER
Forty-Three

Claire

Every fear I've buried deep or thought I'd conquered bubbles to the surface. My mother's warnings that I failed to heed are now playing loud and clear in my head as I watch Trevor's truck drive away. When I turn around, I can tell by the look on Mom's face that she knows exactly what's running through my brain.

This has to be some sort of sign.

My stomach rolls, followed by a thick wave of nausea, and suddenly my mouth becomes overly moist, like it does when I'm about to throw up. Closing my eyes, I take a few deep breaths, willing the feeling to go away.

I can't believe I allowed this to happen. I fooled myself into thinking I could handle something like this, when clearly, I cannot. My heart is racing, nearly exploding out of my chest at the thought of Trevor running into another fire.

Why did I think I could ever do this day in and day out—support him and say goodbye to him, knowing he's running toward danger? I realize now that most days, Trevor leaves for work, and I don't know what kinds of calls he's responding to. I just go by what he tells me at the end of his shift, which usually isn't much more than a brief rundown of what happened. I see now that maybe he was trying to protect me.

My legs are shaky and numb as they carry me back across the yard toward the rest of the group.

Mom stands up and takes a step toward me, but I raise my hand, stopping her. Right now I need to concentrate on holding myself together and not bursting into a ball of tears and snot. If she wraps her arms around me, I'm going to lose that battle.

She takes a step back and sits in her chair, but her back is stiff, and I know she's ready to pounce on me at a moment's notice. I'm not so lucky with Trevor's mom, because as soon as I sit down, she reaches for my hand, and the emotion pushes forward, flooding my eyes.

"He's going to be fine, dear," she says with a smile that tells me he's been called away from family dinner before.

"She's right," Adley says. "This sort of thing happens all the time. We usually don't schedule dinners when he's on call because he inevitably ends up having to leave."

Oh God. Can I do this? Can I handle him leaving mid-dinner every time that pager goes off? And what if it goes off during Easter mass or our kids' Christmas concert? Will he get up and leave?

Who am I kidding? Of course he will, the same way my dad did.

I scoot my chair back and stand up again, looking at Mo. "Could you take me home?"

She glances worriedly between me and Rhett, then stands up. "Yeah, sure. Whatever you need."

I nod. "Let me grab my purse."

I walk away from the table with eight sets of eyes burning a hole in the back of my head, everyone no doubt wondering if

I'm on the verge of some sort of breakdown. They all know my history—the history of my father—but no one but Trevor really understands the internal struggle I've had with my father's death.

The back door slides open, and I step inside the house, grateful for the momentary reprieve. I grab my purse where I left it on the couch and look up to find the TV on. It's muted, so I can't hear what's being said, but there's a picture of a large building on fire, and then it fades to a reporter. I grab the remote from the coffee table and turn it up.

"Authorities in the Dayton area say a fire broke out in this abandoned warehouse earlier this evening. So far nine people are confirmed dead, twelve injured, and several more remain unaccounted for. It is unknown what caused the fire, but crews have been working to contain it for over an hour. We are live on scene and will keep you updated with any new information. Steve, back to you."

"Claire? Are you okay?" Mo asks.

"It looks bad, doesn't it?" I say, staring at the TV.

The reporter may have finished her piece, but the camera is still zoomed in on the fire. There are flashing lights and people running everywhere, and it makes me sick knowing Trevor is among the crowd. Even worse, I don't know where. Is he on a hose in the building, the way he was when he found me? Or is he standing back, manning the crowd the way firefighters sometimes do?

"Come on, let's get you home. Rhett is going to follow us. I've already got Milo in the truck."

I'm on autopilot, painting on a fake smile and overly cheerful voice as I thank Vivian and Sawyer for having me over for dinner. I wave goodbye to everyone else, refusing for a second time to get too close to my mother, and I breathe a sigh of relief when I'm safe and sound inside Mo's truck.

As soon as I'm seated, Milo crawls into my lap. She presses her head against my chest as though she knows how bad it's hurting.

"Drive to the fire."

"What?" Mo looks between me and the road. "No, Claire. I don't know much about fires, but I know that's not something you do."

"Please, Mo. We don't have to get close, but I need to be there if something happens."

"Nothing is going to happen."

"You don't know that," I shout. "Please, Mo. Please, just take me."

"Rhett is going to kill me." She looks in her rearview mirror and side mirror and then executes a perfect three-point turn. A second later we fly past Rhett's truck going the opposite direction. Mo looks in her rearview mirror and flinches when she sees Rhett whip a U-turn in the middle of the road.

Her phone rings through the Bluetooth and she hits the *answer* button on the screen on her dash. "You're on speaker," she says.

"I don't care if the Pope can hear me. Where are you going? Do you know how dangerous it is to turn around like that on the highway?"

"Oh, and your U-turn was so much better?" she counters.

"Mo," Rhett warns. "What are you doing?"

"I'm taking Claire to the fire. But don't worry, we're not going to get close," she adds

Rhett laughs, but it lacks any sort of humor. "Don't worry? Are you two stupid? You know better than to do something like that."

"Don't be mad at her," I tell him. "I asked her to take me."

"And she could've said no."

Mo rolls her eyes.

"Turn around," he orders.

Mo scowls at her dash. "No."

"Monroe Danielle Gallagher, turn your truck around."

"Absolutely not. She needs to be there, Rhett. If the situation was reversed and you were about to run into an inferno, I'd want to be there, too, and I hope to God she'd take me if I asked."

We listen to Rhett sigh through the phone. Mo gives me a tight smile and a thumbs up low enough that Rhett wouldn't be able to see it through the window.

"You don't even know where you're going."

"Dayton. It's a small town. We'll look for the plume of smoke."

There's a long pause filled with lots of white noise, and then Rhett gives in.

"Fine, but do not get close, and do not get out of your car. The last thing Trevor needs is to see you there. He needs his head in the game for this sort of shit, Claire."

"I know. We promise."

Mo disconnects the call and looks at me. "You owe me big time for this."

CHAPTER
Forty-Four

Claire

I'm not ready.

I've been sitting outside the fire in Mo's car for over three hours now, and I've come to that conclusion. I'm not ready to be with a man who risks his life every single day. The amount of fear and anxiety that has raced through my body as I've watched men run in and out the building, pulling out victims and collapsing on the ground beside them, has been immeasurable.

I'd like to think my love for Trevor would outweigh any of this, but I'm not sure it would, and I don't know how to move forward without hurting him. I've tried to think about all the wonderful times we've had together over the years—and particularly more recently—but it only reinforces what I already know: I love Trevor, and it would kill me if something happened to him.

I'm just not sure how I walk away from this taste of his love with my heart intact. I'm pretty sure the answer is I don't. But I also don't know how to move forward. What I do know is I have a decision to make, a decision that will impact my life as well as Trevor's, and I have to make sure we're not only on the same page, but that I'm giving him everything I have to offer. As it stands right now, I'm not sure that's much.

How am I supposed to give someone my whole heart when that heart is weighed down by so much dread?

I'm thinking about what I should do and what I shouldn't, trying to work it all out in my head, when I see a familiar figure walking down the road. It's dark out, but the lights from the streetlamps and emergency vehicles provides enough luminescence, and what I see takes my breath away.

Trevor.

Milo wakes up when I lift her from my lap. I hand her to Mo and step out of the truck to watch him. His helmet dangles from his fingertips, his coat is draped over his arm, and his straps are hanging beside his hips. His hair sticks up in a hundred different directions, and he looks exhausted.

In this moment, my heart fills with so much joy and love, pushing away all of my fear and insecurities, and I take a step forward. The movement much catch Trevor's attention, because his head snaps up, and he stops in the middle of the road.

He stands there, unmoving, as I take another step and then another and another, and before I know it, I'm running full speed, slamming into his chest, and he catches me, because Trevor will always catch me. His arms circle around me in a tight band. I don't care that he's black from soot and smells of smoke, I hold on to him and don't let go.

"I was so worried about you," I breathe into his neck.

"I told you I'd be home."

I nod, unable to get any words out because of the thickness in my throat and the heaviness in my heart. It feels surreal to have him in my arms again, and I'm saddened all over again because I know I have some choices to make. Choices I don't want to make, because I love him, and I want him, and I this is why I have to get my shit together. But I don't think I can.

Trevor makes no move to let me go. He seems content to stand here holding me for as long as I need, but when a car pulls up behind us and honks, I reluctantly step back.

With my hand wrapped in his, Trevor pulls me toward Mo and Rhett's trucks. They get out when they see us approaching.

"What are you guys doing here?" Trevor asks, stopping at the back of Rhett's truck. "It's late."

"Someone insisted we come here," Rhett says, hooking a thumb in my direction.

Trevor's hand tightens on mine. "Come on, baby, let's get you home."

This is it.

I tug his hand when he tries to lead me away. "Rhett, Mo, give us a second, will ya?"

They exchange glances, and then Rhett's eyes linger on mine. I can tell he doesn't want to leave his brother, but I'm not doing this in front of him.

Trevor watches my silent exchange with his brother and then pulls his bunker gear down his body, bunching it over his boots. He steps out and tosses it in the back of Rhett's truck.

"I'm parked two blocks over. Can you toss this in the bed of my truck and bring back my shoes?"

"Yeah, no problem. Come on, Mo." Rhett opens the door for Mo, and we watch them pull away.

Trevor pulls Mo's tailgate down and leans against it. Despite the bunker gear, his clothes are filthy, and my heart flips over in my chest at what a wonderful, brave man he is, which makes what I have to do that much harder.

Milo is awake now, and she must sense Trevor's presence, because I see her tiny head bopping in the window. She's trying to get his attention, but Trevor can't see her.

"Come here." I take his outstretched hand and sit next to him on the tailgate. "Are you sure you're okay?" he asks.

"I feel like I should be asking you that."

Trevor looks back at the mess behind us—the strung-out hoses, pile of rubble where the building used to sit—and I wonder if he's thinking the same thing I am. *He's lucky to be alive.*

"I'm fine," he says. "I promise."

I know he is—I *know* it, but I'm not fine. Far from it.

Rhett and Mo pull up alongside us. Rhett hands Trevor his boots, which he slips on. "We'll be right over here."

Rhett parks down the road, giving us the privacy I asked for.

Trevor squeezes my fingers. "Come on, Claire, let me take you home." He tugs on my hand, but I take a step back.

Trevor furrows his brow and watches me.

"I'm, uh…I'm going to get a ride with Mo."

His face is blank. "Why?"

"It's late, and I'm sure you're drained. You probably want to get home and get cleaned up," I say, unable to look him in the eye.

"Look at me."

I don't.

"Look at me, Claire."

Swallowing, I look up.

"That's better. And yes, I want to go home and get cleaned up, but I also want to be with you."

"I'm tired. Watching all of this has been exhausting."

"Okay, then we'll go home and sleep and talk about it tomorrow."

"No, Trevor."

He shakes his head and runs a hand over his tired eyes.

"Cut the bullshit, Claire, and tell me what's really going on."

"Fine." I take a deep breath and square my shoulders, as if the movement will give me the strength I need. "I have a lot on my mind, and I need to think."

"Does this have to do with the fire?"

"No." I shake my head. "It has nothing to do with the fire."

"You don't want to be around me, is that it?"

"No," I growl. "I just need some space to think, Trevor. All of this—us—has happened so fast, and I need a second to work it all out in my head. I think you do too."

"Work what out? This morning you couldn't get enough of me and we were making plans for the weekend, and now you're asking for space. Excuse me if I'm a little confused."

"A lot has happened this evening, Trevor."

"So this is about the fire." He rubs a hand along his jaw. He tries to reach for my hand again, but I pull back. His face falls— the look pulling me deeper and deeper into the dark hole I'm already in. "What are you doing, Claire?"

I'm ripping my heart out, Trevor, that's what I'm doing. "I'm protecting you."

His jaw clenches tight. "No," he says, shaking his head. "You're protecting yourself. You said you loved me," he whispers.

"I do love you."

"I'm not so sure, Claire. I believe you love the idea of me— of us. But if you loved me, you'd let me take you home, and we'd work through whatever shit is running through your head together."

"Don't you get it? I love you so goddamn much I can't see straight." I shove my fingers into my hair and pace the length of Mo's truck, Trevor's eyes tracking my every move. "When you're around, I feel like I'm standing on the edge of a cliff. I can't think, let alone form words, and I'm seconds away from hurling myself off the edge, and that's terrifying. What if you're not there to catch me?"

"Claire—"

I hold a hand up, stopping Trevor. "I lied. This is about the fire. Watching you tonight made me remember all of the reasons I stayed away from you, and this is it." I wave toward the scene surrounding us. "I thought I could do this, but now I'm not so sure. I need to know that if I jump, you're going be there to catch me. And I don't just mean in that moment; I mean for the rest of our lives. I need to know you're not going to leave me the way my father did."

Trevor takes a step back and stares at me. "So, what? You're breaking up with me? Is that what this is? You want me to walk away and forget everything that's happened between us because you're scared? I can't do that, Claire."

"I don't know what I want. That's the problem. All I could think about while you were fighting that fire is how much it would destroy me if something happened to you. I didn't know what you were doing—if you were inside the fire or fighting it from the outside—and that scared me. I thought about my dad and the pain I went through after his death—the pain my mother went through—and I can't do that again." My voice cracks, along with my heart, and I look down.

"Claire…" Trevor grabs my face and forces me to look at him. "I can't guarantee that I won't get hurt, or that my job won't someday claim my life. But I can promise you I will always use my head. I will follow protocols and approach situations with a clear mind, and I will always do everything in my power to come home to you at the end of the day."

I don't know what to say. I don't know how to feel. I just have so many thoughts, and they're all jumbled, and I can't seem to process them.

Trevor drops his hands from my face. "But this is what I do, Claire. I run into burning buildings when other people are running out. I risk my life because it means saving someone else's. I love you, Claire, and I would do anything for you, but you have to accept that firefighting is a part of my life—a huge part that was influenced by *your* father—and I won't change that. I think you're overwhelmed right now. Tonight was as exhausting for you as it was for me. You need to rest and eat and think about things, and tomorrow you'll look at all of this differently... You'll see it the way I see it."

"And how do you see it?"

"I would rather love you and risk losing you than not have you at all, because my life doesn't work without you in it. But if you don't feel the same way, we're never going to make it. That's the kind of love I want. It's the kind I deserve."

I shake my head. "I don't know, Trevor."

"I do. Life is one big gamble, Claire. You can either play with the cards you're dealt or you can sit out and watch, and I'd rather play. I will always choose to play. I want to do more than play, I want to win. I want the jackpot, and that's you."

I look over Trevor's shoulder, concentrating on a group of firemen loading into a truck because it's easier than looking him in the eye. "You should go, Trevor."

"Don't do this, Claire. If you're scared, don't run away from me, baby, run *to* me."

His words are too much. Closing my eyes, I shake my head.

"You are a lot of things, Claire. You're beautiful, smart, and caring. You're determined and strong and loyal, but you're also a coward, and you better pull your head out of your ass before you ruin the best damn thing that's ever happened to you."

CHAPTER
Forty-Five

Claire

Stunned by his words, all I can do is stand there, and when I don't respond, Trevor curses under his breath and walks away. Off in the distance, I see Mo jump out of Rhett's truck. Trevor stops and says something to Rhett as Mo runs toward me. She grabs my arm, pulling me toward her vehicle, but I can't move. I watch Trevor climb into the seat Mo just vacated, and the moment Rhett turns the corner, I feel empty.

Immediately I begin to wonder if I've made a huge mistake, and I suspect I don't deserve the chance to make it right.

"Come on, Claire. Let's go."

I hop into Mo's truck, brushing Milo off my lap when she jumps from the backseat into the front. "Take me home, please."

Mo worries her lip. "I'm not sure you should go home, Claire. Come back to my place. I'll make some hot chocolate, we can eat ice cream, and we'll talk all of this out...or not. We can get rip-roaring drunk if you'd rather. I just don't think you should be alone right now."

I love Mo, and I love that she cares, but I don't want hot chocolate, the thought of eating something makes my stomach roll, and I sure as hell don't want to talk because she won't understand.

I squeeze my eyes shut, wishing my dad were still here. He would know what to do—though it's not lost on me that if he were here I probably wouldn't be in this situation. My mind drifts back to the look on my mom's face when Trevor got paged earlier this evening. She was watching me, waiting, hoping that I'd come to her. I'm not sure I'm ready to hear what she has to say, but I know in my heart of hearts there's no one more likely to talk me through this than her.

I blink up at Mo. "Can you take me to Mom's?"

"Okay." Mo puts the truck in drive and pulls away. We get about halfway home before she gets enough courage to talk. "What happened back there?"

"I think I broke up with Trevor." The words spill from my mouth, and I cry. I cry because he was right. I am a coward, and I don't deserve him.

Mo doesn't say another word. With one hand on the wheel and the other resting on my back, she makes the drive to my mother's.

The second we pull into the driveway, Mom has her front door open.

I reach for Milo, but Mo stops me. "Go. I'll take care of her tonight."

"Are you sure?"

She nods. "Yeah, you've got enough on your plate. Go do what you need to do."

"Thank you."

I walk up the sidewalk to the porch.

"I thought I might be seeing you," Mom says, holding the door open so I can walk in.

I wave to Mo, letting her know it's okay to leave. I don't

have a car here, but that's okay. Sometimes a girl just needs her mother, and we're long overdue for a sleepover. It's a good thing Phil sleeps in a hospital bed in his own room or it would get a little awkward because I have every intention of sleeping in Daddy's spot tonight.

Mom shuts the door, turns around, and opens her arms. I walk straight into them the way I've always done—the way I should've done tonight at the Allens'. Maybe if I'd given her the chance to talk to me then, I could've avoided all this bullshit tonight.

"Oh, baby." Mom holds me while I cry. She strokes my hair the same way she did when I was a little girl and skinned my knee, whispering in my ear that everything is going to be okay. Minutes pass, maybe hours, but eventually my crying stops, and Mom leads me to the living room and pushes me onto the couch.

Tucking my feet under my butt, I reach for the tattered old afghan on the back of the couch and pull it over my legs. Daddy used to love this afghan. My grandma made it for him when he graduated from the fire academy.

Closing my eyes, I pull the soft material to my face and in-hale. The blanket has been washed more times than I can count, but I can still smell him. Cuddling with me on the couch at the end of a long day, he would tell me about all of the crazy calls he'd gone out on, and I would tell him about school while Mom whipped up a pitcher of warm tea or hot chocolate. And then she would join us. The warmth of the blanket makes it feel like his strong arms are wrapped around me again.

We were a small family of three, but what we lacked in size, we made up for in love.

"Your daddy loved this afghan," Mom says softly, curling up on the couch next to me. I hand her a corner of the blanket, and she tugs it up over her legs.

Shifting on the couch, I rest my head on her shoulder. She pats my leg and sighs. "There's nothing he loved more than curling up on the couch after a long shift with his little girl and this blanket," she says as if she were reading my mind.

I smile to myself. "I was just thinking about that, about all the laughs we had."

"And tears," she adds. "Lots of tears."

I laugh. "And a few fights."

Tilting my head, I look up to find Mom smiling wistfully. "He loved you so much, Claire. You were his pride and joy. He boasted about you to anyone and everyone who would listen. He'd rave about how well you were doing in gymnastics and in your advanced classes. He didn't care what he was talking about, as long as it had to do with you."

When I was younger, I thought it was annoying to stand there and listen to Dad go on and on about whatever was going on in my life, but now I'd give anything to relive those days.

"I miss him."

Mom presses her lips to the top of my head and takes a deep breath. She pauses a moment before blowing it out. "Me too, baby. Me too."

"Do you think about him a lot?"

"Every day."

Over the years I've avoided talking about Daddy too much. Whether it was to protect myself or Mom from an onslaught of memories, I don't know. But I'm ready now.

"What do you miss most about him?" I ask.

"Everything," she whispers. "I miss his arms wrapped around me at night. I miss the way he'd kiss me every morning. I miss the hugs and the way his eyes would dilate every time he told me he loved me. And the way he'd try to cook but would end up ordering takeout because he couldn't follow a recipe to save his life. I miss his smile and laughter, and the stupid jokes he used to tell."

I laugh, wiping the wetness from my eyes. "His jokes were so stupid."

She laughs, but it breaks into a sob, and when I look up she's brushing a tear from her cheek. "I miss the way he'd call every night after you were in bed and ask about my day. Sometimes we would sit and talk for hours about anything and nothing. It was nice having that connection with him when he spent so much time away from home. But most of all, I miss the small things, the things I didn't realize he did until he wasn't here to do them anymore."

I wait for her to continue, and when she doesn't, I urge her on. "Like what? What things?"

"I miss his hand on the small of my back when we'd enter a room, and the way he'd always act as if I was the only woman around—the only woman worth his attention. His eyes never strayed. I miss the feel of his hand in mine while walking down the sidewalk, and the way he used to walk beside me rather than in front of me, and how he used to open a door for me. Any door. The front door, the car door, a door to the department store or movie theater. He always opened the door and never walked in before me. Men these days don't do those sorts of things for women."

Trevor does, I think to myself.

Trevor.

He holds my door and my hand and not once have I caught him looking at another woman. He presses his hand to my lower back and always goes out of his way to tell me how beautiful I look and how much he cares.

Listening to Mom talk makes me realize that maybe I want

all the little things too—cuddling on the couch at night, cooking together and watching movies after a long day of work.

It also makes me realize what I've given up…the chance to have any of that with Trevor.

"I screwed up, Mom," I cry, pressing my face into her neck. She smells the same way she always has, like sunshine and apples and home.

"Talk, Claire. That's the only way I can help you get through this."

I take a deep breath and ask the question that's been on the tip of my tongue for over a decade. "If you had known Daddy was going to die—that he was going to leave you—would you have still married him, or would you have done things differently?"

"What? No, Claire." She shakes her head. "Your father was the light of my life until you came along, and then you two shared the spotlight. Yes, it killed me to lose him, but I wouldn't change a minute of my time with him. He was with me through most of the ups and downs life threw my way, and he gave me you." Her voice wavers and she places a palm on my cheek. "He gave me you, my sweet girl. My Claire Bear."

I laugh tremulously and wipe the tears from my face. "I haven't been called that in a long time. Not since Daddy died."

"I know, and that's my fault. You were his little Claire Bear, and it didn't seem right coming from me. I always sort of felt like it was a thing for the two of you."

"Now maybe it can be a thing between us."

Her face softens. She watches me warily for a few seconds and then asks, "Do you love him?"

I nod, blinking back tears. "With all of my heart."

"Then don't let him go."

Those words from her mouth surprise me. I sort of thought

she would be pleased that Trevor and I broke up. "You mean that?"

"Of course I do. Claire, I just want you to be happy. And if Trevor makes you happy—if he's that guy, then I couldn't be happier for you."

"But what if I lose him? What if he leaves me the same way Daddy did?"

"What if he doesn't? What if you two get married and have babies and grow old together?" she says, squeezing my hand.

What if he doesn't?

What if he doesn't?

Oh my gosh, what if he doesn't?

I've always believed in fate. I might've tried to fight it from time to time, but I've always been a firm believer that we all have a set path we were born to live. What if Trevor is fated to live a long, healthy life doing what he loves and I just walked away from him? I left him behind, along with my heart.

I did that.

I walked away.

He was right. *I* ruined the best thing that has ever happened to me.

And for what? Because I couldn't see the bigger picture from a different angle? What does that say about me as a person?

For most of my adult life, I've been convinced someone like Trevor would hurt me, and here I am the one hurting him.

He told me he loved me, and while I returned the sentiment with words, my actions told an entirely different story.

Christ, he was right. I am a coward. Walking away from him isn't going to make me happy, it's going to make me a sad, lonely woman, and I don't want to spend the rest of my life wondering *what if*.

What if I hadn't walked away?

What if I'd tried?

What if I'd looked past my fears and begged him to forgive me?

I look at Mom. Tears stream down my face. "I love him." I've said those three words to him time and time again, but I've never felt them the way I do now. "I love him." I half laugh half cry and wipe a fresh wave of tears from my face. "Trevor is the love of my life, and I don't want to be without him."

"Then go," she says. Grabbing her keys out of her purse, she shoves them into my hand. "Go to him. Tell him."

"I was horrible to him. He begged me to stay and talk to him, and I walked away."

"You weren't horrible, sweetheart. You were scared, and if he loves you, he'll give you the chance to explain."

"I gotta go."

"Go."

"Are you sure you don't mind me taking your car?"

"I'm sure. Go."

With my heart in my throat, I make the five-mile trek to Trevor's house. His truck is in the driveway, along with Coop's and Rhett's. Great, that's just what I need. For a split second, I wonder if I should leave and come back when he's alone, but I can't get myself to put the car in reverse, and the thought of going another second with him second-guessing my love for him makes my chest hurt.

I put the car in park, and I'm halfway to the door when the porch light flicks on and the front door opens. Rhett steps out onto the porch and shuts the door behind him. He's never looked at me with anything other than love and acceptance, but tonight I see neither of those things in his stormy gaze.

"What are you doing here, Claire?"

I've known Rhett for far too long, which is how I know

there's a giant, soft teddy bear beneath his steely gaze. "You know why I'm here."

"Humor me."

"I want to talk to Trevor."

"I think you've said enough."

I'm frustrated that I have to deal with Rhett when all I want to do is see his brother. But I'm more frustrated with myself for putting all of us into this situation to begin with.

"Really, Rhett? You're going to make me go through you to get to Trevor? I didn't butt into your relationship when you and Mo were trying to work things out, and so I'd appreciate it if you'd stay out of mine."

Rhett walks to the edge of the porch. "He's my brother, and one of the best men I know, and do you have any idea what I told him when he wanted to pursue you?"

I shake my head.

"I told him not to hurt you. I told *him* not to hurt *you,* because I knew that if one of you was going to fuck things up, it was going to be him." He glares at me for a moment. "Damn it, I was wrong. Not once did I think you'd be the one to hurt him, and do you know how that makes me feel?"

"Probably a lot like how I feel right now, if I had to guess."

Rhett pinches his lips together in a thin line and watches me walk toward him.

"I made a mistake, Rhett, and I need to apologize, but not to you, to him." I point toward the door behind him. "I understand you're upset with me. *I'm* upset with me. But I learn from my mistakes, and I try hard not to make the same ones twice, and I promise you I will never hurt your brother again. I love your brother with my whole heart."

Rhett's eyes soften as the front door flies open. "Are you still giving her the third degree? Because if you're done, I have a few things I'd like to say," Coop says.

Sighing, I drop my chin to my chest. "Not you, too."

"Yeah, me, too," he says, joining his brother on the porch. They look so much alike. And while they're both incredibly handsome, they don't hold a candle to Trevor.

Trevor.

My Trevor is somewhere in that house thinking I don't love him the way he loves me.

"Please, guys," I beg. "All I want to do is talk to Trevor."

"So talk," comes the voice I wanted to hear the most.

Rhett and Coop turn around. Trevor stands in the entry-way of his house. Sweatpants hang low on his hips. His hair is still wet from a shower, and his expression is unreadable as he stares at me.

"Are you going to come in, or are you just going to stand out there?"

"I'm coming in."

Stepping over the threshold seems like such a big deal, and when I try to shut the door, Rhett stops me.

"Oh no, we're coming in too."

I roll my eyes and when I turn around, Trevor is gone. Rhett and Coop hang back, but I walk around the corner into the living room.

Trevor is sitting on his couch, his elbows resting on his knees, his hands hanging down. He isn't looking at me, and that can't be a good thing.

"Can I sit?"

He nods but doesn't look up, and rather than take the seat next to him, I sit in the recliner.

"You were right, and I was wrong. I am a coward. I was scared—terrified, really—and it was easier to run away from you when I should've been running toward you. But I've been running my whole life. It's all I know how to do. I ran away from Heaven only to come back. I ran away far and fast from any man who had an occupation I deemed unsafe. I ran from the counselor my senior year when she tried to get me to open up about my father's death. I don't think I ever told you that."

That catches Trevor's attention. He glances up, but doesn't give me much more than that.

"If I could change any moment in time, I'd change that moment because I think if I had sat there and let her pull everything out of me—all of my fears and insecurities—it would've prevented a whole lot of heartache down the road. Not just for me, but for you, because I hurt you tonight, and I don't ever want to hurt you again. I love you, Trevor."

My tears are falling, and I don't bother to wipe them away because they just keep coming. "I love you with all of my heart, and I want every moment with you I can get. I don't want to live in the tomorrow, worrying about what might happen. I want to live today in this moment with you. I want every laugh and fight and tear. I want to get married and have babies. I want to join the ladies auxiliary at the fire department and be there for you when you come home from a long shift. I'm so sorry I did that to you—to us—tonight, and if you give me a second chance, I swear I'll never fail you again."

"What changed, Claire? A few hours ago you were ready to write me off for good. What changed between then and now? How do I know you won't get spooked again and run?"

He has every right not to trust my words, and I hate that I did that to us. I only hope I can fix it. "After the fire, Mo dropped me off at Mom's. We had a long talk, and I realized something while I was there. For years, more than anything else, I've remembered the pain my father's death caused—I've allowed the memory of his death to overshadow his life. I think wanting to keep my heart safe and wanting to honor his memory through the way I lived my life were part of that too. But Mom, she looks at things much differently. She's focused on the time she had with him, all the laughter and tears, and the great memories they made during their years together. I always thought I avoided firefighters and men with certain occupations because I never wanted to feel the pain of losing another loved one. But now I think I stayed away from those men because I was afraid of falling in love. I was afraid of finding the kind of love my parents shared, and I was afraid of what it would do to me if I lost it."

I search Trevor's face, trying to gauge his reaction, but he's giving nothing away. "Falling in love with you wasn't part of my plan. But I did. I fell hard and fast, and I know now that I want what my parents had. I want the nights cuddled on the couch watching movies. I want family dinners and date nights, and I want to cook with you and laugh with you and cry with you. I want the memories—good and bad. What you said during our fight…it got to me, Trevor. I don't want to be a coward. I don't want to waste my life because I'm too afraid to live it. That's not what being safe means. I want you to help me, just like I'll help you. We'll work our way through all of this together. You were right. You are the best thing that's ever happened to me, and I'm not going to let you walk away. I don't want the pain of my past to overshadow my future any more than it already has, and I sure as hell don't want to look back wondering what could've been. I want to do this. I want to live. You're the love of my life, Trevor. You're my first true love, and I want you to be my last." My voice cracks on that final word, and I wipe away my tears.

Pressing his lips together, Trevor looks down at his hands. My heart plummets and my stomach rolls. I don't deserve a second chance, but damn it I was hoping he would give me one.

A moment passes. And then another and another, and then

Trevor stands up in front of me. This time when he looks at me, his bright blue eyes are swirling with intensity, and I have no idea what he's going to do. What I do know is if he doesn't give me another chance, I may very well shrivel up and die from a broken heart.

He holds out his hand. My heart squeezes. I slip my fingers in his, and he pulls me to my feet.

"Say it again."

"I'm sorry."

He shakes his head. "Not that. After that."

"I love you."

He hauls me against his chest and holds me for several long seconds, and when he pulls back, his eyes are still burning.

"I love you, too, Red, and we will work through all of the shit running through your head."

My heart swells in my chest.

"I want that."

"But no more running, baby. I won't survive it. I fear you walking away the same way you fear me running into a fire."

His words hit me with blunt force. I never thought of it like that.

"Never. I will never walk away from you again. This is it, Trevor. You're it for me. That is, if you don't mind putting up with my brand of crazy."

He steps close, so close that all of our best parts align—including our hearts. "I happen to like crazy."

"You do?"

He nods. "I also like hot, sweet, smart, sexy, and kind," he says, ending each word with a kiss. First to my lips and then my nose, each cheek, and my forehead before landing at my ear. "Do you know what else I like?"

It's not just my heart throbbing now, but other places of my body, and I squeeze my thighs together. "No, what?"

"You naked." Trevor kisses the side of my neck. With each touch of his lips against my skin, my body relaxes until I'm nothing but a pile of goo, waiting for him touch me.

"Does this mean you forgive me?"

Trevor cups my jaw, running his thumb along the apple of my cheek. "There's nothing to forgive. You made a mistake, and you apologized. Together we'll move on, and someday you'll make a mistake again, or maybe it'll be me. Either way, we'll get through it—"

"Together," I say, finishing his sentence.

I kiss Trevor with as much passion as I can. I tell him with my lips everything my heart has to say. My tongue plunges deep into his mouth, teasing his in a dance that gets better and better each time we kiss.

Someone, maybe Rhett, clears his throat behind us, but it goes largely unnoticed. Before I know it, Trevor's hand slips under the back of my shirt, his fingers drawing a sensual path up my spine. I shiver and reach for his bare chest. Splaying my fingers out against his abs, I circle them around his waist and up his back, pulling him tight against me in the process.

"You do realize we're still standing here, right?" Coop says.

We don't stop to acknowledge them, mostly because we're too caught up in each other. Hands and moans and whispered promises and—

"I can't watch any more of this," Rhett says.

I should be embarrassed, and I'm sure I've got a pretty good flush going on, but I'm in Trevor's arms, and nothing else matters.

Trevor peels his mouth from mine and looks over my shoulder at his brothers.

"You have about three seconds, and then you're going to get

one hell of a show. Three."

The front door opens.

"Two."

The front door slams shut.

"One."

The front door flies open again and Rhett runs in with a hand over his eyes. "I forgot my keys," he yells, fumbling his way around the living room, peeking through his fingers in fear of catching a glimpse of something he can't unsee.

"Time's up," Trevor says.

Rhett curses, and I laugh. "Give him three more seconds."

Trevor looks down at me and smiles. "You're too sweet."

"Just on the outside. On the inside, I'm wild."

"Praise Jesus! There are my keys." Rhett runs out of the room.

"Wild at heart, huh?" Trevor says, locking the front door.

"You have no idea." Grabbing the bottom of my shirt, I lift it over my head and drop it on the floor, followed by my bra and then my pants and panties, leaving a trail behind me as I walk down the hall.

Trevor catches up to me in his bedroom. We fall onto his bed, and he leans in close, brushing his lips against mine. "Maybe it's time I find out."

Epilogue

Claire

Pie. *Check.* Wine. *Check.* Milo. *Check.* I think I've got everything. I take one last look around Trevor's house to make sure I didn't forget anything, and then I'm out the door.

Trevor and I aren't living together yet, but we might as well be. Sometimes he stays with me, and sometimes I stay with him, and the only time we're apart is when he's at work. And those nights are the hardest.

The last three months have been amazing. We've had several long talks about life and our future and what each of us wants, and I think it's safe to say we're on the same page. It hasn't been easy to make my peace with Trevor's profession, and sometimes I still struggle, especially if I'm staying at his house and hear his radio go off. But Trevor has been a dream, always taking the time to assure me he's safe. After each fire call, he sends me a quick text or gives me a call to tell me he's okay, and at night he fills me in on all the details.

Sometimes I feel like I'd be better off without all of the details. I'm not sure it helps to know the dangerous things he does—like diving into freezing cold water to save a baby or repelling down the side of a building or running into a collapsed parking garage to rescue a family—but he's convinced that the more I know, the better. It's one of the few things we argue about.

My phone rings, and I press the answer button on my dash. "Hey, babe."

Trevor's voices crackles through the speakers. "Hey, are you on your way?"

"Yup." I smile even though he can't see me.

Once a week we have dinner at his mom's. It's usually just the two of us with his parents, sometimes his brothers and sister, but tonight is extra special because my mom and Phil are joining us, and it just so happens that today is my thirtieth birthday.

"Good. And you've got Milo?"

Milo perks up in the passenger seat at the sound of her name. "She's sitting right here. Are you going to run home and take a shower first, or are you meeting me there?"

Trevor is coming off of a forty-eight-hour shift, which means I haven't kissed his soft lips in two days, and I'm practically dying.

"Actually, there's been a small change of plans. Chief asked me to stay and cover the first half of the next shift. Mikey and Todd are out with the stomach flu, so I won't be able to make it to dinner."

"Oh." My heart falls to the pit of my stomach.

"Are you upset?"

"No."

"Want to try that again?"

"Fine. Maybe, but not at you. I'm upset with the situation. I just miss you, that's all."

"I know, baby, me too. And I know tonight was special because your mom was coming to dinner, and I swear I would be there if I could, but my crew needs me. I promise I'll make it up to you."

Actually, tonight was special because it was the first birthday I'd get to spend with you. "It's okay. I understand."

"You're not going to cry, are you?"

Maybe. "No." I pull into his parents' drive and park on the pad in front of the garage. "Mom and Phil aren't even here yet. I probably have time to cancel."

"What? No," Trevor says. "You've been looking forward to this, and you should go. My mom is making that lasagna you loved so much."

Vivian makes the best lasagna, and it does sound good, but... "It's not going to be the same without you. I might feel out of place."

"What are you talking about? You could never be out of place, because my family is your family. Now go and have a good dinner, and tomorrow morning you can tell me all about it."

"Fine." I put my vehicle in park. "Will you come to my house when you get off?"

"It's the only place I would go when I get off. Tell my mom I'm sorry I can't make it."

"I will."

"Bye."

The phone disconnects without a happy birthday, and I feel a ping of disappointment.

"This has been the worst birthday in the history of birthdays."

"Arf!" Milo tries to follow my voice by crawling across the console. She trips when her foot lands in the cup holder, but she eventually falls into my lap.

"Let's get this over with." With Milo in one hand, the pie in the other, and the wine squeezed tight under my arm, I walk along the sidewalk toward the front door. "Maybe if you're good, I'll open a tub of Ben and Jerry's when we get home."

"Arf!"

"See," I say, kissing the top of her head. "This is why we're friends. You support emotional eating."

"Arf!"

I stop in front of the door and stare at the doorbell, which I can't exactly reach because of all the things I'm holding. I reach for the small round button, but fall short.

"Screw it." Using the toe of my shoe, I give the door three solid kicks.

"It's open," Vivian hollers from the other side.

"Uh…" I look down at stuff in my hands and then at Milo. "You do have four legs."

Milo tilts her head at me.

"Don't cock your head at me. You're more than capable of walking in yourself." I squat down, loosen my grip on Milo, and she reluctantly jumps toward the ground.

"Thank you," I say, reaching for the front door. It opens easily, and I use my foot to nudge Milo into the house.

Vivian and Sawyer have a beautiful home, full of so much warmth and love. It's the sort of home I hope to have someday—the kind where memories of laughter live in the walls, where every nick, dent, and paint chip tells a story.

The fireplace is on, bathing the room in a soft, orange glow, and the smell of food wafts through the house, causing my mouth to water.

"Vivian?" I holler, shutting the door behind me.

"In the kitchen, dear."

Milo takes off through the house. She's been here enough now that she knows which obstacles are in her way and has learned to maneuver through the rooms.

The closer I get to the kitchen, the more delectable the smell becomes, and my stomach growls.

"It smells so good in here." My nose follows my stomach into the kitchen, and when I round the corner there's a chorus of "Surprise!"

I jump nearly a foot off the ground and almost lose the pie and wine in the process. "Oh my gosh!" I say, looking around at everyone.

The room is full. Mom is standing next to Phil's wheelchair, which is parked next to Mo and Rhett. Coop, Lincoln, Adley, and Tess are all smiles by the stove next to Vivian, who is holding a birthday cake, and Sawyer, who has an arm draped around his bride.

And then there's Trevor, and the sight of his gorgeous, bright smile brings tears to my eyes. "What are you doing here? I thought you were at work!"

He smiles, takes the wine and pie from my hands, sets them on the island in the middle of the kitchen, and he reaches for me. Drawing me into his warm embrace, he kisses the side of my head and laughs.

"You didn't really think I'd forget your birthday, did you?"

"No," I say, wiping a tear from my eye. "Okay, maybe."

His arms tighten, and I melt against him. "Claire, I promise I will never forget your birthday or our anniversary or the birthday of our fur babies."

"Baby."

"Huh?"

"You said fur babies, but we only have one, so it's fur baby."

"About that…" Trevor turns around and nods toward Mo.

She opens the door to the back patio, and in stumbles a lanky puppy—a mutt from what I can tell, maybe a German Shepherd mix. His ears flop in front of his face, and he trips over his too-big paws. He has a giant bow tied around his neck, and he runs straight for Trevor.

Trevor bends down and picks the puppy up. He holds the fur ball near my face, and a slobbery, pink tongue darts out, licking my cheek.

"Happy birthday."

"You got me a puppy?" I say, taking the wiggly body from his hands. "What's his name? Or is it a she?"

"Definitely a he," Trevor laughs, wrapping an arm around me. He runs his fingers through the fuzzy coat. "And I got him more for Milo."

"Milo?"

Mo steps forward. "I found a guy who trains dogs to be seeing eye dogs for other dogs."

I look from Trevor to Mo and back to Trevor. "You did this…"

I shake my head and hand the puppy off to the first person who reaches for him, and then I step up to Trevor. I push up on my toes and kiss him right here in front of everyone.

I probably shouldn't, but holding him is heaven, and the comfort of knowing he's mine is overwhelming. We indulge in a deep, languid kiss, only breaking apart when he dips his head to my neck.

"You're killing me, Red," he whispers.

Smirking, I pull back just enough to look into his eyes. "You are the very best part of my life, and this is the best gift you could've given me."

"Just wait. I've got more for you at home," he whispers.

"I don't need more. I just need you."

"All of this lovey-dovey crap is great, and happy birthday, Claire, but can we eat now?" Cooper asks.

Trevor laughs.

Vivian scoffs. "Cooper Allen."

"What? I've been waiting all day for this. I'm starving."

"Me too," Rhett adds.

"Let's eat," I say, keeping my eyes on Trevor's.

The room erupts in chatter. Milo and the puppy hop around, already the best of friends, and Trevor and I stay in our little cocoon for a few more seconds, relishing the peace we've found in the midst of chaos.

"Happy birthday, baby."

"Thank you." I giggle and look down when the puppy trips over my foot. "We need to name him. How about Bob?"

Trevor wrinkles his nose. "Bob? For a dog?"

I nod, and he shakes his head. "You are the absolute worst at naming things. When we have children, you will not be in charge of that task."

I blink. "You just said *when* we have children."

"I did."

"Not if, but when."

He nods and smiles.

When we have children.

I smile back like a doofus.

Trevor's eyes soften and he pulls me closer. "When," he whispers across my lips.

Rhett pokes his head into our personal space. "Are you two going to stand here and gush over each other all night? Because the rest of us are hungry, and the birthday cake Mom made is calling my name."

Mo sticks her head in the conversation as well, smiling sweetly. "Normally I'd slap him upside the head for interrupting such a tender moment, but he's right. We're all hungry, and since you're the guest of honor, we can't really start without you."

"Then by all means..." I step out of Trevor's arms and pull out a chair at the oversized table. "Let's eat."

An hour and a half later, the dirty dishes are piled up in the sink, the leftovers put away, and my belly is as full as my heart. Everyone has migrated to the back deck. Mom and Phil are sitting at the table with Vivian and Sawyer. Cooper, Mo, Tess, and Trevor have taken each other on in an intense game of horse, Lincoln and Adley have disappeared to I don't know where, and Rhett is standing beside me, taking it all in.

I don't know what's running through his head, but all I'm thinking about is how perfect all of this feels. I've managed to move on and forgive myself since the tutoring fire, and my memories of my father are warm and supportive—a source of courage for me now, not guilt. It was hard to overcome all that, and some days the fire still floats to the surface of my mind, but I try not to let those moments take over my life the way they once did. And they've begun to happen less often.

"I don't think I've ever seen you this content."

Smiling, I look up at Rhett. "I could same the same about you."

He nods and looks out at Mo. "It's her fault."

Mo squares her feet up to the basketball hoop, raises the ball, and shoots. The basketball swirls around the rim before falling through the net. She raises her arms, dancing around Coop and Trevor like the champion she is while the men hassle her.

Rhett chuckles, and as I watch him watch her, I can't help

but wonder what he's waiting on. I can't help myself. I nudge him in the arm. "So when are you going to pop the question?"

Looking at me, Rhett frowns. "He told you, didn't he?"

"Told me what?"

"Trevor. He told you I bought a ring."

"*What*?"

Rhett puts a hand over my mouth and glances at the people around us. "Would you keep it down?"

I cringe. "Sorry." I can't keep the excitement at bay for long, and I dance around on my toes. "Tell me everything. What does it look like? How long have you had it? When are you going to ask her?"

"You'll see it when I give it to her. I've had it for months. And I don't have a freaking clue."

"Months?"

He looks at me cautiously and nods.

"What are you waiting for?"

Blowing out a breath, Rhett shakes his head. "I don't know. The perfect moment, I guess."

"The perfect moment doesn't exist, Rhett, and tomorrow isn't promised. If you want to marry Mo, you should do it." My eyes travel across the yard to Trevor. He slaps the ball from Mo's hand, dodges left, and sinks a layup. For all those years I looked at Trevor as nothing more than Rhett and Coop's little brother, and then came the years I forced myself to ignore the crush I had on him... I would give anything to rewind time and see things as I do now.

I turn back to Rhett. "Maybe the perfect moment does exist. Maybe the perfect moment is now."

The lines on his forehead smooth as my words sink in. "You mean right here...right now?"

"Why not? This is a perfect moment, surrounded by the

people you love. Your family is here, along with Linc—although I don't know where he went. Mo's family is here, as are two of her best friends. What could be more perfect than this? Just think, you could go home tonight and make love to your fiancée."

"My fiancée," he says, with awe in his voice. "You're right. I shouldn't have waited this long."

I clap my hands together and try to come up with something encouraging to say, but it's not needed because Rhett is already striding off the deck with purpose.

Mo is standing at the back of the concrete pad, which I presume to be about as far away from the basket as a free-throw line. Coop, Trevor, and Tess are off to the side, waiting on her. She bounces the ball three times and shoots. The ball swishes through the net just as Rhett goes down on one knee behind her.

Everyone else sees it before she does, and there's a collective gasp as she tosses her arms into the air and spins around. "Rhett, baby, did you see—*ohmygod.*"

Her hands fly to her face when she sees the man she loves kneeling in front of her, and good Lord, I wasn't prepared to cry today.

I blink up at the sky, trying my best to keep from bursting into tears—something Mo is failing horribly at. My heart races as Rhett pulls a black velvet ring box from his pocket.

He casually lifts the lid and pulls the ring out.

"Oh my," Mo breathes, looking down at the sparkling diamond.

Rhett takes Mo's trembling hand in his, and although I can't see his face, I know he's looking at her as though she's the most precious thing in the universe.

"Monroe Gallagher, I love you more than I've ever loved another human being. You are my heart and soul. You are my home. I want to go to bed with you every night and wake up with you every morning. I want to cook for you and spoil you. I want to watch your belly grow round with our babies. I want to grow old with you. But mostly, I don't want to go another second without knowing that you're mine forever. Please, Mo, say you'll spend the rest of your life with me. Will you marry me?"

"Yes."

There isn't a dry eye in the backyard as Mo throws herself into Rhett's arms.

"Didn't see this coming," Trevor whispers. He places his hands on the railing in front of me, caging me in. I have no idea when he moved across the yard; I was too engrossed in my friend's engagement, but I'm happy he's here.

"Liar. Rhett told me you knew he bought a ring."

"I did, but I didn't know he'd pop the question on your birthday."

I smile. "I don't mind."

Vivian squeals, throwing herself off the deck so she can shower her soon-to-be daughter in law with as much love as she can, and I laugh when Rhett pushes his mom away.

Trevor lowers his head, and I expect him to make some offhanded comment about his mom, which is why I'm startled when he says, "Move in with me."

The breath seizes in my lungs. Tilting my head back, I look up at him. His big, blue eyes are steady, warm, and full of so much love. This decision is one of the easiest I've ever made.

"Okay."

He beams at me. "Yeah?"

I nod and smile as I look back at Mo. She tackles Rhett to the ground, peppering him in kisses, friends and family be damned.

"Soon," Trevor adds.

"I'll pack a bag tonight."

I pull his hands from the banister in front of me and wrap his arms around me.

"I love you, Claire."

Dropping my head back against his shoulder, I sigh. For so long I've looked at my life as one big missed opportunity, but not anymore. Now I have Trevor, and I'm going to seize every moment I can.

"I love you, too."

"One day soon that's going to be us. I'm going to ask you to marry me."

I try to turn in his arms, but they tighten around me, holding me in place as we watch our closest friends and family celebrate.

"You're going to say yes, right? When I ask you?" he says, his warm breath blowing against my ear.

I nod. "Yes."

I feel his body relax against mine. I hate that I ever walked away from him, that even for a moment I led him to believe I wasn't in this for the long haul. Forgiving myself for that night outside the warehouse fire has also been a struggle, but Trevor has been so supportive, and I've made a silent vow to show him each and every day how much he means to me. I want to prove to him that I'll never hurt him again—which I won't, because hurting Trevor is like hurting myself, and my pain tolerance is ridiculously low.

This time when I try to turn, he allows it. Draping my arms around his neck, I pull him toward me. "Just don't make me wait too long, okay? Because I am getting old."

"That's right. You're thirty now." He gives me a look, and I slap his arm. "I'm just kidding, baby. Don't worry, by the time *I'm* thirty, you'll be my wife, and I'll have you barefoot in the kitchen with one kid on your hip and another on the way."

A year ago that image would've made me nervous. Today, it makes me hopeful. "Is that what you want? Me barefoot and pregnant?"

"I just want you, Claire, however I can get you."

"I'm already yours."

"Forever."

"Forever's a long time."

"Not nearly long enough." But Trevor barely gets the words out because I'm kissing him, happily losing myself in the man who loves and understands me, and wants me forever.

And he's right; forever isn't nearly long enough.

ACKNOWLEDGEMENTS

First and foremost, I have to thank my husband, Tom. The endless amount of support and encouragement you give me while writing is truly amazing. Thank you for making sure the house stayed clean, the laundry got done, and the kids were fed. Thank you for taking over nighttime duty so that I could stay up late and write. Your love and support is what gets me through the day and I'm so incredibly thankful for you.

Mom and dad. Thank you for always supporting me and encouraging me to follow my dreams. And thank you for watching my kids when I'm desperate to hit a deadlines. I love you both more than you'll ever know.

Keshia Langston, Kristen Proby and Rebecca Shea… 'Thank you' seems so insignificant. You've encouraged me, supported me, and laughed with me. Your kind words and friendship has been the highlight of many of my days. Thank you for always being there, no matter the question or concern. Each of you mean so much to me and I love you <3.

Jessica Royer Ocken, my amazing editor. Thank you for being patient with me, and for taking my often scrambled prose and transforming it into something beautiful. Your opinion means the world to me, and I am so grateful that you edited this book. You're stuck with me forever.

A big huge thank you to Kari March for creating such a beautiful cover. You know my vision better than I do.

Stacey Ryan Blake, aka the best damn formatter in the world, thank you for making the inside of my books look beautiful. And, thank you for putting up with all of my last minutes changes. You're amazing and you're never getting rid of me ;)

To the staff with Give Me Books... THANK YOU for taking me on and cheering for my books. I appreciate all of the hard work and dedication that you put into each and every project. Your love of the book world shows and I'm proud to be part of it.

Last and certainly not least, thank you to every single one of my readers and all of the bloggers. Thank you for taking the time to read my books and share them. I hope you swooned over Trevor and Claire as much as I did. Your support means so much to me and without you and I wouldn't be doing what I love.

ABOUT THE AUTHOR

Photo by Perrywinkle Photography

K.L. Grayson resides in a small town outside of St. Louis, MO. She is entertained daily by her extraordinary husband, who will forever inspire every good quality she writes in a man. Her entire life rests in the palms of six dirty little hands, and when the day is over and those pint-sized cherubs have been washed and tucked into bed, you can find her typing away furiously on her computer. She has a love for alpha-males, brownies, reading, tattoos, sunglasses, and happy endings...and not particularly in that order.

OTHER BOOKS BY
K.L. GRAYSON

A Touch of Fate Series
Where We Belong
Pretty Pink Ribbons
On Solid Ground – a Harley and Tyson Novella
Live Without Regret

Dirty Dicks Series
Crazy Sexy Love

Other Titles
A Lover's Lament
The Truth About Lennon
Black

Made in the USA
Middletown, DE
26 July 2019